APPEARANCE AND ILLUSION

Appearance and Illusion

Published by The Conrad Press in the United Kingdom 2019

Tel: +44(0)1227 472 874
www.theconradpress.com
info@theconradpress.com

ISBN 978-1-911546-69-6

Copyright © Rob Stuart, 2019

The moral right of Rob Stuart to be identified as author of this work has been asserted in accordance with the Copyright, Designs and Patents Act 1988.

All rights reserved.

Typesetting and Cover Design by:
Charlotte Mouncey, www.bookstyle.co.uk with thanks to Liane Stuart
for photographic inspiration.

The Conrad Press logo was designed by Maria Priestley.

Printed and bound in Great Britain
by Clays Ltd, Elcograf S.p.A.

To Sue
Much love
[signature]

APPEARANCE AND ILLUSION

Rob Stuart

Also by Rob Stuart:
A Place in the Country
The Conrad Press (2018)

To all those who laboured at the chalkface in IFCELS,
2000-2016

Part One

1

Dr. Wendy McPherson drags herself into the open-plan office she shares with eleven other underpaid minions and slumps down in her carrel. She sinks down in her seat and holds her head in her hands. Her long red hair falls forward over her hands, covering her face. She sighs.

Another bloody Friday afternoon, she thinks, and what have I got to look forward to? I'm thirty-nine, not in a relationship since that bastard Tony walked out two years ago. I'm overweight, drink too much, spent three sodding years working on my PhD thesis (*Berkshire Hunts: An examination of the Origins of East London Rhyming Slang in the Mid Nineteenth Century*), live in a crummy flat with a mortgage I can only just afford and all for this – trying to teach English for Academic Purposes to a load of pre-undergrads who always have an infinity of excuses for not turning up to classes. I bet they all have better lives than I do, better things to do with their time than study Western History and Culture on a wet Friday in November. I've had it!

She is painfully aware that the best she has to look forward to is a drink (or seven) with some of her female colleagues in the pub after work. She will get nicely oiled and take the tube home to Acton in a pleasant alcoholic haze. No doubt she will finish off the bottle of Pinot that sits in her fridge waiting for her.

I haven't even got a bloody cat to kick, she thinks bitterly. They say a pet is a great comfort for the lonely. Fat bloody chance! And then what? A cold and empty desert of a double bed.

She fires up her PC to check her email. A page of departmental announcements scrolls onto the screen. Meetings, details of in-house training seminars, emails from students excusing themselves from her classes. The best is from a student who says she has locked herself *into* her room and can't get out until the halls of residence maintenance men arrive to free her. That's an anecdote for the pub later.

The one nugget of gold amongst the dross is an email from Frank Brice, who teaches on the Politics and International Relations course, and spends his days surfing the internet looking for amusing stuff to forward on to a select group who he thinks might do with a laugh. Wendy is high on his list of recipients. Right now she could do with cheering up so she opens the email in anticipation of a chuckle.

The subject line says *Lost in Translation*. She scrolls down the page. There follows examples of literal translations taken from, amongst others, Chinese restaurant menus and public notices.

Beware of missing foot; Cock soup; Nanometer silver Cryptomorphic condom. What the hell is that one about? *Fuck the duck until exploded.* Some kind of Chinese culinary method, obviously. She makes a mental note to give the crispy duck a miss next time she is in a Chinese restaurant. *Soup for sluts.* Ditto. Although given the barren state of her my life, chance might be a fine thing, she thinks. And then she sees a picture on the screen that makes her stop and her heart gives a little flutter. It is a photograph of a lawn. At the edge of the lawn is a small sign and written on the sign are the words: *Do not disturb – tiny grass is dreaming.*

She sits back in her chair and closes her eyes for a Zen moment, contemplating the image of the dreaming grass. Make the most of it, she thinks, some bastard is sure to turn up with a lawn mower to give you a nasty wake-up call.

She moves on to the last image. A hand-written sign offers *Engish Lessons*. She lets out an audible groan.

Dr. Sheila Jones, seated in the next carrel, leans over. 'That bad?'

'Have a look at this,' Wendy says, indicating her screen'

'See what you mean.'

'You up for the pub later?' Wendy asks.

'Can't tonight. First assignments are in: *Globalisation has a positive impact for developing countries. Discuss.* Preferably in English rather than Engish! Although I'm not holding my breath.'

The two women teach in a unit of a red brick university in central London that specializes in foundation courses for international students hoping to apply for undergraduate and postgraduate courses at British universities and paying large fees for the tuition, foreign students being very useful milch cows to the coffers of British Higher Education.

For many international students the idea of having to think for themselves arrives as a bit of a shock, coming as they do from educational backgrounds where cramming for exams is the norm, as is the expectation of being spoon-fed by their teachers with the 'right' answer. Getting free-flowing discussion going in seminar groups, Wendy reflects, is about as much fun as bashing your head against a wall. The girls are often too shy and too culturally conditioned to speak up and the boys, released from their pressure cooker secondary schools, don't bother with the required reading.

And then there is the question of language skills. While the unit does have strict language competence guidelines, commercial pressures from competing, and less scrupulous academic institutions, means that there is a steady erosion of standards to ensure bums on seats. English lessons play a major role in the curriculum alongside academic units. It can be an uphill struggle of the sort that might give Sisyphus pause for thought.

Class sizes are relatively small, ten to twelve students on average, but David Rhys, the Head of Department, is in discussions with Jim Smythe, the Society of University Lecturers rep, to increase to fifteen, a move that Smythe is resisting at the moment but he will, inevitably, have to bow to financial imperatives. None of the staff relish the idea of an increased marking load and there is muttering in favour of strike action.

The student body is solidly behind the staff on this issue as it means a break from classes and the university authorities don't mind because it means they can dock the strikers' pay and save money. The reality for the staff is that they will have to turn up and man picket lines in the rain, lose pay and, in the long run, end up teaching the bigger classes.

Unrest is rife in the ranks. And the general consensus is that things will only get worse.

2

Wendy stands in front of the mirror in the ladies' loo, putting on her make-up ready for the night out with her colleagues when Jamila Khan (Development Studies) comes in. She is a pretty, young woman in her early thirties whose family came to England from Uganda during the Idi Amin expulsions of Asian families from that country. She is always cheerful and gives Wendy a beaming smile.

'Are you joining us for the weekly booze-up?' asks Wendy.

'I'm just coming out for one drink.' Jamila replies. 'Hubby and son to look after. He can't boil an egg, even with written instructions.' She laughs and enters one of the cubicles. 'See you outside.'

Ten minutes later, Jamila joins the four other women huddled out of the rain at the entrance to the building.

As well as Wendy, there are Annabella Rossi (forty-eight, plump and comfortable, with dyed red hair); Pauline Queen (fifty-two, thin rather than svelte, blond hair turning to grey); and Mary Bowyer (forty-four, dark-haired, tall and always reminding Wendy of Morticia Addams, or perhaps Cher).

'Right, ladies,' says Mary, 'are we hot to trot?'

'Ready and willing!' says Annabella.

'Bring on the Chardonnay!' says Wendy.

'Slug and Lettuce here we come,' says Pauline. 'God, I need a drink after the week I've had. Talk about battering your head against the wall!'

'Let's go. I can taste it already,' says Mary.

The Slug and Lettuce on Northampton Road is a brightly-lit wine bar, all pine tables and classical piano music with a long bar with bottles of wine in racks from floor to ceiling behind the bar. By six o'clock, it is packed with punters enjoying an end-of-the-week drink with workmates and friends and the place is buzzing. The five women manage to find seats by the loos and away from the speakers. They shake the rain off their coats and hang them on the back of their chairs, carefully covering their handbags away from the sharp eyes of casual thieves.

'Kitty?' asks Annabella.

'I'm only staying for one glass,' Jamila says.

'Everyone else?' asks Annabella again.

'Tenner each?' Wendy suggests to general agreement.

'Good start,' says Mary. 'I'm up for getting hammered. What a week!'

By nine o'clock, with Jamila long departed, the four remaining women are much the worse for drink, having disparaged the University management, bemoaned the state of their love lives (although Pauline is married and Annabelle lives with her long-term partner, a solicitor called Carol; Mary is divorced) and discussed the foibles of their students.

Pauline, who lives in Tooting Bec and Annabelle, who lives in Clapham Common, decide to stagger off together to catch a Northern Line tube home and set off into the night and the rain, leaving Wendy and Mary to finish up the last bottle.

The wine bar is still heaving as some drinkers leave and others arrive; the two women have been nibbling from dishes of olives and slices of ciabatta with dipping oil but have not eaten anything more substantial and their heads are beginning to spin.

At first, they are unaware of the two young men hovering near their table.

'Are these seats free?' asks one of the men. He is in his late twenties, tall, dressed in denim, with his hair cropped around his ears and a gelled topknot.

'Wha…?' says Wendy, when it sinks in she is being addressed.

'I was asking if these seats are vacant,' says the young man. 'We saw your friends leave.'

'Sit down, sit down.' Mary slurs.

The two men pull out the chairs and sit. The second is shorter than his friend and wears a tee shirt and cargo pants. He, too, is in his mid-twenties, with carefully trimmed stubble and floppy dark hair.

'I'm Lucas,' the taller young man introduces himself, 'and this is Richard. Can we get you lovely ladies a drink?'

Mary and Wendy look at each other in mute interrogation and reach an unspoken decision.

'Why not?' says Wendy. 'The others have gone home. No stamina. I'm Wendy.'

'And I'm Mary. We're drinking Chardonnay!'

3

The next morning Wendy wakes up with the mother of all hangovers and struggles to recall the events of the previous night. She drags herself upright in her bed and sees her clothes strewn on the bedroom floor. Memory hits like a blow from a fist: Lucas! She came home with the young man from the Slug and Lettuce. Oh God! She had a one-night stand with a total stranger. And what she can remember about the sex was that it was perfunctory and not at all satisfying. Is he still in the flat?

She climbs out of bed and wraps herself in the dressing gown that hangs on the bedroom door in a sudden and arguably inconsistent attempt to protect her modesty, although why she bothers she is not sure – he has, after all, seen her in her naked glory and jumped her bones.

The flat is empty, as is her purse. All her cash, her plastic and her smartphone are missing from her handbag. The shock is beginning to dissipate her hangover but she runs herself a large glass of cold water from the kitchen tap and swallows a couple of aspirins.

Her new laptop has gone as have the pieces of jewelry she inherited from her mother and the black pearl necklace that she treated herself to on her trip to China last year.

She sits down on her sofa in the living room and gives in to tears. What a fool! What a stupid, gullible, *old* FOOL. What did she imagine a young man like Lucas – was that even his *real name*? – could see in her? She is the victim of her own loneliness. That and *way* too much white wine.

Her landline phone rings, biting into her misery, slicing into her hangover. She wipes the tears off her face and gropes for the receiver.

'Wendy?' It's Mary. 'I feel so stupid. I've been robbed. It was that Richard from last night. I took him home.'

'I took Lucas home too,' says Wendy bitterly. 'He robbed me as well.'

'What the hell were we thinking?'

'We were thinking with our vaginas and far too much wine.'

'Have you lost much?' Mary asks.

'Enough,' Wendy replies. 'Plastic, my smartphone, a laptop. Bits of jewelry.'

'Have you reported it to your bank? Stopped the cards?'

'I'm still not thinking straight. I've got the hangover to end all hangovers. How much did we drink?'

'I lost count after we switched to cocktails.'

'Oh God,' says Wendy, shuddering at the memory of the enormity of their excesses.

'Look, I'll get off the phone to let you phone the bank and cancel your cards.'

'Mary?'

'Yes?'

'Let's keep this as our little secret. Don't mention this to anyone at work.'

'No chance. We'll be a laughing-stock. Can you imagine?'

Wendy can imagine only too well. *Put this one down to experience. Learn your lesson and never speak of it again.*

Mary rings off and Wendy rummages around in the drawer

where she keeps all her important documents. In her academic life she is a meticulous record-keeper but her private papers are a mess and the hangover is not helping.

She finally locates the relevant information on her bank details. Her living room floor is strewn with piles of paper she has flung out of the drawer in her search.

With her hand shaking from all the toxins in her bloodstream, she keys in the number of her bank's helpline.

The number rings.

'You have reached the helpline of Wadham's Bank,' a foreign-sounding voice informs her. *'Press one, followed by your sort code, account number and date of birth and the hash tag for a statement; press two to make an enquiry about opening an account; press three for information on overdrafts; press four for enquiries about our financial services; press five to speak to an agent.'*

Wendy viciously stabs five.

'All our agents are very busy today dealing with other customers' problem; you are being held in a queue.

A recording of Vivaldi's *Four Seasons* starts to play. Wendy cannot be sure but she thinks it is *Winter*.

After three minutes, a voice tells her: *'Please hold; your call is very important to us.'*

'Just answer the sodding phone!' she grinds out through clenched teeth and wishes that the aspirins would kick in.

Vivaldi is going great guns and probably thinking it was time for Spring when a human being comes onto the line.

'Philip speaking. How may I help you?'

She is tempted to ask him how the weather is in Manila, for that is surely where the call centre must be, but swallows her frustration. Getting angry with him will solve nothing.

'I want to cancel my credit and debit cards, please.'

'Are you unsatisfied with the service of Wadham's Bank, Madam?'

'No, not especially. My cards have been stolen.'

'I'm afraid you've come through to the wrong department. Just let me transfer you to a colleague who deals with this.' There is a click and music starts up again. This time it's The Mavericks blasting out 'Dance the Night Away'. She feels like bursting into tears again.

Just when she decides she is losing the will to live in the face of the irrepressible cheeriness of The Mavericks, a new voice announces itself.

'Hello, my name is Gregory. How may I help you?'

'I want to report my cards stolen.'

'OK. I need to ask you a few questions for identification purposes. Can you give me your full name?'

'Wendy Anne McPherson,' she tells him.

'And is it all right if I call you Wendy?'

You can call me anything as long as you stop that scumbag going on a spree with my cards, she thinks, but agrees he can call her Wendy.

'And when did this happen, Wendy?'

'Last night some time.'

'Where did you lose your cards, Wendy?'

This is awkward. She decides to fudge.

'I think they must have been stolen from my handbag. In a wine bar.'

'Do you have your card details to hand?'

'No,' she says. Who has their card details when they haven't GOT the cards?

'Oh, that is a shame. Never mind, I'm sure I can find them.' She hears him tapping away on his keyboard. 'Ah, yes,' he says. 'Got you.'

'Oh, that's good then.'

'Yes. When do you think you last used your card?'

'Just before six o'clock last night. I withdrew fifty pounds from the ATM.' And whatever was left after last night, that bastard stole!

'So you haven't been using it since then?'

'No. MY CARDS HAVE BEEN STOLEN.' Perhaps he doesn't understand. That's what you get from outsourcing.

'Because we have a record of your card being used in a number of liquor stores since three a.m. this morning. Your time,' he adds in case she is unsure of her time zone.

'Well, it wasn't me. I was in bed fast asleep.' Passed out, if I'm honest, she thinks. And I'm NEVER going to buy or consume alcohol in any shape or form EVER again, she promises herself.

'Almost five hundred pounds worth.' Can she detect a note of disapproval in his voice. 'In amounts of less than thirty pounds. Using your swipe card.'

Oh, you sly shit, Lucas or whoever you are. You cunning little sod.

'Can you stop the cards? Right away. Now, please. It wasn't me!' Why can't he believe me.

'Don't worry, Wendy. I'm doing it now.' He tap taps at his keyboard again. 'There,' he says, 'all done.'

'What about the money that was stolen?'

'Have you reported it to the police?'

'Not yet, that's my next job.'

'Do that and then get in touch with your local branch. We will send out replacements as soon as possible.'

'But,' says Wendy in desperation, 'I haven't got any money NOW. How am I going to buy food for the weekend?'

The line has gone dead and Gregory has disappeared back into the ether; not his problem.

She sits in stunned silence, then leaps to her feet and attacks the piles of papers in her drawer and on the floor looking for her insurance details. When she finds them, she has to squint to bring them into focus.

The instructions are clear: before she can make a claim, she must report the robbery to the police and get a crime number to submit to the insurers. She thinks about the possible scenario.

It's like this, officer. I was pissed out of my mind and got picked up by a total stranger, half my age and brought him back to my flat for a shag, because I'm a lonely, middle-aged woman who, just for a change, fancied waking up next to a warm body No, I don't know his name or address or, in fact, anything at all about him except, from what I can remember, he wasn't that good in bed. Anyone like that in your files?

That, she thinks, is a bit of a non-starter.

She goes to see what she might find in the cupboard or the freezer to keep body and soul together until her new cards arrive.

4

It is Wednesday in the second week of December, the penultimate week of the autumn term. Wendy has just finished trying to teach a lesson on Globalisation of Multinational Business to a class of evidently mainly uncomprehending Chinese students. Despite their parents having paid large sums of money in university fees, the students seem spectacularly uninterested in the subject and have talked amongst themselves in Chinese for most of the two-hour session; some young men have engaged in burping contests, much to the amusement of the young women and much to Wendy's frustration.

She opens her email and finds a summons from David Rhys for her to come and see him asap.

'Bloody hell,' she mutters aloud, 'what does he want? Have the students been moaning again?'

'What's up?' asks Sheila Jones.

'I've been summoned by David Rhys.'

'What have you done now?'

'God knows! I expect I'm in for a bollocking for something. Best get it over with.'

She takes the stairs up to the second floor where David has his office and knocks on the door, ready to defend herself against anything he might tax her with.

'Come in,' says a voice from behind the door and she enters, her fists unconsciously clenched by her sides.

David looks up from whatever he has been doing and smiles at her; she is instantly on her guard.

'Ah, Wendy. Thank you for coming so promptly,' he says. 'Close the door, please.'

Here we go, she thinks and waits for him to start.

'How is everything?' he asks.

Is this a trick question? Wendy is not sure and pauses before she answers to give herself time to prepare a defence against whatever is coming.

'So, so,' she replies, not committing herself to anything.

'Take a seat.' He waves her to the chair facing him.

Ah, she thinks, we are in for a long session. She sits and resigns herself to losing a chunk of time in her life that she will never get back. She is quite prepared to sit and tune him out if that is what it takes.

'I've got a proposition for you,' he says unexpectedly.

'Oh please, not extra language support classes,' she says. She will argue vehemently against picking up more classes; her timetable is stretched as it is and the students taking the extra classes are the worst of the bunch.

'No, no, nothing like that. Well, not exactly.'

She can hear a big BUT hovering and doesn't like the prospect.

'So what have you got in mind?' Whatever it is, she thinks, I'm not doing it.

'What do you know about Kesheva?'

'Kesheva?' echoes Wendy, pronouncing it as he did; 'Ker–shee-*vah* with an emphasis on the 'vah'.

'Yes.'

'Isn't it somewhere in Central Asia?'

'Exactly!'

'What about it?' *What the hell is he going on about?*

'We've had a request from the President.'

'What kind of request?' Wendy asks. And, more importantly, what has it got to do with me? she wonders.

'He has a young teenage son whom he wants to send to a university over here. Wants him to study Law and then go on to Harvard.'

Wendy thinks she knows where this is going: 'And I suppose he needs one-to-one tuition to get him up to scratch?'

'You've hit the nail on the head!'

'I can't take on one-to-one classes with the teaching load I've got, if that is what you are thinking. Sorry, David.' She starts to rise out of the chair.

'Hear me out. The President doesn't want him to come here; he wants someone to go to Kesheva and tutor him *in situ*.'

Wendy just stares at him.

'You must be joking!'

'No, Wendy I'm not joking. The President is prepared to be very generous in extra remuneration on top of your salary here. And there is a new wing to the library on offer if and when his son is accepted on a course in the UK.'

Ah, thinks Wendy. That's the hook. *The university is strapped for cash and a nice new addition to the library building is one hell of an incentive.*

'OK. Why me?'

'Well, because you are a very valued and experienced member of the teaching team. We want to send our best.'

Flattery is not going to get you anywhere, she thinks.

'Also, it's partly a question of language skills. I went over your CV from the files. I see you taught in Turkey in the early nineties.'

'Yes. For about six months.'

'But you *do* speak Turkish?'

'A bit, yes, but I'm hardly fluent.'

'And you have an 'O' level GCSE in Russian.'

'That I've not used in twenty years.

'Nevertheless, you are the best qualified for the job.'

'How... how long is it for, exactly?' Despite her misgiving, Wendy's interest has been piqued.

'About six months,' says David, sensing that his victim is sniffing around the hook.

'What are the terms and conditions? I'm not saying yes, mind you.'

'You'll have your own commodious and comfortable accommodation in the old city. Staff to look after you, a local salary to meet your needs and a hard currency salary of three thousand pounds a month tax-free paid directly into the bank of your choice. First-class flights to and from Kesheva and a termination bonus, depending on results, of ten thousand pounds. *Tax free.*'

'That *is* very tempting,' Wendy concedes. A wodge of cash in the bank would certainly not go amiss at this stage of my life, she thinks. And can it be any worse than trying to teach these ingrates here? 'Can I think about it?' she asks David.

'Of course. I don't expect you to make your mind up here and now. It's a big decision. Take a day or two to think about it and then get back to me. But I need an answer by the end of the week, please.'

No pressure, then, Wendy thinks but she is already half sold on the idea. Why *not* take a break away from her lack luster life here in London? After all, it's hardly what you might call a bunch of roses. And then there is the money! She would be mad to turn her nose up at a windfall like this. How bad can it be? Maybe the boy is highly motivated and a pleasure to teach. Thirsty for knowledge; what she went into teaching for in the first place. And the chance to experience a new country and culture.

'Give me a day or two, then, David. I'll give you my answer by Friday.'

'I honestly don't think you'll regret it if you decide to go. And I hope you will decide yes. You'll be ideal for the post. Give you a break from the daily grind here!'

Wendy gives a nod of tentative complicity. She makes her way back to her shared office and seeks out Frank Brice, who is sitting at his desk trawling the internet, which is all he seems to do between classes. He gives the same series of lectures year upon year and sees no need to waste time updating them.

'Frank,' she says, 'what do you know about Kesheva?'

'Kesheva? Central Asia. Used to be a Soviet Republic but struck out on its own in 1992, along with all the other Stans in that area. Run by a bod called Aslan Dargan and his family. Floating on oil. Why?'

'David Rhys has just offered me a secondment to go and teach the President's son for six months.'

'Really? Make a bit of a change from here, won't it?

'Do you think I should go?'

'What's the dosh like?'

'Tempting.'

'Do you have any problems with a one-party dictatorship?'

'No. I work here don't I?

'Seriously. Would you be likely to cause a revolution?

'Hardly. I'd be there to teach Dargan's son'

'So you'd be well in with the powers that be?'

'I expect so. I wouldn't be involved in local politics or anything like that.'

'Just as well; the usual career path for opposition is the cemetery. Dargan's not big on dissent. Critics of the regime have a record of disappearing in the night. Old habits learnt from the KGB.'

'What else do you know?'

'Not a lot more. Why not check it out on Google or Wikipedia.'

'Thanks, I'll do that. Would you go?'

'If the dosh was right. I could do with a change from this lot.' Next she consults with Mary, Pauline and Annabelle. The consensus is 'Go. Give yourself a break from here. You're single, no ties. What have you got to lose? Wish he'd asked me!'

She goes home that evening to her empty flat and pours herself a drink and reviews her life, such as it is...

What have I got here? I'm sick of the work; sick of the students; sick of the weather; sick of the commute; sick of being lonely.

The next morning, she tells David Rhys that she will do it. *When do I start?*

5

Wendy spends Christmas with her older brother, Jamie, a forty-four-year-old recording engineer, and his GP wife Rosemary.

Jamie has collected their mother, Jane, who is seventy-five and beginning to slide into dementia, from her nursing home (which Wendy and Jamie jointly fund) for her annual visit to her children, although both of them regularly make the trip to Hertford to see her when they have time.

Jamie and Rosemary's two grown-up children, Frank, twenty-three, a computer programmer and Belinda, twenty-two, a post-graduate biochemist, are also home for the festival. Frank would rather be spending the holiday with his new girlfriend and Belinda has reached a crucial stage in her research; neither of them really want to be there and both feel a little uncomfortable around their grandmother. Rosemary feels a touch of resentment that her parents, who live in York, have decided to spend Christmas with her sister although Jamie has pointed out that her sister lives in Halifax and it is much more convenient for them than making the long trek south to Hampstead. Jamie promises Rosemary that next year they will *definitely* celebrate Christmas in Yorkshire but Rosemary is sceptical.

Christmas dinner is a subdued affair despite the crackers and paper crowns, the turkey, parsnips and Brussel sprouts and Christmas pudding and brandy butter to follow.

Into this setting, Wendy lobs her bombshell.

'I'm going abroad for six months,' she announces.

'*What?*' says her brother. Her niece and nephew seem totally indifferent to their aunt's news; her mother smiles at her and says nothing. Wendy wonders if she has understood. Probably not.

'Where?' asks Rosemary.

'Kesheva,' Wendy replies.

'Where the hell is that?' Jamie asks.

'In Central Asia,' she tells him.

'Why?' asks Rosemary.

'The University's sending me on a secondment. To teach the President's son.'

'What about your flat?' asks Rosemary, the practical member of the family.

'I'll just lock it up for six months. It'll be fine.' *There's very little left to steal, she thinks.* And whatever there is, I'll claim back on the insurance. New for old! Deal!

'When are you going, dear?' her mother suddenly and unexpectedly asks.

'On Tuesday, Mummy.'

'*This* Tuesday?' asks Jamie, aghast.

'Yep. Tuesday the twenty-eighth. They want me to start in the New Year.'

'Where will you live, dear?' her mother asks again.

'They have arranged somewhere for me to live. Probably a spare palace or something,' she jokes to lighten the mood.

'That's nice,' says her mother. 'You'll be like the Queen of Kesheva.'

'Queen of Kesheva,' says Wendy with a wry smile. 'I like

the sound of that.'

'Are they paying you?' Jamie wants to know.

'Yes, and very well. Also, I still get my salary from the University. It's a really good deal. I'd be mad to turn it down.' *And I really, really do need a break. My life is completely shit at the moment.* But of course, she does not tell them that.

'Well,' says Rosemary, 'I hope it all turns out for you.'

'Do they drink alcohol?' asks Jamie, pouring himself another glass of red wine.

'It is Islamic but from what I could see on Wikipedia, they seem to be fairly relaxed. Must be the Russian influence. All that vodka.'

'I went to Dubai,' says Frank, looking up from his smartphone from where he has been texting his girlfriend. 'Plenty of booze there!'

'I'm not going on a boozy stag trip, Frank,' says Wendy and realises she sounds just like the maiden aunt they must take her for.

'No worries,' Frank tells her.

'*I* think it sounds cool,' Belinda chimes in, pushing away her empty plate. 'What's the weather like? Better than here, I bet.'

'It can be quite cold in the winter, I believe,' says Wendy. 'But the summers are hot.'

'Cool,' says Belinda again and then appears to lose interest.

This girl is going on to do a PhD, Wendy thinks. God help us all and here's to dumbing down. She takes a healthy swallow of wine. *I'll go on the wagon when I get to Kesheva,* she promises herself. *My New Year's Resolution.*

6

At nine o'clock on Tuesday, 28th of December Wendy, somewhat self-consciously, is the only passenger so far in the first-class line at the Air Kesheva check-in desk in Terminal Four in Heathrow Airport.

She has never flown in anything but economy class, shuffling down the aisle with her carry-on and hoping there will be space in the overhead lockers somewhere in sight of her seat. The superior beings sprawled in their armchairs that convert to beds and already being served chilled champagne by super-attentive cabin crew live in a different world. At the economy counter, a line has already formed and people are manipulating bags and children who run around their parents excitedly.

Wendy hands over her passport to the smiling woman at the counter. Wendy does not have a ticket but an email message from the Keshevan Embassy has informed her that all travel arrangements have been made for her and there is no baggage limit for her.

'Dr. McPherson?' the check-in lady enquires, looking up from her computer, 'you're early for check-in. First-class passengers don't have to check in until an hour before departure. Have you come far?'

'No, not really,' Wendy tells her, loath to admit, now she is a first-class passenger, that she came on the Piccadilly Line from Acton Town tube station.

The check-in lady hands Wendy her boarding pass and processes her two suitcases without bothering to look at the scales. 'Please feel free to use our First-Class Lounge. There is a shower if you want to freshen up and complimentary drinks and light refreshments are available. And you have plenty of time if you want to use the spa facilities. Boarding for first-class passengers is at 11.30 for take-off at 12.15. Enjoy your flight with Air Kesheva.'

I could get used to this, Wendy thinks as she makes her way through security and passport checks.

She finds the Air Kesheva First Class Lounge and pokes her head around the door. Attendants in Air Kesheva uniforms stand around looking bored but apart from them, the lounge is empty. The staff spring into action when they see her.

Wendy is ushered to a seat and offered a range of drinks, tea, coffee, champagne, Buck's Fizz or Mimosas for a healthy option. Smoked salmon or a light snack of caviar and blinis.

She opts for the champagne and caviar. After all, it is not yet the New Year and she doesn't have to start detoxing *just* yet. Enjoy it while you can, she tells herself.

'Towels and a complimentary robe and slippers are available if you wish to use the spa, madam,' a bright young woman informs her when she has finished her food.

Oh, yes, I could get very used to this, Wendy thinks. Beats schlepping in to central London for a nine o'clock Monday morning class.

An hour later, Wendy is feeling refreshed and invigorated after a sauna and hot shower. Other first-class passengers start to drift into the lounge. The men are dark-haired, wear black suits and shined shoes and carry expensive looking briefcases and are all speaking into their smartphones. The women come in two varieties: small, dumpy and middle aged or young, blond and willowy – trophy wives and girlfriends. But without exception all of the women are loaded down with shopping bags from the posh shops in the departure area concourse.

At 11.30 on the dot, one of the uniformed staff announces that boarding is commencing for first-class passengers and could they all please make their way to the departure gate?

Wendy enters the Airbus A380 and is guided to a self-contained little world with a wide seat that slides down to make a bed. She has online access, a video screen showing a selection of several hundred entertainment choices and a sliding door that she can close to cut out the world. If she needs a change of scenery, she can stroll across the aisle and sit on a leather bench next to a bar where the barman is hers to command and she has fellow travellers to chat to. The set-up puts her little flat in Acton to shame.

The flight to Kesheva will take nine hours and Kesheva is four hours ahead of UK time so they will arrive in the middle of the night. Wendy is not usually a good sleeper hunched up in an economy-class seat but does not anticipate a problem stretched out in the comfort of her bed/seat.

A young woman in Air Kesheva uniform introduces herself to Wendy as Katerina. Wendy noticed she has a distinct Oriental cast to her eyes and cheekbones, bringing home to Wendy that she is bound for the exotic world of central Asia.

'I shall be your attendant for this flight, Dr McPherson. If there is anything you need, please let me know. You are an honoured guest of our country and our President.'

How come everyone knows who I am and what I'm here for, Wendy wonders but chooses not to pursue it. *Let's just have a bask in the pampering,* she thinks. It's been a long time since anyone gave a damn about me.

Her meal, when it comes, is served on china with silver flatware and a half bottle of a good hock. Wendy selects a movie, called *Living the Dream,* that she had planned to watch over the Christmas holidays but had not got round to.

Katerina comes to clear her table. 'Can I get you a drink?' she asks Wendy.

'Do you have something typical of Kesheva? What do people drink there? Or *do* they drink alcohol?' She suddenly remembers Kesheva is an Islamic country and is afraid she has made a faux pas.

'We drink vodka,' Katerina replies. 'We were a part of the Soviet Union in the old days and had many Russians living in our country. They brought a taste for vodka with them and it stayed after they left.'

'Vodka sounds nice. What have you got?'

'We have Grey Goose, Zubrowka Bison Grass, Stolichnaya and Absolut. And many locally distilled vodkas.' She counts them off on her fingers. 'We have many flavoured vodkas: caramel, lime, peach, raspberry, pepper and peach.'

'Wow!' Wendy exclaims, 'I'm spoilt for choice.' She mulls over the options. 'I'll try pepper, please.'

'I'll be right back, Dr McPherson,' Katerina promises and true to her word reappears shortly carrying an ice bucket containing a full bottle of spirit which she places on Wendy's table, cracks the cap and pours Wendy a measure into a shot glass. Wendy takes an exploratory sip. The vodka is cold but then the pepper sends a stream of fire down her throat. She coughs.

'Is it all right?' Katerina asks anxiously.

'It's fine,' Wendy gasps. 'I've never had anything like it.'

'Please call me if there is anything else you need,' says Katerina, retreating and leaving the bottle.

Katerina is shaking her shoulder for some reason that Wendy cannot fathom. She realises she is lying in bed with a blanket over her and a pillow under her head.

'We will be landing soon, Dr. McPherson, and you need to put your seat upright.'

'How did I get into bed?'

'I put your bed down and covered you. You had fallen asleep and were snoring. Some of the other passengers complained but when I told them you were a guest of the President, they stopped.'

'How long have I been asleep? Wendy asks. For some reason her head feels muzzy.

'I think since just before we entered Russian airspace.'

Suspicion rears its head. 'How much of that vodka did I drink?'

'Oh, I'm not sure,' says Katerina diplomatically. She had removed the half-empty bottle from Wendy's grasp before putting her to bed. The remains of the bottle had been surreptitiously poured into a water bottle, which Katerina will give to her father when she gets home. The perks of the job.

Bloody hell, Wendy thinks. I'm arriving at my new job half-pissed.

7

Aslan Dargan International Airport does not have air bridges for passengers to embark and disembark their flights and so the pilot has to taxi to the hard standing and wait for the portable stairs to arrive before the passengers can leave the aircraft.

Wendy, as befits her status as a first-class VIP, is among the first to exit the plane. As she stands on the platform at the top of the stairs, a number of impressions hit her.

Firstly, the cold. She knew it was the middle of winter and that temperatures would be colder than London but she is not prepared for the wind chill. She had the good sense to buy a quilted puffa jacket before she came, but the cold stings her face and cuts through the thin material of her trousers.

Secondly, the whole airport is floodlit and she can see groups of armed soldiers in long trench coats and fur hats patrolling the perimeters with automatic weapons cradled to their chests.

Thirdly, there is the huge portrait of a man in his thirties, his hand raised in apparent blessing, erected over the airport terminal building. As far as she can work out from her limited knowledge of the language, the portrait bears the legend, in Cyrillic and Latin script:

Long Live Aslan Dargan
Beloved President for Life!

That's funny, Wendy thinks, he must be a lot older. Then she realises that dictators throughout history love to present a young and virile image of themselves.

Finally, she registers a black Mercedes salon car parked at the foot of the stairs. A tall young man, bundled up in a long black coat stands by the car. He, too, is wearing a fur hat and she can see his breath condense in the freezing air.

As Wendy descends the stairs, he moves to their foot.

'Dr. McPherson?' he asks.

'Yes,' she replies.

'Welcome to Kesheva. How was your flight?'

'Fantastic!' says Wendy with genuine enthusiasm. From what I can remember of it, she thinks.

'My name is Rustram Abdulin. I'm an aide to His Excellency the President. I've been sent to take you to your accommodation. Then I am sure you will want to rest. I'll introduce you to your staff and then leave you in peace. Tomorrow I will show you around our lovely city.' As he speaks, he ushers Wendy to the car.

'Staff?'

'Yes, an elderly couple. They have worked for the His Excellency for many years. They speak a little English.'

Wendy gets into the car and feels a welcome blast of heat. Rustram gets into the front, next to the driver. With what Wendy thinks is remarkable efficiency, two baggage handlers arrive with her luggage and stow it into the trunk of the car.

A line of disembarked passengers from the aircraft make their way towards the terminal building, escorted by soldiers who flank the column. Wendy notices that the younger men among the passengers are being detached from the line and led to a separate entrance. She comments on this to Rustram.

'Nothing to worry about,' he says. 'It's just to speed up the immigration process. We let the families go first at this time of night. Get the children tucked up in their beds.'

'How thoughtful.' She decides she is going to like Kesheva. 'But what about me?' she asks as the car speeds off to an access road, 'I haven't been through immigration and customs.'

'You are a guest of His Excellency; you do not need to be checked.' Rustram sounds hurt at the very suggestion that she might have to join the common herd.

The car skirts the terminal building and joins the main road. She sees a number of armoured vehicles parked adjacent to the road, their occupants lolling behind the machine guns in the turrets.

'Why are there so many soldiers around the airport?' she asks Rustram.

'Security, Dr. McPherson. We all live in troubled times. I believe you have armed police in your own airports and train stations.'

Wendy has to concede the sad truth of this as the limousine circles the roundabout and then shoots off along the six-lane expressway. The car's powerful headlights illuminate the immediate surroundings, which seem to consist of flat, treeless desert.

'How far is the city?' she asks.

'Ten kilometres. We won't be long.'

But after about only one kilometre, they slow down to pass a roadblock. Concrete bollards block off two lanes on both sides of the expressway and again the soldiers are backed up by armoured cars. The car stops and Rustram winds down his window, letting a blast of bitter air in. He speaks briefly to the soldiers, who step back and snap sharp salutes at him and raise the striped barrier to let them pass. They go through the same procedure three more times before the city looms out of the night.

The suburbs of Kesheva are lined with monolithic apartment buildings. At this time of night, they are mainly in darkness but some have dim lights still burning, hardly making an impression on the blackness of the moonless night. The streets are deserted and unlit by streetlights, with not a car or bus in sight, very different to the twenty-four-hour vibrancy of London that Wendy is used to. Anyway, she thinks, it's too bloody cold to be out and about.

They turn off the expressway and take to more normal-sized urban streets. The houses here are smaller with tiny gardens with trees, bare now in the middle of winter. She sees a small park with swings, slides, and climbing frames that shows a more human, friendlier face to the city. On a plinth in the centre of the park stands a statue of a figure she recognises from the airport: Aslan Dargan stands with his arm raised in heroic pose, blessing his people.

The car stops outside a pair of wrought-iron gates set in a high wall and the driver gets out to open them. A short drive along a tree-lined avenue leads to a two-storey villa that is brightly lit. As the car draws to a halt, the double doors are thrown open and a man and woman emerge.

The woman wears a headscarf and a baggy dress with bright lozenges of red and green. Her face is brown and lined and Wendy guesses her age to be in the late fifties. The man wears a felt pillbox cap with a black waistcoat over a faded shirt and loose brown trousers tucked into black felt boots. He is older than the woman and his face, too, is lined. Like Katerina on the aircraft, their features show a distinct central Asian origin, with the high cheekbones and slight slant to their dark eyes.

They hold their ground just outside the door as Rustram alights from the car and opens the back door for Wendy.

'This is Ruthinna,' says Rustram, indicating the woman, who curtsies, and smiles with a flash of gold teeth, 'and her husband, Oybek. They will look after you while you are in Kesheva. Ruthinna is a good cook and Oybek is,' he pauses for a moment, trying to find the right word, 'a handy person,'

'Handyman,' Wendy corrects automatically.

'As you say, a *handyman*.'

'Pleased to meet you,' Wendy says politely.

'We are honoured to have you in Kevesha,' Oybek says in heavily accented English.

'Let us go in out of the cold,' says Rustram. Oybek helps the driver unload Wendy's cases as Rustram takes Wendy into the building, which she finds is warm to the point of stifling.

A wide entrance hall, paved with ceramic tiles in geometric patterns with dark wood-panelled walls and ending in an impressive staircase is bisected by a number of doors. Ruthinna bustles past them, opening the doors as they come to them. Wendy has an impression of comfortable reception rooms carpeted by rugs and filled with armchairs and sofas. How many people live here? she wonders.

Oybek and the driver carry her cases in and up the staircase and disappear onto the first floor, where she assumes her bedroom will be. The heat is getting to her and she shucks off her puffer jacket, which is immediately whisked away by Ruthinna.

'It's lovely and warm in here,' she comments rather inanely to Rustram.

'A legacy from our late Soviet friends,' he explains. 'All the buildings in Kesheva are heated by a central power plant that sends super-heated steam along pipes to every building in the city, free of charge. Our winters are cold, as you may have noticed, so we need to keep warm. Nowadays, of course, all the power plants in the country are oil-fired so we are quite environmentally friendly. No more coal!'

Ruthinna is back, bearing a tray with a teapot and small bowls for the tea and leads Wendy and Rustram into one of the sitting rooms. She places the tray on a small table, inlaid with mother-of-pearl.

'Please,' she says shyly. 'Welcome to your home. Drink.'

Wendy sinks into an armchair, realising that despite her vodka-induced sleep on the plane, she is very tired.

Rustram takes a polite sip or two of the tea and takes his leave.

'I will return tomorrow, or later today,' he laughs, 'when you are rested and show you the old city. It is a World Heritage Site,' he says proudly. 'You have the day off. His Excellency is expecting you on Thursday. Good night and sleep well.'

Wendy drinks her tea, yawns and stretches.

'Please, I take you to your bed,' says Ruthinna and leads Wendy upstairs to a room containing a massive bed, a dressing table and a wardrobe large enough to fit every item of clothing that Wendy possesses, both here and what is left in her Acton flat.

'Oybek has put your clothes in cupboard,' Ruthinna tells her. 'Bathroom here.' She opens a door on the side of the room and Wendy sees a room with a bathtub she can do lengths in, a large throne of a WC, a bidet, a shower stall and a small table with a vase of flowers. Where did they get the flowers from in the middle of winter? she thinks. Do I really care? No! Time for bed.

Ruthinna shows her a bell-button by the side of the bed. 'You want, you ring, I come.'

'Thank you. Thank you for making me so welcome,' Wendy gushes.

'Is no problem. Welcome to your home. In morning, you ring, I make breakfast. Sleep well.'

'Oh, I will,' says Wendy to Ruthinna's departing back and goes to try and find where Oybek has hidden her pyjamas.

It has been a long and strange day.

8

Wendy wakes up when Ruthinna enters the bedroom bearing breakfast on a tray. The tray contains a teapot and bowl, two boiled eggs, fresh buttered bread and yoghurt and Wendy's mouth starts to water in anticipation. She pulls herself upright in the bed and Ruthinna places the tray on her lap.

'Sleep good?'

'Wonderfully,' Wendy replies, her hangover a thing of the past.

'Tonight I make *plov*,' Ruthinna announces.

Wendy mishears 'love' and has a sudden picture in her head of Ruthinna and Oybek writhing in wrinkly congress. Too much information, she thinks and is at a loss how to reply. Instead she gives Ruthinna a weak smile, perhaps at her good fortune to have an active sex life at her age.

'Is national dish of Kesheva,' Ruthinna tells her proudly.

'Sorry,' says Wendy, feeling ashamed of her thoughts. 'What did you say?'

'*Plov*. Is national dish. Is very good.'

'Oh, *plov!* What is it?'

'Is sheep and carrots and rice.'

'Sounds yummy,' says Wendy with feigned enthusiasm.

'Please to eat now. Mr Rustram is here to show you city.'

Wendy makes short work of her breakfast, has a swift shower

– careful not to get her hair wet, pulls on as many layers of clothing as she can and goes downstairs.

Rustram is waiting for her, clad in a long, black coat and holding a fur hat in his hand.

'This is for you,' he says, handing her the hat. 'It's quite cold today. You will need it.'

'What about you?' she asks.

'I was born here,' he laughs and then pulls a fur cap out of his pocket like a conjurer with a rabbit. 'Did you sleep well?'

'Yes, I did. Ruthinna tells me she is going to make *plov* tonight.'

'Ah, the national dish. It is very good.'

'I look forward to it,' Wendy says dubiously.

'Let us go. I want to show you our city. Are you ready?'

'Looking forward to it. Let's go!'

'The best way to see the city is on foot. Some of the streets are too narrow for a car. If you get too cold, we can stop at a tea house.'

'OK.'

They set off along the drive, pass the gates and turn in the direction of the city. Now that it is day, the streets are crowded with people going in all directions, walking briskly in the cold air, their breath streaming in clouds around their heads. Wendy thrusts her hands into the pockets of her puffa jacket and makes a mental note to try and buy a pair of gloves asap.

Rustram slips into tourist-guide mode as they stride along.

'Kesheva is a very old city. It was an important trading post on the Silk Road and has a long tradition of silk weaving and carpet making. Tamerlane held his court here from time to time in the fifteenth century and after his death it was ruled by a minor branch of his descendants who styled themselves Khans until it attracted the attention of the Russian Empire.'

'Oh, why was that?'

'They had the unfortunate habit of either enslaving foreigners or murdering them. The lucky ones were flung off the minaret of the Hasan Murad mosque.'

'The *lucky* ones?'

"The Khans were very inventive when it came to killing people,' says Rustram laconically.

'So what happened with the Russians?'

'The tsarist Government sent a small delegation to Khan Mahmud to ask him to stop his anti-social ways towards travellers; he had them rolled up in carpets and trampled to death by camels in the Maidan.'

'Ah, I can see why that didn't go down to well with the Russians.'

'The next thing Khan Mahmud knew there was a small Russian army armed with modern weapons sat outside the walls demanding his surrender. That ended the rule of the Khans rather abruptly. A group of his ministers hauled him up the minaret and pitched him over and then opened the gates to welcome our Russian liberators from tyranny.'

'And then the Russians stayed until the collapse of the Soviet Union?'

'You've got it.'

Their walk has taken them to the massive ochre walls of the old city. The walls tower thirty feet over their heads, great sloping masses of sunbaked mud, many feet thick, topped with ramparts. They enter the old city through the Ota Davorza Gate, a long tunnel cut through the wall.

The old city of Kesheva seems to Wendy an architectural jewel of what she supposes are late Medieval Islamic buildings. The road from the gate cuts through tiny, winding streets of mud-brick houses to the central Maidan Square, which is surrounded on three sides by beautiful blue-tiled buildings, which Rustram tells Wendy were madrassas, boarding schools for Islamic scholars. Wendy recognises them from a holiday in Iran she had three years ago. Their size and scale are impressive; each is capped by a massive dome topped by a crescent moon. The tiles gleam in the weak winter sunlight and Wendy can only imagine what the effect must be in the full glare of summer. The Maidan is crowded with people, Keshevans of all ages and knots of tourists following the little flags of their guides. Policemen in pairs patrol the crowds.

'Wow!'

'It is impressive, isn't it?' says Rustram proudly. 'This is a UNESCO World Heritage site.'

'I'm not surprised. It's fabulous.'

Rustram leads them on to another square.

'This is the Hasan Murad mosque.'

'And this must be the infamous tower,' says Wendy, looking up a cylindrical tower covered with geometric blue, green, black and white tiles. At the apex of the tower, an inscription in Arabic writing curls around.

'Yes. Let us go in. I want to show you something.'

They step over the raised doorstep and into the gloom of the building. The building is long and low, the ceiling supported by a great number of wooden pillars.

'We call this the forest of Kesheva; there are over two hundred pillars. Most are hundreds of years old.'

'Wow!' Wendy says again.

'That building on the other side of the square is the Kukhna Ark, the principal residence of the Khans and also the citadel of the city. The building to the right of the Ark is the harem with the baths for the ladies. The story goes that the Khans used to sit on the balcony over the pool and watch the ladies bathe. The Khan would toss down an apple and the lucky lady that caught it would be his companion for that night.'

'Lucky girl,' says Wendy, drily.

'Yes, it was considered a great honour. At times the Khans had two hundred and fifty ladies in their harems.'

'Did they know all the girl's names?' asks Wendy, a proud feminist.

'Probably not,' Rustram admits. 'But I think it didn't trouble the Khans over much. Come on, there is much more to see. Unless you want to stop for some tea?'

'No, let's go on. I'm fascinated. It's like stepping back in time.'

They enter a maze of streets lined with small shops; most of which are now given over to selling tourist tat with groups of tourists bravely trying to bargain down the prices, which have been set at three times the actual asking price. It is a game the Keshevan shopkeepers have learnt to love to play since the country has opened up to visitors.

Wendy and Rustram enter a vaulted building crowded with more stalls selling everything under the sun. Chinese electronic goods are sold next to traditional Keshevan textiles; fruit and vegetables are being purchased by Keshevan matrons, their heads covered by bright headscarves, and heaped into thin plastic bags; a row of butchers' shops have carcasses of sheep and lambs hanging from hooks (at this time of year there are no flies – in the summer it is a different story); clothes shops have racks of quilted jackets and trousers to fit all sizes; knock-off copy handbags with slightly mis-spelt names of famous designer labels are being thrust at tourists and touts are trying to entice the unwary to visit their cousin's carpet shop. Everyone seems to be shouting and waving their arms in the air and the racket reverberates back off the arched ceiling.

'This is the bazaar,' Rustram yells into Wendy's ear.

'No kidding!'

The presence of so many people in the enclosed space has raised the temperature. Wendy unzips her jacket and removes her new fur hat. A stall heaped high with circular loaves of bread (called, with what Wendy regards as strange culinary negativity, *non*, according to Rustram) sends off steaming temptation, like the smell of fresh bread pumped out by supermarkets, and is doing brisk business.

Each stall in the bazaar has a small portrait photograph of Aslan Dargan hanging up in a prominent position and a large poster photograph of Dargan giving his now familiar blessing is displayed high over the entrance to the bazaar. Wendy comments on this to Rustram.

'The people all love His Excellency,' Rustram replies, deadpan.

'They must do.'

'Tomorrow you will meet him. You will love him too.'

Wendy is not sure whether this is a straightforward comment or an order but decides she will make her own mind up.

'Does the President live here in the old city?' she asks.

'No. His Excellency lives in the Peoples' Palace outside the city. It used to be the residence of the Russian governor but has been extensively modernised over the last ten years. It is also the seat of the government of Kesheva where the ministers consult with His Excellency.'

'Handy,' Wendy murmurs.

'Are you hungry?' Rustram asks, abruptly changing the subject.

The smell of the freshly-baked bread has worked its magic and Wendy realises that she is, indeed, ready for a spot of lunch.

They leave the bazaar and Rustram leads them to an old caravanserai adjacent to the bazaar that has been converted to a guesthouse with a restaurant on the ground floor. The restaurant is small, crowded with tables and has high, arched ceilings. The air is redolent of grilled meat. They find a table and sit down under the inevitable gaze of Aslan Dargan..

'Please allow me to order for us,' says Rustram and barks a stream of words to the middle-aged waitress, who, like Ruthinna, is the proud owner of a set of gold teeth. Wendy, with her basic knowledge of Turkish tries to follow what is being said but many of the words are completely foreign to her.

'What's with the gold teeth?' she asks.

'It is a tradition here. People did not use banks. It was a way of protecting the family's wealth. If times were hard they could always pull a tooth and sell it.'

'I don't notice many men with gold teeth.'

'No. Traditionally it is the women who have them.'

'So if times are hard the woman loses her teeth?' Wendy's feminist sensibilities are shocked.

'Yes,' says Rustram in a tone that implies he sees no problem.

'Are you married?'

'Yes.'

'And does your wife have gold teeth?'

'No. I use a bank. This is the twenty-first century. Kesheva is a modern country. But my mother did.'

The food arrives: a hearty soup with large mutton dumplings floating in it; a bowl of yoghurt with chives and cucumber; *samsa* pastries baked in a clay oven like a tandoor and skewered mutton kebabs from a charcoal grill. All this accompanied by copious mounds of *non* bread and tea.

'How many people did you order for?' Wendy gasps at the steaming piles of food.

'This is just for the two of us. A little lunch. Ruthinna is making *plov*. I didn't want to spoil your appetite.'

'You *are* joking?'

'No,' he says, in all apparent seriousness and starts to rip in to the loaves of bread. 'Please, what do you say? "tuck in"'

She is surprised at how the frosty air and the long walk through the old city has sharpened her appetite and thirty minutes later lolls in her chair, replete, and surveys the jumble of empty plates on the table.

'That,' she says with emphasis, 'was good.'

'Now I will take you back to your lodgings. I am sure you will want a little sleep.'

'Sounds like heaven.'

9

Thursday. Wendy's second day in Kesheva. She wakes up convinced she has put on at least a couple of kilos. Ruthinna's plov was a mountain of rice and carrots with what looked like half a sheep. 'Eat, Dr McPherson, eat!' And Wendy dutifully did until her eyes bulged and her stomach groaned. At this rate, by the time she goes home, she will look like a blimp. She takes a shower, gets dressed in a neat little formal suit, pencil skirt, white blouse, jacket and court shoes. How much longer will this fit me, she thinks. At this rate, I'm going to end up in a kaftan or a Mumu.

She goes downstairs where Ruthinna produces a breakfast of tea, toast, yogurt, boiled eggs and honey. In for a kilogramme, in for a kilo, thinks Wendy as she tucks in. She is aware of having eaten more in the last thirty-six hours than she eats in a week in London.

At ten o'clock on the dot, Rustram arrives in the Mercedes to take her to meet the President.

They drive through the twisting streets of the Old Town until they hit a four-lane highway and are stopped at a checkpoint manned by soldiers. Rustram shows a pass and they are ushered through.

'What's with all the security?' Wendy asks him. 'I noticed it at the airport and then all the way on the drive to the city. And there were police everyway in the city yesterday. Is there some kind of security alert?'

'No, no. Nothing to worry about. Kesheva is perfectly safe,' Rustram reassures her.

But Wendy is far from reassured. 'Come on! All these check points and armed soldiers and police in the streets. That's *not* normal! At least, it isn't where I come from.'

'But then, you have terrorist attacks in the West, don't you? London, Paris, Brussels, Nice, Germany. And 9/11 of course.'

'So are you expecting a terrorist attack?'

'No. We have security to make sure it cannot happen here.'

There seems to be no answer to that logic so Wendy looks out of the window. They are driving through open, flat countryside of what looks like desert. She notices that there are no other cars on the road and comments on this.

'It's a restricted road. It is only used by government ministers. And the President, of course.'

'It's good to be king,' Wendy mutters to herself.

They stop at another checkpoint. In the distance, she can see a group of buildings surrounded by a high wall that seems to stretch for a kilometre either side of a gate flanked by watchtowers. Other watchtowers rise over the wall at regular intervals.

They slow down as they hit a long row of speed bumps. A triple line of concrete dragon's teeth litter the desert.

This guy is seriously paranoid, she thinks.

Two T-14 Armata battle tanks are parked guarding the gates; she sees more soldiers in the watchtowers.

'Not taking any chances, then,' she says to Rustram.

'Are your leaders not guarded?' he replies.

She tries to imagine Chieftain 2 battle tanks parked by the gates of Downing Street. Nah!

'They do have police body guards,' she concedes.

'Well, there you are!' Rustram says, triumphantly.

'Yes, but…' She has seen a machine gun in the tower swing in their direction and is now pointing directly at the car. Rustram does not appear to be fazed.

The car crawls to the gate, Rustram shows his pass and a soldier retracts the row of metal teeth designed to rip the tyres off a speeding car. They enter the compound.

Inside, it resembles a small town. A large four-storey building, clad in white marble and dazzling in the winter sunshine looms ahead.

Rustram is back in tour-guide mode. 'That is the Peoples' Congress building. They meet once a year to discuss matters of national interest. The members are elected by the people of Kesheva in free and fair elections every ten years,' he says proudly. 'They can make suggestions for the good of the country.'

'Uh-huh,' says Wendy, trying to keep the scepticism out of her voice. She is beginning to get the feeling that Kesheva is not exactly a Peoples' Paradise.

To either side of the Congress building are a series of two-storey low-rise buildings painted in a pastel yellow to blend with the desert.

'Those are the ministries,' Rustram tells her, as they make their slow progress. 'The ministers themselves and their families live in comfortable villas, also in the compound. There are stores and leisure facilities and also housing for workers. The main ministries are outside Kesheva. So only the ministers and their top advisors live here.'

Wendy is reminded of the Japanese shoguns who kept their

friends close and their rivals closer.

They have come to another wall and another gate and another tank.

'This is the President's own compound,' Rustram explains, presenting his pass again. A soldier peers closely into the car and writes something down on a clipboard, checking his watch as he does so.

Through the gates and they are in the Land of Oz. The desert has turned into green lawns studded with trees and sprayed by lawn sprinklers that shimmer in the sunlight. A small herd of oryx graze on the verdant grass and a fountain erupts in a small ornamental lake.

'The lawn is heated in the winter, so grows all year round.'

'I was wondering.' Wendy says. 'It was bitterly cold this morning.'

The building that sits in the middle of this fairyland is an appropriate sugar-coated copy of a Loire chateau, all white marble and pointed turrets, only about three times the size of the original. Outbuildings nestle around like chicks around a mother hen.

One final security check and they pull up into a courtyard. A soldier appears and opens the car doors for them.

'His Excellency is expecting you,' he says in English.

'Then we must not keep him waiting,' Rustram says. 'Let us go.'

10

Inside, a vestibule that would not look out of place in a five-star hotel, Wendy thinks. Pink marble cladding on the walls; mirrors that cast a faint rosy glow. In the distance, a staircase ascends to the upper floors. At its foot, two bearded soldiers stand to attention, shiny stainless steel helmets on their heads and sub-machine guns slung at port arms across their chests. Rustram leads the way.

They climb the stairs to the next level. High double doors, white with gilding, give on to rooms off a landing the size of a helipad. More soldiers stand guard. Rustram obviously knows his way around as he heads straight for a pair of doors on the right hand side of the landing and nods at the two soldiers standing there. They nod back, but Wendy sees them surreptitiously slip a finger inside the trigger guard of their weapons. She feels she ought to spread her arms wide. 'Look! Not armed. Harmless. *He* wants to see *me*.' But, of course, she says nothing.

Rustram knocks softly at the doors, which are immediately opened, as if someone was standing just inside waiting for his knock. As, it turns out, they were.

Wendy and Rustram enter the room. It is smaller than Wendy might have imagined, not on the same scale as the spaces she has seen so far. Tucked discreetly to one side (safely away from the window) is a desk of polished mahogany upon which papers are scattered. A beautiful hand-woven carpet depicting a stylised garden with flowers and birds covers most of the floor. Three sofas are placed in an open square with small occasional tables by their sides. In a corner, on another small table, stands an exquisite silver samovar.

Aslan Dargan rises from behind his desk to greet them. He looks twenty years older than his ubiquitous portrait. She guesses he is in reality about sixty. He is also shorter than the impression given by his picture, five foot eight or so. His bushy black hair is swept back in a pompadour and Wendy has an impression that black dye has been skilfully employed to make him look youthful. His body is compact, but again, that might be the result of the skilful tailoring of his grey business suit.

Dargan strides across the room, his hand extended in welcome.

'Dr. McPherson, please let me welcome you to Kesheva.' His handshake is firm and warm.

'I'm honoured to be here, Your Excellency,' she replies. 'From what I have seen, Kesheva is a beautiful country.'

'And you shall see a whole lot more during your stay with us,' he assures her. 'Please, take a seat.' He waves his hand in the direction of the sofas. As if by magic, a young woman enters the room carrying a tray bearing a silver teapot and the tea bowls Keshevans use to drink tea. She crosses to the samovar, fills the pot with hot water and places the tray on one of the small tables before gliding silently from the room.

'Tea?' asks Dargan, preparing to play mother. Wendy nods; 'My son, Jamshid, is going to study Law in the UK,' says Dargan, cutting to the chase. 'He does not want to go but he will do as he is told. After that, he will go to Harvard to do an MBA. It will be your task to prepare him for his academic studies in the West.'

Oh great, Wendy thinks, another student who does not want to study but has been told by his father that he must. *Plus ça change.* She forces a smile and tries to look enthusiastic.

Perhaps Dargan senses her feelings. He says: 'I know the task might prove difficult. The boy is not, what is the expression? "over the moon" but he will do as he is told. The alternative is a stint in the army. In a frontier unit. As a private soldier.'

'If I may say so, Your Excellency, your own English is *very* good.'

Dargan beams at the compliment. 'I am a graduate of the Moscow Institute of Foreign Languages. Our erstwhile Soviet overlords had their uses.'

'When would you like me to start? I'd like a preliminary meeting with Jamshid to do a number of diagnostic tests.'

'You shall meet him this very morning. He is waiting and probably sulking here in the palace. Try and get him to put down his games console and don't let him use his smartphone. The kids of today! When I was his age, I was in the Young Communists helping out in the cotton fields in all weathers. It did me no harm. How is your tea?'

Wendy's mind is spinning; the task promises to be daunting. Dargan gives the impression of being down to earth but the few scions of Middle Eastern ruling families she has taught have not always been easy. Accustomed to getting their own way and growing up in total privilege and unlimited wealth can have a certain effect on the character of the young: 'Daddy, I've totalled the Lamborgini, buy me another!' 'What colour would you like, son?'

'The tea is delicious,' she says.

'Excellent! Now, perhaps you would like to meet Jamshid. My very good aide, Major Abdulin, will take you to see him.'

Ah, so Rustram is military, is he? Well, what did you expect? After only two days in the country, Wendy is beginning to realise that Kesheva is a military/police state.

'It would be my pleasure, Excellency,' Rustram announces, getting to his feet, clicking his heels and bowing his head.

Dargan also rises and drifts back to his desk. The audience is over.

11

Major Abdulin, as Wendy now thinks of Rustram, takes her along a corridor to a less ostentatious, but still guarded, staircase.

'His Excellency's private family quarters are on the second floor. It is here he relaxes with his family away from the cares of state.'

They have certainly got you sprouting the party line, Wendy thinks as she follows him up the stairs. The entrance to the second floor is barred by a heavy door and another helmeted soldier. Rustram flashed his pass and the soldier rings a bell set next to the doorframe. A moment passes and then a spy hole in the door is opened from the inside. Rustram holds his pass up to the spy-hole and there is the sound of bolts being drawn back. The door swings open heavily. Wendy gets the impression that it is reinforced by sheets of metal set into the door itself. No one is going to get in here uninvited in a hurry.

'Major Abdulin and Dr McPherson to see Jamshid Dargan. He will be expecting us.'

A clipboard is consulted and Wendy and Rustram are admitted and escorted down a corridor leading off to the left. Doors bisect the corridor to left and right, but they are closed and give no clue as to what lies behind them. As they proceed along the corridor the sound of hip-hop music gets ever louder. Wendy makes out the words:

Yo' ma bitch
Go get the switch
'Cos I gotta itch
Yo' gonna need a stitch

'I believe that is very popular in the West,' Rustram replies drily as they come to a halt outside a door that is positively vibrating from the bass line of the music. Rustram hammers on it with his fist to make himself heard.

After two minutes of beating, the music level drops to the decibel level of a 747 taking off and the door inches open and a face peers out of the gloom. Jamshid Dargan is seventeen; his face is pale as befits someone who lives in their room with the drapes drawn most of the time. He is taller than his father, but thin, almost gangly. His hair is shaved at the sides of his head and topped by a thick cascade of dreadlocks on the top. Wendy is reminded of Sideshow Bob from the Simpsons. Incongruously, he is only clad in a pair of Y-front underpants.

'Yo,' he says, by way of a greeting.

'This is Dr McPherson. From England,' Rustram introduces Wendy.

'My father said you were coming,' Jamshid admits grudgingly.

'Good of you to dress up,' Rustram mutters but his words are lost under the racket of the music. 'Can we come in? And, please, turn the music off,' he yells.

Jamshid turns on his heel and disappears into the interior. The volume lowers until it is possible to have a shouted conversation. 'A little more, please,' Rustram insists. With a pout, Jamshid addresses the banks of speakers, twiddles a knob and the music stops. 'And, perhaps, some daylight?' Rustram suggests.

Jamshid presses a button on the wall and the drapes slide open. He blinks as the winter sunshine floods the room.

It is the room of the archetypal teenager if they lived in a room the size of a tennis court and had limitless pocket money; posters of music stars and football teams cover the wall and discarded clothing covers the floor. The sound system would not be out of place in an Ibizan nightclub; state-of-the-art electronics are banked up on desks and tables, crowned by a 62-inch television screen. Armchairs and sofas are scattered about and a table holds a tray with the remains of a meal abandoned on it. Wendy notes a number of empty beer bottles (imported) strewn amongst the clothing.

Jamshid flings himself into an armchair and hugs his knees to his chest, his face going into its default mode of sulky pout.

This is going to be a challenge, Wendy concedes to herself but screws on her brightest smile.

'I believe you are going over to England to study Law,' she says in her most cheerful tone.

Jamshid does not reply.

'Your father has brought me here to help you get ready,' she continues undaunted.

'I don't want to go,' Jamshid says.

'Why not?' Wendy tries.

'Waste of time.'

'I believe the alternative is a spell in the Army,' Rustram points out.

'Nobody asked you, *Major*!' Jamshid snaps, his anger and resentment flaring up. 'Why don't you go away and leave us alone? Go and find someone to torture.' Wendy likes the fact that he speaks English for her benefit.

Rustram flushes red. (Anger or embarrassment, possibly both. This is a new side to Rustram Abdulin. *Torture?* He seems so *nice*, Wendy thinks. I can't imagine him pulling toe nails out or sticking electrodes to people's genitals.)

Rustram does the clicky heels, bowing thing again and strides out of the room.

'I'll wait for you, Dr. McPherson,' he calls over his shoulder.

'Your English is very good. Did you go to the Moscow Institute like your father?'

'No. I've had home tutors since I was very young. You are just the latest in a long line. I speak Keshevan, of course, and Russian and some Farsi as well as English.'

'Then why does your father think you need me?'

'Beats me!' Jamshid gets up and goes over to a small refrigerator built into a desk, roots around inside and pulls out a bottle of beer, opens it and takes a swig. Suddenly remembering his manners, he asks Wendy if she would like one.

'Bit early for me,' she declines his offer.

'Fuck all else to do around here.' Jamshid takes another pull at the bottle.

Wendy tries another tack: 'So, what do you do with yourself all day?'

'Listen to music. Play games. Get drunk.'

'What about your friends?'

'What friends?'

'Surely you must have friends. Everybody has friends.'

'Not really,' says Jamshid. 'Sometimes I hang out with the kids of the ministers that live in the compound but mostly they're bores. Their parents make them hang out with me to cosy up to my father.'

'Oh, you poor kid,' says Wendy involuntarily. Her own childhood was a happy time. Despite being bright, she had a gang of mates that she did all the usually things with; parties, boyfriends, dancing, going to gigs, getting up to mischief in the town centre, underage drinking, throwing up, sports. She cannot imagine a life of isolation growing up in a gilded cage.

'I'm all right,' says Jamshid, defensively. 'I can have anything I want. I've got a sports car that I can drive around the compound. And horses in the stables.'

'Do you go into Kesheva much?'

'About as often as I go to the moon. My father says it is too dangerous unless I go with armed guards. People like Major Abdulin.' He gives a shudder and drains his bottle. 'That man is *creepy*. He is one of my father's hatchet-men.'

'I see you like football. What team do you support?'

'I like Barca and Liverpool and Juventus. I watch the matches on satellite.'

'What about the local teams? Do they play football in Kesheva?'

'Yeah. My brother is the captain of the national team.'

'Wow! Really? Is he good?'

'Not really, but he is my father's eldest son. He'd be the captain if he only had one leg and was blind.' A little bit of sibling jealousy? A touch of bitterness?

'So,' says Wendy, getting back to the matter in hand, 'what can I do to help you?'

'Like I said: beats me.'

'Have you heard of the IELTS test?'

'No. What is it?'

'The test British universities ask non-native students to take to determine their ability to study in the UK.'

'And?'

'We could work on that. I've got some materials with me we can work through.'

'Why?'

'So you can take it and get admission,' Wendy explains slowly.

'Waste of time!'

'And just why is that?'

'Don't you think I can just get someone else to take it for me? Some professor from the University here.'

'You mean *cheat* your way in?' Wendy, the professional academic, is scandalised.

'Why not? They'd be pleased to do it if they thought they were doing my father a favour.'

'And once you got to England? Who'd do your work for you?'

Jamshid laughs at Wendy's naivety.

'Really, Dr. McPherson? Even living here in this compound in Kesheva I have heard on online sites that produce essays ready-written for students with money. Any subject.'

Wendy is forced to admit the truth of this but is surprised Jamshid has heard of them. Perhaps there is more to this boy than meets the eye.

'What about day-to-day living? How will you manage?'

'*If* I go, my family has property in London. A place called Knightsbridge. We have year-round live-in staff. I will manage.'

'Don't you *want* to go to London? It's a wonderful city.

Vibrant. Multi-cultural.'

'You really don't get it, do you? My father has enemies. I will be surrounded by bodyguards at all times. It won't be any different to living in this, this *prison*! What kind of life do you think I have? Nothing!' Jamshid is on the verge of tears. Without thinking, Wendy moves over to him and gives him a hug.

At first he stiffens, rebuffing her but then gives in and sinks into the embrace. For all his bravado, he is just a lonely, lost little boy.

He pulls away and wipes his face.

'Don't you dare pity me,' he says.

'I'm sorry,' says Wendy, 'I thought you needed a hug. I've got a nephew and a niece not much older than you and I always gave them a hug when they were feeling down.' They probably resented it too. At least, after the age of ten when hugs from Auntie Wendy were even less cool than hugs from their parents. How independent we are in our teens when we need support the most, she thinks sadly.

'Perhaps we could just talk?' Jamshid suggests shyly. 'I think I would like that. You can tell me all about London and being a student. 'If I have to go, then I have to go. I might as well be prepared for it.'

'That could be a good start. Now, it's nearly twelve o'clock. I think I'd like a beer right about now.'

'I think we might be friends,' says Jamshid, heading for the fridge.

12

Rustram has procured a chair from somewhere and is sitting in the corridor like a naughty schoolboy waiting for Wendy to finish with Jamshid. They descend to the ground floor in silence, Jamshid's accusation is the elephant in the room between them.

Once in the car they both speak at the same time:

'How did you find our young prince?' says Rustram and

'Are you really a torturer?' asks Wendy, not really expecting him to answer her honestly; if she were a wielder of thumbscrews she *certainly* wouldn't admit to it.

'Of course I'm not a torturer,' Rustram answers vehemently. 'I'm an engineer seconded to His Excellency as an aide.'

'Honestly?'

'Honestly.'

'I'm very relieved to hear that, Rustram. You don't know how much.'

'Any way, how did you get on with young Jamshid?'

'Quite well, I think. Eventually. I think he is suffering from isolation. He needs to get out more, meet people of his own age.'

'It is difficult. He is the son of the President, after all, not a normal boy. He cannot mix with ordinary people for his own protection.'

'That's going to screw him up. What about when he goes

to the UK? He will have to mix then.'

'Even there he will be protected.'

'What about if he meets someone and he wants a bit of, you know, *privacy*?'

'The girl will be carefully vetted.'

'What about if it is a boy?' Wendy's university proudly flies the rainbow flag on its roof.

'That is, of course forbidden, both in Islam and the laws of Kesheva.'

'But not in the UK,' Wendy points out.

'It will not be an issue,' Rustram insists. 'Let us please change the subject. What did you talk about?'

'Oh, this and that. Student life in the UK. What he might expect from his studies.'

'That is good. His Excellency will be very pleased. Jamshid was being very difficult. If you can bring him round to the idea, you will have done your duty.'

'I aim to please,' says Wendy with a touch of sarcasm in her voice that Rustram chooses to ignore, or perhaps he does not pick up on it.

'What is your programme?'

'My programme?'

'Yes. What hours of classes have you arranged and what is your curriculum?'

'Well, I brought some materials with me. Materials for the IELTS exam, for example. But we have a problem there.'

'Oh, what?'

'Jamshid told me he can get a substitute to take the exam for him. I presume the British Council here will be the testing centre?'

'This is not a problem. If Jamshid has to take an examination then he *will* take it in person. I will make sure of that.'

'OK. Then I have access to my department's banks of materials online. I've got plenty of stuff to keep him busy.'

'The internet is monitored in Kesheva. Pornography is banned, as is subversive political content.'

'I wasn't planning to introduce him to *Hot Honey dot com!*' says Wendy indignantly. 'I'm absolutely not in favour of the exploitation and degradation of women.'

'No, no,' says Rustram hastily, 'I am sure you are not. And as there are no restrictions on the internet inside the Presidential compound, I am sure he has managed to find those sites for himself.'

'Well, then,' Wendy says, 'What's the problem? He will have to learn to examine and evaluate evidence for himself if he is to be a successful student in the UK. That's perhaps the most important function of our higher education system. Despite what the students think,' she adds ruefully. 'But there is also the question of learning to be independent.'

'I'm not sure I understand what you mean,' Rustram says.

'When a young adult goes to university it is, in most cases, the first time they have lived away from their homes and their parents. It is a bridging stage between school and the great big cruel world of work. They have to learn to live in the world for the first time. To budget their time and money. To make their own routines. To accept responsibility for their studies rather than be directed by their schoolteachers. They make friendships that may last their whole lives. This is even more so in the department where I work. Not only are these students leaving home, they are coming to a foreign country, studying in a foreign language in a foreign culture. This is what Jamshid will come to. He will need space to develop. He can't do that if you try to keep him in a bubble. Have you thought of that?'

'His Excellency will have thought of that,' Rustram said with complete conviction.

'I believe Jamshid has a brother. Did he study abroad?'

Rustram does not reply immediately. Then he says 'Stas Dargan did spend some time in the United States.'

'And?' Wendy feels there is something Rustram is not telling her.

'There was an unfortunate misunderstanding.'

'Are you going to tell me about it?'

'I'm afraid this is a state secret that you do not have any clearance for.'

'That bad, eh?'

'It was nothing bad; I am not allowed to speak of it.'

Wendy resolves to quiz Jamshid about his brother's doings in the United States. Perhaps that is why Aslan Dargan has decided to send Jamshid to study initially in the UK.

They are entering the outskirts of the city again, having negotiated the checkpoints along the highway.

'You still have not told me about your arrangements for your classes with Jamshid.'

'I thought two hours in the morning and two hours in the afternoon, if that is agreeable?'

'That sounds very acceptable. With a break at the weekend?'

'Yes. I don't want him to get sick of the sight of me,' she laughs.

'And weekly progress reports and details of the subjects covered and the topics discussed, please.'

So that's *my* weekends out of the window.

'Fine,' Wendy agrees.

'And copies of your lesson plans.'

Now you are pushing it, she thinks. I haven't written a lesson plan in years. Not as such. I always know what I want to cover but you have to allow for spontaneous discussion. Although, perhaps not in Kesheva!

'I'll see what I can do, but my lessons are very loose.'

'Nothing *too* unstructured. And absolutely no discussion of religious matters or politics.'

'Can we discuss the price of fish?' she asks in seeming innocence.

'I'm sorry, I do not understand?'

'I'm teasing you!'

'Ah. Please do not. This is a very sensitive matter. Jamshid will go on to have a very important role in the Government of Kesheva one day.'

'If he gets elected, surely.' Wendy is in a skittish mood.

'He will be,' replies Rustram in all seriousness.

Yes, Wendy thinks, I am sure he will be. It's the family business.

They arrive at Wendy's accommodation. Oybek is hovering in the driveway looking very excited. He rushes up to Wendy as she leaves the car.

'You have letter,' he announces. 'Delivered by hand. Please come see.'

Rustram makes to come with her but she has had enough of being minded.

'I'll see you tomorrow then. Same time?'

A look of annoyance flashes over his face for a moment and

then his smile returns. He can check with Oybek later who delivered it.

'Yes, same time. Enjoy the rest of your day. Will you go to the bazaar?'

'No,' she says, 'I'll be *far* too busy writing lesson plans and preparing our lessons for the week.'

Indoors a letter in a stiff white envelope sits on a table in the hallway. It is addressed to:

W. McPherson PhD

She opens it. It contains an embossed card bearing the seal of HM Government and carries the message that Her Britannic Majesty's Ambassador to the State of Kesheva requests her company at the Embassy's New Year function.

Wendy has managed to lose all track of time. Of course, tomorrow is New Year's Eve.

The invitation (or summons?) goes on to inform her that a car will collect her at eight p.m. and that dress is formal.

She remembers she forgot to pack her ball gown.

13

'By the way,' says Rustram when he calls for her the next morning, 'who was your letter from? I was unaware you knew anybody in Kesheva.' He knows the answer; after leaving Wendy yesterday he checked with Oybek.

'It was from the Embassy. I've been invited to a New Year's Eve party. Trouble is, it's formal wear.'

'And that is a problem?'

'I wasn't expecting to have to dress up. Anyway, here are my notes for today and next week,' she says, handing Rustram a bundle of papers. 'I don't think you will find anything to object to. I'm going to talk about things like topic sentences and argument and counter-argument. He likes football so we can start with discussing the merits of the Premier League versus La Liga. I've no idea what I'm talking about but I'm sure he does.'

'That's very good, Dr. McPherson,' Rustram laughs.

'For goodness sake, call me Wendy. All my students do. Dr. McPherson is for my official email. Otherwise I will have to refer to you as Major Abdulin.' She pauses: 'I can call you Rustram, can't I?'

'Of course, Wendy.' He says her name tentatively, as if trying out for size in his mouth. 'Thank you for these notes. I will make sure His Excellency sees them and pass on any comments to you.'

'They are pretty harmless.'

'And do you plan to go the Embassy party?'

'Yes. Perhaps I can keep my coat on.'

'Are you making a joke?'

'What do you think?'

'I am not sure. Sometimes I have trouble with the famous British sense of humour.'

'I'm joking. Don't worry. I'll dig something up.'

Although Friday is the most important day of the week for Muslims to attend the mosque, Kesheva has adhered to the old Soviet custom of a Saturday/Sunday weekend, today is just another working day. Wendy is whisked off to the Ministerial compound to resume her sessions with Jamshid. She has made it a rule that she'll avoid beer until lunchtime, and then only drink in moderation. She spends the morning trying to encourage Jamshid to take the session seriously and write a short piece debating the respective values of Barca and Liverpool FC and by midday has succeeded in getting Jamshid to produce a couple of paragraphs praising both teams. It's a start, she thinks. But we have a long way to go.

At precisely twelve o'clock, there is a knock on the door and the young woman who served the tea at Wendy's audience with Aslan Dargan pops her head around the door and asks them what they would like for lunch?

Jamshid settles for burger and fries.

'Perhaps something Keshevan?' the young woman asks Wendy.

Wendy remembers the vast quantities of local dishes she consumed on the first day and the piles of grilled lamb chops and rice Ruthinna made her last night.

'Just something light for me, please.'

Wendy and Jamshid are drinking their lunchtime bottle of beer when the young woman returns wheeling a trolley on which are half a dozen plates covered by silver cloches. A plastic bottle of tomato ketchup stands out incongruously.

She clears away some of Jamshid's mess of a table and sets out the plates, lifting the cloches to display the dishes beneath.

'I have brought you a selection: mutton kebab; *nakhot shurak* – chickpeas stewed with onions and meat; a *mastava* soup of rice and vegetables and *chalop* – yoghurt, chives and cucumber. And *non* bread, of course. There is also water and a local wine. I'm told it is very good.'

So much for a light lunch. If she eats even only a mouthful from each dish she will be fast asleep for the afternoon.

'Have Keshevans ever heard of a salad?' Wendy asks Jamshid.

'It is our tradition to feast our guests,' he tells her as the young woman backs out of the room.

'Jamshid, this is just too much. I'm contracted to be here for six months. I won't be able to fit into any of my clothes after a week; in six months I'll be wearing a tent!'

Jamshid thinks this is hilarious and opens another beer on the strength of it.

'Don't worry, I will speak to the kitchen staff. I, too, prefer simple food.' His simple lunch consists a half a dozen cheeseburgers and a huge pile of French fries that he proceeds to slather in ketchup.

How does he stay so skinny, Wendy wonders.

As they set about eating their lunch, Wendy says 'I believe your brother studied in America?'

'Yes. But he didn't stay there long.'

'Oh? Why was that? Didn't he like it?'

Jamshid is silent for a moment.

'They won't tell me but I think it something to do with a girl.'

'Fell in love, did he?'

'Please do not repeat this, Dr. Wendy, but I have the idea he was with a group of his friends who attacked and had sex with a girl against her will.'

Wow! That would NOT play well here at home in an Islamic country if it were to become widely known. Definitely a black mark. Another reason for keeping this boy on a tight leash in the UK.

'I won't say anything. Don't worry.'

'Thank you. I hope I can trust you?'

And I wonder how many people you *can* trust, she thinks. She finds herself feeling increasingly sympathetic towards this boy she has only known for two days. What must his life be like, trapped as he is by his family and his privilege?

No real friends; no real life; no freedom to be a normal teenager. She determines to do all in her power to enable him to escape to the normality of student life in England.

'Right, back to work. Listening comprehension. I will read a passage to you and I want you to answer the questions on this worksheet. I will read the passage twice. You have two minutes to read the questions before I start. Ready?'

On the drive home Rustram keeps grinning to himself like a little boy with a secret he is itching to let slip.

'What's up with you?' Wendy demands but he shakes his head and remains tight lipped. Then it starts to snow and within a matter of minutes visibility is down to the front of the vehicle. The driver slows the car to a crawl. The soldiers on the checkpoints huddle inside rain capes that are immediately caked with snow, making them look like sinister killer snowmen with their guns black against the white.

Good, Wendy thinks, I can wear my smart new puffa jacket tonight to the reception. Probably with a pair of jeans and a scarf!

Oybek is lurking in the drive again. He must have come out of the house when he heard the car pull in because he is only covered in a light dusting. Light shines out of the open door where Ruthinna stands guard. Oybek, too, has a silly grin plastered across his face. Must be catching or is the whole population of Kesheva in on a secret that no one has let on to me. Perhaps it is New Year fever; next year promises to be better than this.

Oybek opens the door for Wendy and she gets out, immediately hit by a gust of snow.

'You have big surprise,' Oybek tells her with a huge grin. In the light of the doorway, Wendy can see Ruthinna's gold teeth flashing in another soppy smile.

'You come quick out of snow. You have surprise,' Ruthinna calls.

Wendy makes a dash for the door and hears Rustram shout 'Happy New Year!' from inside the car. Oybek slams the door and the car disappears into the swirl of dancing snow.

'Is in bedroom,' Ruthinna beams.

For just a wild moment, Wendy speculates whether Keshevan hospitality runs to providing a super stud to keep her warm in the blizzard. I could think of worse ways to enter the New Year. My last shag hardly ignited any fireworks. She dismisses the idea as ridiculous wishful thinking. God, I must be getting desperate.

She goes up to her room. There, laid out on the bed is not a hunk wearing nothing but a smile and clenching a rose between his teeth, but four evening dresses. As well as a classic little black number there is a burgundy sleeveless with matching bolero jacket; a long, blue satin dress with three-quarter length sleeves and a stunning creation in cream silk, trimmed with what looks like antique lace.

Ruthinna is standing in the doorway grinning fit to burst at Wendy's surprise.

'Is gift from President. For party at Embassy.'

Cinders, you *shall* go to the ball!

14

With her hair washed and brushed until it shines like polished copper, Wendy puts on the last touches of make-up in front of the bathroom mirror.

'I can still scrub up nicely,' she says to her reflection, 'when all is said and done.' She has a flash of memory where she is standing in the ladies' loo in the university putting on her slap on that dreadful Friday in November and shudders. But that was another time and place and here she is waiting to be whisked away to a reception in the British Embassy, a VIP working for the ruling family of Kesheva. Whodda thunk it?

At half past seven, she waits in the sitting room on the ground floor of the villa. She has chosen the formal black evening gown that fits perfectly and shows just enough of a cleavage to be interesting. That bastard Tony always said her boobs were her best feature. Didn't make him stick around though, did it? Ruthinna fusses around her, paying her compliments.

'You will be best pretty lady. You see. I sure. Dress is lovely. Very sexy.'

'It was so kind of His Excellency. How did he know?'

'Maybe little bird tell him. Maybe little bird called Major Abdulin?'

'But how did he know? I only told him this morning.'

Ruthinna winks 'No secrets in Kesheva. Everyone know everyone business.'

Wendy is not sure if she is exactly comfortable with this knowledge but what the hell, she is not planning to overthrow the state.

The muffled sound of a car horn is heard from outside. Oybek comes in.

'Is car from Embassy. For you.'

Outside the blizzard shows no sign of abating. Through the curtain of falling snow, Wendy can just make out the shape of a boxy, little grey car with a three-inch layer of snow on the roof. The front window is wound down and an arm waves at her. She pulls on her puffa jacket, braves the elements, and slides her way to the car through the snow that is beginning to bank up in the drive. The court shoes that she has chosen to wear immediately fill with cold, wet snow. Thank God I didn't wear the glass slippers, she thinks flippantly, I'd have broken my neck by now.

The passenger side door swings open and she dives into the car, pulling the door closed behind her, collapsing into her seat in an undignified heap.

'Dr. McPherson?'

'The very same.'

'I'm Patrick Winterslow.'

'And you've brought it with you,' she says in an attempt at humour to detract from her loss of dignity.

'I'm sorry?'

'The winter! Never mind. Attempt at a joke.' She squirms around in her seat to get a better look at her companion. Her first impression of Patrick Winterslow is of Peirce Brosnan as James Bond. He has the same glossy black hair, brushed back from his forehead, blue eyes, a tight mouth and firm chin. He rings all the cliché buttons of a movie leading man. Scrunched up in the tiny Masda 2 she cannot properly judge his height but guesses he is over six feet tall. He is wearing evening dress complete with black bow tie. Straight from Central Casting. Happy New Year, Wendy.

'Shall we start again? Wendy McPherson.' She holds out her hand.

'Patrick Winterslow, Cultural Attaché. Pleased to meet you. Call me Paddy,' he says, taking her hand in a firm but not crushing grip and shaking it politely. He puts the car in gear and drives slowly and carefully towards the gate.

'I expected something a bit grander in the way of transport,' says Wendy, just for something to say.

'Austerity, Dr. McPherson. Cuts. Belts tightened all round in the Foreign and Commonwealth Office. The Ambassador drives around in a second-hand Lexus Hybrid. The Rolls is a thing of the past. We've got one, but it mainly lives in the garage. Comes out for ceremonials. Anyway, we are only a small station here. Half a dozen of us Brits and a few locally-employed staff. All of them spies for the Internal Security Service.'

'The what?'

'Internal Security Service. It's what the Keshevans renamed the KGB after the Soviets pulled out.'

'There *does* seem to be a lot of security about. We have to go through checkpoints all the way to the Ministerial Compound. And there are armed guards everywhere inside.'

'What do you know about Kesheva?' asks Paddy, his voice suddenly serious.

'Well, I researched the history, of course, before I came. How it used to be a Soviet Republic; that it is an Islamic country but that Islam is worn lightly; that Aslan Dargan took over after the Russians left; that he is President For Life; that the country is floating on oil.'

Winterslow is driving into a district Wendy has not yet seen, around the old walls and out to the suburbs. Through the snow, she can make out the shapes of villas nestling behind gated walls.

'This is the diplomatic quarter,' Paddy explains. 'We are all here. The Russians and the Yanks in great big compounds, us and the other Europeans in smaller ones, the neighbouring 'Stans something in between. The Middle Eastern countries are beginning to take an interest and are starting to snap up property and set up stations. South Americans aren't interested. Our friends the Chinese are getting very interested and are planning a big affair. At the moment, they are only represented by a legation but all that is going to change. It's all going to make a big difference to our social life,' he says with a laugh.

'What's happening tonight? At the reception?'

'Oh, usual sort of diplomatic bash. They come to us, some of us go to them. Lots of bubbly and snacks on crackers. Mingling and schmoozing. A bit of dancing. Have you got your glad rags on?'

'President Dargan sent me a selection of dresses. I wasn't expecting to attend any grand functions, so I didn't pack any of my extensive wardrobe.'

Paddy laughs, a flash of perfect white teeth. Wendy goes a bit weak at the knees.

'You've made a hit with His Excellency. Anyway, as I was saying, what do you know about Kesheva?'

'Only what I've just told you. I've not exactly been out and about meeting people. I've met the President and his son Jamshid and my minder, Major Abdulin and the old couple who look after me and that's about it. I've been a busy little bee teaching Jamshid and writing lesson plans and eating and that's about it. This is only my third day in the country, for Heaven's sake.'

'Fair enough. Look,' he says, turning the car into a drive, 'we are here now. I'll take you in and introduce you to the Ambassador and his wife and then let you mingle with the great and the good of the Diplomatic Corps and then catch up with you later once you have a glass in your hand.'

Her Britannic Majesty's Embassy to the Republic of Kesheva is housed in a villa building much like the one she is staying in herself. It is a two-storey building of white stucco with the Embassy coat of arms over the doorway which is framed by a portico and two plain pillars. The double doors stand open, welcoming. Yellow light shines from the ground floor windows, softly diffused by the falling snow.

A flunky with an open umbrella makes his way to the car and covers Wendy with it as she alights. An array of cars, some grand, some modest, are parked in the forecourt of the building and she can see people moving through the windows. From the opened doors, she can hear the faint sound of a string quartet playing something she does not recognise.

She enters and another flunky relieves her of her puffa jacket and vanishes off somewhere with it. Paddy has parked the car and joins her, taking her by the elbow and steering her into the reception room.

A man in his late middle age and a woman of similar vintage

stand stiffly just inside the room. Paddy propels Wendy towards them.

'Allow me to introduce his Excellency, the British Ambassador to Kesheva. Sir, this is Dr. McPherson who is in Kesheva at the request of the President to educate his youngest son.'

'Call me Jim,' says the Ambassador, shaking her hand. 'And this is my wife, Phoebe. We know all about you. The FCO told us you were coming. That's how we knew to invite you this evening. Precious few of us Brits in Kesheva. Glad you could make up the numbers.'

'How do you do?' says Wendy, formally.

'I'll be pleased when this blessed snow clears off. Hate the winters here.'

She can feel herself warming to this man who seems devoid of the airs and graces she imagined a high ranking diplomat would have.

'Don't think you have to stand here talking to me just to be polite. Go and get yourself a drink. We've got some decent stuff. British sparkling wine. Grown on the south coast. Planning to set up a vineyard ourselves, aren't we, old girl? When we retire. Can't come soon enough, eh?' The last part of this appears to be addressed to Phoebe, who has so far not spoken.

'We've bought a couple of acres in Hampshire, near Ringwood,' Phoebe confirms. 'Do you know it?'

'I'm afraid not,' Wendy confesses.

'Never mind,' says Phoebe.

'Off you go, then,' says Jim. 'There's food doing the rounds. Dig in. I can see the Head of the South Korean Legation coming in. Nice chap but a bit formal. Have to say hello.'

'I'll see you later, sir,' Paddy says as he escorts Wendy further into the large reception room where the string quartet saw away on a small raised dais. Yet another flunky floats past, carrying a tray of drinks. Paddy snags two glasses and hands one to Wendy. She sips the chilled wine and pronounces it to be good.

The guests appear to be an eclectic mix of nationalities and ages. Some are dressed in the national costumes of their countries but most are in formal Western evening dress. There is a low hubbub of conversation as people chat and mingle.

'I'll just introduce you to some of the more interesting folk and then I'm afraid I will have to leave you to your own devices for a while. I'll catch up with you later.'

Wendy quite fancies the idea of being caught up with by Paddy Winterslow.

15

It is nearly the magic hour when the Old Year will change into the New. Wendy has danced and chatted and even flirted the hours away. Food and strong drink has been consumed and she feels pleasantly mellow. Tomorrow she will go on the wagon but tonight she will party and bugger the consequences for tomorrow is another breakfast. Paddy Winterslow has been conspicuous by his absence. What duties does a cultural attaché have at this time of night to keep him away from an official bash? But then, here he is, like Prince Charming, at her elbow requesting the pleasure of a slow dance. The string quartet have been dispatched to another function and a mixture of oldies and soft rock is playing; Ray Davis is thanking someone for the days as Paddy takes her in his arms and gently swings her around the dance floor. Wendy is conscious of experiencing a Mills-and-Boon moment.

As the song ends, Paddy says 'Can I take you away for a moment for a chat?'

Take me, take me. Take me anywhere but take me now, her loins are shrieking.

He takes her to a small, windowless office furnished with a desk, an impressive-looking computer set-up and steel filing cabinets.

This is not quite what I had in mind, Wendy thinks, but, hey-ho, I've never done it on a desk before. Something new for the New Year.

Her erotic bubble is burst when Paddy asks her to sit down on the chair facing the desk and firmly plants himself on the other side. If he is aware of her disappointment, he gives no indication; he is sober and down to business.

'I asked you earlier what you knew about Kesheva.'

'Kesheva?' This is not the romantic foreplay she wants.

'Yes. I'd like to fill you in on the realities. Let's start with the Dargan family.'

'It's New Year's Eve. I was enjoying myself!' she protests.

'Dr. McPherson, this is important! Please pay attention.'

'Why now? Can't we have fun?'

'Later. Now listen! Try and take this in. Aslan Dargan runs this country with an iron fist. There is no opposition to speak off, and what opposition there was are now in jail if not 'disappeared'. His first wife, Deniza, is the mother of Kamilla. Kamilla is the Vice-President of the Kesheva National Oil Company and milks the revenues into the Dargan family bank accounts scattered around places like the Cayman Islands; Switzerland became a little too opaque as the banking centre of choice for dictators. Stas, her son, is a playboy of the old mould and also a thug; he has the concession for all imports of foreign cars, electronics and telecommunications.'

'I've heard of him. Didn't he get into trouble in the United States? Jamshid said something about a girl.' Wendy is fast sobering up.

'He was involved in a vicious gang rape. He and some friends abducted a girl from the campus where they were studying, raped and beat her. They were all arrested and charged with rape and aggravated assault. His father pulled diplomatic immunity for him, said he was the First Secretary at the Embassy and got him out. He's been persona non grata in the States ever since but that doesn't seem to worry him over much. He gets up to pretty similar tricks here at home. Dargan's second wife, Muattar, is the mother of your lad, Jamshid. They keep him wrapped up in cotton wool so he doesn't go off the rails like his step-brother,'

'So I've noticed. He's desperately lonely.'

'Dargan has plans for the boy. Stas is a dead loss. Oh, he is ambitious, right enough, but Dargan is a savvy old bird. He would not have lasted this long if he wasn't. Young Jamshid is the Dargan's best bet to continue the dynasty. He is an unknown entity and, as yet, not universally loathed in Kesheva like his brother.'

'How do you know all this?' Wendy asks. 'I thought you were the cultural attaché? Art shows and Morris dancers and stuff.'

'I'm in the Diplomatic Corps. It is part of my job to know what is going on in my posting.'

Wendy is beginning to have her suspicions about Paddy Winterslow. Why is he telling her all this? Where is it leading?

Winterslow is off on another tack: 'Kesheva is a predominantly Islamic country, but not exclusively so. During the Soviet era religion was frowned upon, while it was tolerated. Dargan is not about to make the same mistakes the Shah made in Iran. He allows religious freedom but stamps down hard on the more militant sects. There was a very nasty incident four years ago when the army fired on a religious demonstration that cost over sixty lives. It's been quiet ever since, but there is a festering undercurrent of fundamentalism. He throws the odd mullah in jail whenever discontent gets too close to the surface.

Again, unlike the Shah, he is not about to let his opponents go into exile in the West.'

'That explains all the security everywhere,' Wendy realises.

'Exactly. But there is a problem.'

'Which is?' Wendy's lustful impulses towards Paddy have, for the moment, subsided as her academic interest is piqued.

'Although Kesheva is floating on oil reserves, youth unemployment is high. Forty per cent of the population is under thirty years old and there is very little work to be had. Dargan makes sure nobody starves by paying a state stipend to all Keshevan citizens but the young want more. Do you know what Kesheva's second largest export after oil is?'

'No.'

'Young men.'

'What do you mean? Young men?'

'Young men emigrate to work in Russia. Mostly as unskilled labour but some of the luckier ones get good jobs and send money home to their families. However, far more worrying to Dargan are the ones who leave to become Jihadis.'

'Jihadis!'

'They go to fight in Afghanistan, Iraq, Syria, Libya. Anywhere where Islamic organisations need fighters and are willing to pay for them. Some go because they are true believers in the cause; others go because they can earn a fast buck. But for whatever reason, they all become radicalised and Dargan is terrified of them coming home, trained and hungry for change. Just like we in the West are leery of letting our wayward souls back in. The difference being that only a handful have left from the West. In Kesheva they have left in their thousands to fight the good fight.'

'I had no idea,' Wendy says.

'This is where you come in.'

'Me? What's it got to do with me?'

'You have unique access to the potential next ruler of Kesheva.'

'Jamshid?'

'Got it in one. You can talk to him, influence him. Keep him on side. Fill him up with Western liberal values. A little more democracy here, a little more equal distribution of wealth there. HM Government would be *very* grateful indeed!'

The scales fall from Wendy's eyes. She is being recruited to be, what? An agent of influence. A spy. Paddy Winterslow has more than a passing resemblance to James Bond: he works for the same organisation!

'So,' she accuses, 'you're a "cultural attaché" from Vauxhall. And I don't mean the Young Vic.'

He winks but doesn't confirm or deny.

'We would like you to submit reports on your dealing with young Jamshid. The sort of things you talk about. What he thinks about the ideas you discuss; his attitude to life. Any political leanings. That sort of things. Anything and everything about Jamshid is of interest to us.'

Oh great, Wendy thinks. First, I have to write copious notes for Rustram and now the British Secret Service want me to submit reports as well! When the hell do I get to *sleep*? But the idea of being a spy *does* have a certain frisson. I was getting fed up with my humdrum going-no-where life back in London and look at me now. A regular Marta Hari. But perhaps without the exotic dancing and the sleeping with military men. Chance to *actually* sleep would be a fine thing!

'Will you do it?' Paddy asks.

'Will I be in any danger?' Wendy replies, the reality of what he is asks sinking in.

'None whatsoever,' he assures her, glibly. 'We can always get you out if we have to.'

'Good man!' Paddy tells her. So, Wendy thinks, he hasn't noticed that I'm all woman. So much for my romantic fantasy. He's not interested in my body, he's interested in my reports! What is it with me and men?

'It's nearly midnight. Shall we go back and see in the New Year?'

A New Year and a new career, in espionage.

16

Two o'clock in the morning of Saturday January the first and Paddy Winterslow is driving Wendy home. The snow has stopped falling but lies heavy on the houses and streets of Kesheva. The snow ploughs are not yet out, their crews no doubt fast asleep in their beds after a heavy night on the vodka greeting the New Year.

Paddy is giving Wendy a crash course in basic spying tradecraft.

'Always write your reports out in longhand on paper. Do not write anything on your laptop. Even if you think you have deleted something a good IT tekkie can retrieve it. And the ISS have some good tekkies.'

'ISS?'

'Internal Security Service. Remember?'

'Oh yes.' Apart from toasting in the New Year with a glass of English sparkling white, Wendy has not touched another drop since being recruited to spy for HM Government. She takes her new role very seriously. At least, for now.

'I will be in touch later about where you are to leave your reports. You should not be seen calling in at the embassy too often.'

'A dead letter drop,' says Wendy, who has read her share of John Le Carré.

'Yes,' Paddy confirms. 'Somewhere that does not arouse suspicion.'

'This is exciting.'

'But also very, very serious. It is NOT a game.'

'You said I wouldn't be in any danger,' Wendy accuses.

'Nor will you be, if you take basic precautions. Trust no-one.'

'I told you, I don't know anyone here.'

'Your minder, as you call him, Major Abdulin. He is an ISS officer.'

'Rustram? He told me he was an engineer!'

'He would hardly come out and say he was an officer of the Security Service, now, would he?'

'I suppose not.'

'And be wary of the old couple who run the place you are staying. They would not be put in charge of a foreign visitor with direct access to the Dargan family if they were not completely trusted to report your every move.'

'You make this spying malarkey sound so much fun!'

'Wendy, what I'm asking you to do is of vital importance to HMG's geopolitical policies. We need all the friendly regimes we can get in this part of the world. The threat of Islamic extremism is very real and very serious. Not to mention the oil. Just be careful and nothing untoward can happen to you. Talk to the boy, get him onside and make him a friend of Britain. We are talking long-term strategy here. Aslan Dargan is not going anywhere in the near future. We are not asking you to steal state secrets. Just gently persuade Jamshid into our way of thinking.'

Wendy feels reassured. It's just what I was planning to do, anyway, she thinks. If Jamshid is to study in the UK he needs a liberal outlook on life, an open mind. He is going to have to fit in with the idealism of the young, before the young get jobs in the multinationals or the City and become hard-line conservative capitalists.

They arrive at Wendy's villa and she decides to see if she can rescue anything from the evening.

'Would you like to come in for a coffee?'

'Have you actually *got* any coffee?' asks Paddy, greatly amused.

'No,' she confesses, 'but would you like to come in anyway?' Please don't let him laugh at her and reject her.

'Yes,' he says, much to her relief, 'I think I would.'

MI6 must run courses in seduction and follow-through, Wendy thinks, or perhaps Paddy is just a natural. He is a warm and considerate lover, taking his time and concentrating on her needs before his own. Wendy is conscious of not having had like this in years, not even with the bastard Tony, who she always thought was pretty fair in the bedroom department. She falls into a contented and sated sleep.

When she wakes up in the late morning Paddy is long gone and his side of the bed is cold.

Part Two

17

It is the last week of February, still very cold but with the distinct promise of warmer days to come. Wendy has only seen Paddy Winterslow once more since New Year's Day and that was at the Burns' Night dinner on the twenty-fifth of January held at the Embassy when she was given instructions on how to pass messages on.

Paddy made no mention of their lovemaking so Wendy, not wishing to appear needy, does not say anything either. She suspects that their tryst was no more than a professional sweetener to get her on side and relegates it to just a pleasant memory; a one-night stand in her otherwise barren love life. Hey-ho, Wendy thinks; well, it was good while it lasted.

When she can spare the time from her seemingly endless lesson preparation and report writing, she has taken to wandering the alleyways and streets of the Old Town, which, by now, she knows quite well. Her walks serve a more nefarious purpose. At the Burns' Night Supper, Paddy inducted her into the mysteries of dead letter drops. She was instructed to visit the National Museum and look for a tiny mark in blue chalk on a case displaying a collection of ancient small arms. Taped underneath the case was a tiny scrap of paper instructing her to leave her report, folded as small as possible, behind the mihrab pulpit of the Aga Mehmet mosque.

Her heart beating fifteen to the dozen, Wendy makes her

way to the mosque, which at this time of day is empty apart from a few tourists. Taking her shoes off, and trying to act as casually as she can, she circles the inside of the building, stopping to admire the inlaid Koranic inscriptions on the walls and sneaking glances. When she is satisfied that she is not being observed by legions of secret policemen, she slips behind the steps to the pulpit and hides her single page report in a crack between the steps and the wall. There is another blue mark on the lip of the mihrab that reveals another message with the location of her next drop. Despite the chill inside the mosque, she finds that she is sweating profusely. She pulls her fur hat down over her head, snuggles down inside her puffa jacket and performs another casual circuit of the building, before heading back out. She realises that her legs are trembling and briskly walks to a coffee shop.

In the coffee shop she sips her coffee and nibbles at a pastry and waits for her breathing to settle down. She wonders how *real* spies can go on doing this year after year; the burn-out rate must be tremendous from the strain on their nerves. She dreads to think what conditions must be like in a Keshevan prison and then entertains a mental image of being led out on a cold dawn and being stood up against a wall. Will she laugh at her executioners and distain the proffered blindfold, or will she pee herself in terror? Best to have a wee before they take her out, she decides, feeling sorry for herself.

But nothing happens. There is no heavy hand descending on her shoulder, only the waitress at her elbow asking if she would like another cup of coffee? She would, and perhaps another of those tasty little cakes.

And now she is a hardened agent of three drops. Her reports

contain details of her progress in turning Jamshid Dargan into a convinced Anglophile.

It has not been that onerous a task. Trapped inside his restricted little world, Jamshid was bored out of his mind and totally receptive to the pictures Wendy painted of university and London life. Jamshid loves music, yet has never attended a live concert; he loves football but has only ever watched the Keshevan national team play – a team that would not last long in an English non-league competition and always goes out in the first round of any regional qualifiers. He has never been on a date with a girl, although he hints that he has had conquests amongst the female servants. Wendy gets the impression that the girls in question did not have much of a say in the matter. He has never travelled outside Kesheva, indeed, rarely left the Ministerial Compound.

Wendy extols the joys of student societies and activities, of mixing freely with people of his own age, of riding the Tube system while carefully omitting to mention the hell of rush hour – but what student is actually awake and commuting at that hour of the morning? - of seeing the bustle of a great city from the top deck of a bus. She obliquely explores the idea of the Rule of Law and the guiding principles of the democratic system, being very careful to take a neutral stance. She includes this in her lesson plans for Rustram Abdulin, justifying its inclusion under International Law 101. So far, neither Rustram nor his master have raised any objections.

Jamshid soaks all this up enthusiastically and is making great efforts with his written work. He sits at his computer late into the night, researching material for the next day's lesson, preparing and defending his position on the given topic. Wendy is very pleased with his progress and his new-found enthusiasm. She is sure that he will be ready and able to attend university by the coming October.

Since the end of January, Rustram has stopped collecting her in person; she has been issued a pass to allow her to pass through the checkpoints and is now well known to the guards in the Ministerial Compound, who now greet her by name every morning, so it comes as a surprise to find Rustram waiting in the car.

'Hello, stranger,' she greets him, 'long time no see.'

'His Excellency wishes to speak to you,' says Rustram, getting straight to the point.

'Oh,' Wendy replies in what she hopes is a flippant tone, 'what have I done?' Her stomach is churning. *Are they on to me?*

'A very good job, by all accounts,' Rustram assures her. 'His Excellency is very pleased with Jamshid's progress. He wants to thank you in person and discuss your future direction.'

'That is good news. I think Jamshid is doing very well.'

And so, instead of going straight up to Jamshid's rooms, Wendy is taken to Aslan Dargan's office. As before, he is ensconced behind his desk, the picture of a man dedicated to the service of his country. He rises as Wendy is ushered in and grips her hand in both of his. He is smiling broadly.

'Dr. McPherson! Dr. McPherson! What can I say?'

'Good morning, Your Excellency.'

'Yes, I could say "good morning"'

Wendy realises he is trying to make a joke and smiles to show she appreciates the effort.

'I have asked you to come and see me before you start your

class with my son. I wish to discuss his progress. Please,' he gestures to the armchairs, 'sit down.'

The young woman, who, Wendy decides, must be psychic, slips into the room and proceeds to brew a pot of tea. Dargan seats himself opposite Wendy, still smiling broadly. Does he smile like this when he is signing death warrants, she speculates.

'I have, of course, read your reports and your lesson plans. As you may be aware, Jamshid is destined to play an important role in the future of Kesheva. To do this he must be educated in *some* of the ways of the West. This is why we are sending him to study abroad. Before you came, he was resisting the whole idea. Frankly, I don't know what was wrong with the boy. At his age, I would have jumped at the chance. But you seem to have made an impression on him. He is now much more amenable to the idea, even enthusiastic. And for this, I thank you. You will find a small token of my gratitude in your bank account.'

How small? Enough to pay off the mortgage?

'That's very kind of you, Your Excellency.'

'Think nothing of it. Good work deserves a reward. Now, in your honest opinion, will Jamshid be ready to travel abroad in October? Will he pass the entrance examinations?'

'Yes, I'm pretty sure he will. He is trying very hard and we still have plenty of time. He needs to send in his applications by the end of May and sit the exam round about the same time. May I make a suggestion?'

'Of course, Dr. McPherson. I welcome any suggestions you make.'

'You, or perhaps your Embassy in London, have already been in contact with my own university. That's how I came to be here. We run foundation courses. A sort of one-year training for non-native students to accustom them to the norms of British university expectations. It would be perfect for Jamshid. It would mean an extra year of study, of course, but it would do him no end of good.'

'And add another year of fees to your, no doubt, excellent establishment?' Dargan says but Wendy can detect a distinct twinkle in his eyes and knows he is teasing her.

'Well worth it,' she replies. 'If I may be permitted to say, Your Excellency, Jamshid lacks any real-life experience. I understand the reasons,' she adds hastily, 'but some of the work I have been doing with him is to try and teach him about living as a student in a strange city and a strange country. He is an intelligent boy but is sadly lacking in knowledge of the real world.'

'I fully agree with you. He needs all the help he can get. It is not easy for him. I have enemies. All leaders do, as you must be aware. It is too dangerous for him to roam freely in this country, safe as all citizens are in Kesheva. But political opponents might strike at him to strike at me. You *do* see that?'

'Yes.' But she cannot help thinking about the children of Western establishment figures who lead normal lives; the children of royalty and the children of prime ministers who attend local schools and universities without undue fuss.

As if reading her mind, Dargan says: 'We are very different from the West. I have two other children from my first wife. They both lead independent lives as successful business people but they are both much older and wiser that Jamshid. He is my baby and I love him very much. I want the best for him. Perhaps I have, what is the word? Mollycoddled? Him.'

'And now, maybe, is the time to let him go?' Wendy says gently. She is amazed that Dargan is opening up like this to her, and a little touched at his confiding in her.

'You are right. But it is not an easy thing for a father to do. I have great faith in you, Dr. McPherson. I think your suggestion is a good one. I will have someone contact Dr. Rhys about a place in your university for Jamshid. You do have a faculty of Law?'

'Yes. Quite a good one. Perhaps not the *best*, but nonetheless, a good one.'

'Then it is settled. I have one more favour to ask of you, Dr. McPherson.'

'If I can, I will.'

'Look after Jamshid when he is in London. I'm asking this as a father. Keep an eye on him. Not just his progress academically but his well-being. He will have all the resources of the Embassy behind him. That goes without saying. But he will need a friend and a mentor. I would like you to be that friend and mentor. You will be paid for your trouble.'

Once again, Wendy is touched. She wrestles with her conscience. What I'm doing for Paddy Winterslow is not *really* so much at odds with what Dargan wants for his son. I'm only laying the groundwork for the future relations between the UK and Kesheva. Where's the harm? It's a win-win situation.

'Of course I will keep an eye on Jamshid. I like him very much. He has potential. And I don't need paying. I'd be glad to help him find his feet in London.'

'I and Kesheva would be in your debt. You will always be welcome here as an honoured guest.'

This is turning into a love-fest, she thinks.

'Then I must not keep you from your pupil any longer.' He rises to return to his desk and the cares of state. As Wendy reaches the door Dargan says: By the way, are you still seeing the very charming Mr. Winterslow?'

'I'm sorry?'

'From your Embassy. I hear he brought you home from the New Year's Eve reception and stayed with you. I expect he couldn't get back because of the snow?'

Wendy feels her ears burn.

'Yes. It was kind of him. I did see him at the Burns' Night Supper.'

'A handsome man. A woman needs a handsome man.'

Wendy is flustered: what message is Dargan sending her? That she is being watched? That he knows everything that happens in Kesheva? That he knows she is spying? Or just that he condones her extra-curriculum activities?

'Good day to you, Dr. McPherson.'

And the interview is over.

18

On the Saturday after her meeting with Aslan Dargan, Wendy rises late. She enjoys a long breakfast and a chat about the weather with Ruthinna, who promises her that spring is just around the corner. She takes a pot of coffee up to her room and sits at her desk working on next week's lessons for Jamshid. She intends to examine the United Nations Charter and the Declaration of Human Rights, to which Kesheva is a signatory. So far, Rustram, and by extension, Dargan, has had little to object to in her programme but she wonders if she might be stepping onto sensitive ground. What the hell! This is the stuff the boy will be exposed to when he studies Law in the UK.

Suddenly she hears a loud bang. She saves the material on her laptop, shuts it down and goes downstairs to see if she can find out what the noise was.

Oybek and Ruthinna are both outside. She joins them. They are speaking in Keshevan, a language vaguely akin to Turkish that Wendy had successfully began to pick up and which she studies a little most evenings using a book she does not imagine competes with J.K. Rowling for bestseller status: *Keshevan in Twenty Lessons*. But they are speaking quickly and Wendy can only catch the odd word. It is clear that something is wrong, though. The old couple's body language is agitated and animated.

Ruthinna points to a black plume of smoke rising to the north. Wendy cannot grasp the significance.

'Is bomb,' Oybek says excitedly. 'I was in army. I know.'

'A bomb?' Wendy cannot believe what she is hearing.

'Maybe in car. Like in Afghanistan.'

'A bomb!' she says again. 'Who would do that?'

'Bad people. People who hate us,' Oybek explains as if he were talking to a child.

'In Kesheva?' Wendy is being particularly dense. She is having trouble coming to terms with what she is hearing. 'But the security? How?'

'I not know. But I know is bomb.'

Ruthinna has started to cry softly. She dabs her eyes with the hem of the apron she is wearing. 'Now it starts,' she sobs.

'What? What starts,' asks Wendy.

'Trouble,' Oybek says gravely. 'Trouble like Afghanistan.'

The sound of sirens fills the air, police and ambulances are rushing through the city.

'Maybe it was natural causes,' says Wendy, grasping at straws. 'People use propane gas to cook. Maybe a gas cylinder blew up?'

'No,' Oybek tells her firmly, 'is bomb. I know.'

'How can you be sure?'

'I was in army. I know.'

Through the gateway, they can see people streaming in the direction of the smoke plume. A moment later, there is a second loud explosion, dispelling all doubt. It is a classic terrorist attack: set off one bomb, wait for the security and emergency services to converge and then set off a second, maximising casualties.

'I must phone the Embassy,' Wendy says and rushes into

the house to use the landline.

The Embassy phone lines are busy. Wendy hangs on, redials and hangs on.

Eventually the call is answered.

'British Embassy.'

'Oh, hi. I'm Dr. McPherson. There have just been two explosions in the Old City. Can you tell me anything?'

'I'm afraid not, Dr. McPherson. We are just as in the dark as you are. We have heard a report about a bomb attack in the Old City but we do not know exactly where. The advice from the Embassy is to avoid the Old City at all costs. We will be contacting all British nationals in the area with further advice when we are in a position to do so. I repeat, for the present, avoid the Old City. Thank you for your call.'

Wendy does not know what to do. Should she try and phone Rustram Abdulin? Is he likely to know any more than she does? She knows he does not live in the Old City but out in the suburbs somewhere. She decides against it and goes back outside. Oybek and Ruthinna are standing by the gate and peering along the street. More sirens sound.

'What do we do?' Wendy asks, a note of desperation in her voice.

'We do nothing,' Oybek tells her. 'Is nothing we can do. Leave to police. We go back inside house and drink strong tea. Is good for nerves. Perhaps also drink brandy. Is also good for nerves.'

A brandy sounds just the job. Wendy lives in London, which has had its share of terrorist outrages over the years, and like all Londoners does not let terrorism impinge on her daily life. But this is in some way different, more serious. She has seen the horrors of terrorism in the Middle East on the nightly news programmes. At home, in London, she somehow knows how to react. She is on home ground. But here? What to do? How to behave?

Ruthinna has taken her by the hand and leads her into the house. Wendy realises she is in shock. Oybek pours three stiff glasses of cherry brandy. Wendy knocks her drink back in one, hardly aware of its burn down her throat. Ruthinna bustles off to make a brew of tea.

How can they be taking this so calmly? Wendy wonders. But then, what can you do? What was the famous morale-boosting slogan during the Blitz? *'Keep calm and carry on!'* That is *precisely* what she would do at home. Don't let the bastards win. They want you to panic – that is the whole purpose of terrorism. Fuck 'em!

They drink Ruthinna's tea and drink another brandy and Wendy feels a lot calmer. There *is* nothing she can do so she goes back to her desk and tries to concentrate on her lesson plans. She reaches the section of the UN Charter that has the provisions for a just war and self-defence of nations. With her students in the UK she might open up a discussion on the justification of the Allied invasion of Afghanistan after the 9/11 attack on the Twins Towers or the humanitarian interventions in Kosovo and Libya or perhaps even whether the UK was justified in the policy of internment in Northern Ireland but she has the distinct feeling that an attack in Kesheva was, however indirectly, an attack on the Dargan family. Jamshid might be taking this personally and the topic might be too sensitive at this time.

She hears the phone ring downstairs and hears Ruthinna answer it.

'Is for you, Dr. Wendy. Is Embassy.'

Wendy runs down the stairs and grabs the phone from Ruthinna's hand.

'Yes? Hello!'

'Wendy? It's Paddy.'

'Paddy! Thank God. What's happening?'

'Things are a bit confused at the moment. As you can imagine. Are you all right?'

'Me? Yes, why?'

'I thought you might be out and about in the Old Town. You often go out for a walk at the weekend.'

Yes, she thinks, to deliver your bloody reports.

'I was at home. Working.' On your bloody report!

'Good. I'm glad you are safe. As far as we can tell, there were two explosions spaced about ten minutes apart by the Uhlan Beg Mosque, the one near the bazaar.'

'Yes, I know it.'

'Lots of casualties. We don't have exact numbers at present but the numbers are high.'

'Who did it?'

'No-one has claimed responsibility as yet but an educated guess would say that it was some religious fundamentalist group. It was too co-ordinated to be a lone wolf. The Embassy's advice to all Brits is: stay away.'

'I wasn't planning to go and rubberneck. Scenes of carnage are not my thing.'

'Good. Look, I'm going to be terribly busy in the next few hours but I will try to get over to see you later, if I can. I expect that the security forces are going to lock the city down for the foreseeable future but the diplomatic plates might get me through.'

'I'd love to see you. I feel so *helpless*.'

'There is absolutely nothing you can do. Just sit tight. I'll be there when I can.' He hangs up.

Wendy puts the phone down, goes back upstairs and lays down on her bed. Thoughts swirl around in her head. She would love to see Paddy again. She knows she will feel safe just to be in his presence, to hear him reassure her and allay her fears. She understands now the reason for the omnipresent security in Kesheva. They have been expecting this. What was it the IRA are supposed to have said: "You have to be lucky one hundred per cent of the time; we only have to be lucky once". And now the terrorists have been lucky. But will it stop here? How many years has the terrorism in Iraq dragged on? And how many people have died? Is it time for her to cut her losses and go home? But if she does that, then the terrorists have, in a tiny way, won. Fuck 'em! I'm going to stay! Jamshid needs me. Now more than ever.

19

It is past ten o'clock that evening when Paddy Winterslow finally arrives in his little Mazda.

'Sorry to be so late,' he says. 'It's been hectic at the Embassy. All hands to the pumps. We have been trying to contact all the Brits registered with us to see if they are OK.'

'Has anyone been hurt?' asks Wendy, all concerned. The waiting has been stressful; Oybek and Ruthinna have tried to find out the extent of the mayhem but have not been successful. The city is in shutdown. All day the sirens have been wailing and troops are swarming on the streets, nervous and trigger-happy. Oybek has prescribed vodka and Ruthinna disappeared into her kitchen to make comfort food. Wendy is now stuffed to the gills and more than a little drunk.

'As far as we know,' Paddy tells her as she gets into the car, 'there have been no British casualties. Thank God you weren't out and about.'

Wow, Wendy thinks, perhaps he does *actually* care for me. Since they spent that night together on New Year's Eve, Wendy has allowed herself to dream about a future with Paddy, a future that went beyond the Spymaster and his Joe. The fact that they have not met since the Burns' Night dinner has dampened her spirits; in recent years she has become accustomed to rejection, resigned herself to loneliness and a single life. Paddy Winterslow offered her hope.

'So,' she says, 'are you gathering all the expats into the Embassy?'

'No. We have been advising people to stay put unless it is essential to go out. The city is crawling with security. I had a hell of a time just getting here. The Dip plates help, of course, but even so...'

'Then why have you come for me?'

'I want to be sure you are safe. The best place for you is with me in the Embassy.'

She feels her legs go weak. Good job she is sitting down in the car. He *does* care for me whispers a little voice somewhere deep inside.

'I have a small flat in the Embassy compound. You can stay there until all this unpleasantness resolves itself. Where you are now is too close to the scene.'

She is sure that her heart has actually skipped a beat.

He is driving slowly through streets deserted by civilians but with checkpoints manned by armed police and soldiers at every intersection. Armoured personnel carriers block the roads. The Mazda appears to be the only car moving. Their passage is slow as they creep from roadblock to roadblock.

'Do you know what happened?'

'We are getting more of a picture. The Keshevan authorities have imposed a news blackout but our sources tell us that up to fifty people have been killed and there are hundreds of wounded. The hospitals can't cope with these sorts of numbers, so the death toll is bound to rise.'

'It's so horrible. I thought Kesheva was safe.'

'Nowhere is safe, Wendy,' he tells her gently, as if explaining the facts of twenty-first century life to a child. 'We live in a difficult world.'

'But who could have done such a thing?'

'We think it might be an offshoot of Isis or Al-Qaeda. That seems the most likely.'

'But they are Islamic movements!'

'And?'

'You said the bombs were outside the Uhlan Beg Mosque.'

'Yes. We have confirmed that.'

'But it was outside a *mosque*!'

'What's your point?' asks Paddy, puzzled.

'A mosque where Muslims worship. They were targeting their own.'

'Oh, I see. What do you know about the likes of Isis and Al-Qaeda?'

'They are terrorist organisations that hate the West and its values and want to establish an Islamic Caliphate throughout the world. To take the world back to the early days of Islam and the rule of Sharia law.'

'That is essentially true. But, first and foremost, they are Salafists.'

'Salafists?'

'A movement inspired by the teaching of Muhammad ibn Abd al-Wahhab, an eighteenth-century religious teacher who lived in what is now Saudi Arabia. He advocated a return to what he saw as the basic principles of Islam. A return to the fundamentals of the community founded by the Prophet Muhammad in Medina.'

'OK,' says Wendy slowly, 'so why target other Muslims? Surely that goes against everything they stand for?'

'Wrong kind of Muslims!'

'*What?*'

'The Salafists are Sunni, the mainstream of Islam. The Uhlan Beg Mosque is a Shia mosque. The Salafist see their first duty is to eradicate heresy and to establish the rule of orthodoxy – i.e., Sunni Islam.'

'Right,' says Wendy. 'Like the struggle between Catholicism and the Protestants in Europe during the Thirty Years War.'

'The same!'

'Why is it,' Wendy muses, 'that whenever someone comes up with an idea for mankind to live together in peace and harmony, subsequent generations have to take the message and twist it. It has happened to all the great philosophies.'

'Beats me,' says Paddy. 'That sort of thing is above my pay grade.'

They are entering the diplomatic quarter. Concrete barriers have been set along the approaches so the car has to slow even more to negotiate the zigzags. Here there are tanks with turret-mounted searchlights tracking their movements.

'I guess we will be safe enough here,' says Wendy.

'I certainly hope so. I don't want anything to happen to you.'

'Oh, Paddy,' says Wendy in a slightly mocking tone to mask her true feelings, 'I didn't know you cared!'

He turns to face her, making eye contact and holding her gaze. 'I know what I have asked you to do for me and, indeed, your country.' He stops and laughs at himself. 'Christ, I sound like a real pompous prat, don't I? What I'm trying to say is that I genuinely worry about you. I keep replaying that night we spent together and want to get to know you better; to spend more time with you. But the nature of our work meant I had to keep my distance. For your own safety. I could not draw attention to us. There are eyes everywhere in Kesheva. Your friend Rustram Abdulin for one. And the old couple who are looking after you. You even said that President Dargan commented on me.'

'He said I needed a handsome man.'

'Well, I'm flattered. But don't forget, nothing is as it seems in Kesheva.'

'But I could do with a handsome man,' says Wendy wistfully. And you fit the bill very nicely, Paddy Winterslow.

'It's an ill wind,' says Paddy. 'Now I have the perfect excuse to spend some time with you.'

They pull into the gates of the British Embassy, having shown their pass one final time. The journey has taken over forty minutes and Wendy is tired, perhaps from the effects of the alcohol and food Oybek and Ruthinna have plied her with all evening. She finds her head dropping onto Paddy's shoulder as he manipulates his way behind the main Embassy building to a small cluster of buildings behind.

'Here we are, Marm. Home sweet home!'

'I haven't brought anything with me,' Wendy suddenly realises.

'Don't worry,' says Paddy. 'I keep a spare toothbrush in case of emergencies.'

And how many of those have you had, Mr. Winterslow? she wonders cynically and then knows that she does not care.

He takes her hand and leads her to one of the small, two-storey buildings and opens the door with his key.

'I'm on the ground floor and the First Secretary is on the top,' he explains.

His flat is neat, almost minimalist, with stark white walls

unadorned by any pictures. There is a large carpet on the floor of the sitting room, a coffee table and a sofa and a wall unit with a few books and two or three knick-knacks on the shelves.

'Bits and pieces I've picked up from my various postings,' he explains. 'The nature of the job does not require me to accumulate many possessions, I'm afraid. I live a bit of a Spartan existence. You know, here today, persona non grata tomorrow!'

Wendy, with the curiosity of an academic, has wandered over to the bookshelves to examine Paddy's books. There are four recent political biographies, a couple of well-thumbed Terry Pratchetts and a pristine copy *Catch 22*.

'Can I get you something to drink?' he asks. 'I usually enjoy a rather fine Oban single malt before bed. I've had a really shitty day and I could do with one. You?'

'Sounds good to me!'

'And, er, the bedroom is over here.' He points to a door leading off from the left of the sitting room. 'There is only the one, I'm afraid. I can bunk down here on the sofa.'

'Don't even think about it, Paddy Winterslow,' she says as she kisses him.

20

Wendy wakes up alone in the bed on Sunday morning. For a moment, she wonders if she has been loved and left again – par for the course, she thinks – but then hears noises coming from what she assumes is the kitchen. She stretches, her body still resonating to the lovemaking in the night. Paddy really is *very* good. She yawns and swings her legs out of the bed. The bare floor is cold on her feet as she pads in the direction of the sounds. She finds Paddy, in, of all things, a paisley pattern silk dressing gown, making coffee and bacon sandwiches.

'Sleep well?' he asks, flashing his white teeth at her in a smile.

'Mmmm.'

'Breakfast?'

'Where *did* you get that bacon? I've never seen it here.'

'Diplomatic bag. A trick I learnt in the Middle East. Can't have breakfast without a bacon buttie, can you?'

'What time is it?'

'Still quite early, but I think I'm going to have another busy day. Make yourself at home, if you can. You know where the bathroom is.'

Wendy is bursting for a pee and heads in the direction Paddy has indicated. Given the sparseness of the rest of the flat, she is surprised by the size of the bathroom, which has a freestanding tub and a wet-room shower area. Later, she thinks. Loo first!

Then breakfast. She realises that she is hungry and the aroma of brewing coffee and frying bacon permeates the flat. She finds a white towelling bathrobe hanging on a hook on the back of the bathroom door and wraps it around herself. It is too big but better than nothing.

'Grub's up!' Paddy calls from the kitchen.

Perched on a stool at the tiny breakfast bar that serves Paddy as his dining table, munching her bacon sandwich and sipping at her coffee, Wendy thinks she just might be falling in love with Paddy Winterslow. She feels a warm glow every time she looks at him, a tingling in her whole body, not just confined to her loins. Might they have a future? Does he feel the same or is she just an available shag?

Her brain tells her that they live in different worlds; her future is back in London and the University while he is a career diplomat/spy. Might she be prepared to give up her London life and follow him around the world? Her heart shouts YES! But her brain whispers a cautious "but is that what *he* wants?'

'I've got to go,' says Paddy, puncturing her thought bubble. 'Will you be OK here by yourself? There's not much in the way of entertainment, I'm afraid.'

'I'll be OK.' She reassures him. 'I'll have a long shower and a browse through your copy of *A Very English Scandal*. Should be good for a laugh.' She is trying to be flippant, not giving her emotions away. looking for a sign from him; he is giving nothing away, like the good spy that he is.

'I'll pop back when I can,' he says as he leaves. Then he stops, comes back to her and kisses her. She feels all swoony, like the heroine in a Mills and Boon. Get a grip, you daft old trout, she tells herself. You're a middle-aged woman, not some dippy teenager with a first crush. But still, it *is* rather nice.

She runs a shower and hums as she soaps herself and washes her hair. In the trauma of yesterday she neglected to pack a bag with spare clothes (Oybek's vodka might have had something to do with it), so she rinses out her undies and hangs them to dry on the radiator that is going full blast in the living room and settles down in her bathrobe with a towel wrapped around her wet hair to read.

Her mobile phone, tucked away in her handbag, is ringing. It is the phone Rustram issued to her once she started teaching Jamshid, with a Keshevan SIM card and paid for by the Keshevan government. Paddy has warned her that it will definitely be bugged and that she should be circumspect when she uses it. So far, she has only used it to confirm travel arrangements to the Ministerial Compound and once to phone her brother to tell him she has arrived in Kesheva and how fascinating it is. All harmless stuff.

She fishes the phone out of her bag and checks the caller ID: it is Rustram.

'Hi, Rustram,' she says.

'Dr. McPherson? I trust you are well? You are in the British Embassy, I believe?'

'Yes.' She does not ask him how he knows where she is. Oybek will have told him. There seem to be no secrets in Kesheva.

'There really is no need. You are perfectly safe in your villa.'

'The Embassy wanted to check up on all British citizens,' she explains.

'So, are *all* the British expatriates in Kesheva hiding in the Embassy?'

'Not that I know of,' she admits.

'And is the handsome Mr Winterslow looking after you?'

Is that the merest hint of jealousy she can detect in his voice? Come on! He's a married man. There again, when has that ever stopped a married man showing an interest in a woman? She decides to evade the question.

'Do you want me to come to the Ministerial Compound tomorrow?'

'No. Not for the moment. I will tell you when you are to resume your teaching.'

'Rustram, what the hell happened yesterday?'

He does not answer immediately. She imagines he is choosing his words carefully, what to tell her, what to omit.

'There was a terrorist outrage aimed at innocent people,' he says, finally.

'I know that. But what is it all about? Who are these terrorists? What do they want?'

'They are terrorists,' he says simply. 'They want to destabilise the democratically elected government of this country. They have no popular support and they cannot succeed.'

'But who are they?' she persists.

The phone goes silent again as he considers what to tell her.

'We think they may be a radical Islamic group. Without doubt foreign agitators from across the borders.'

'So, not Keshevans, then?'

'Absolutely not!'

'How many people were killed?'

'Fortunately, not many,' he lies.

'The Embassy heard it was a great number and that the hospitals were full to overflowing.'

'There are all sorts of rumours. You must not believe everything you hear.'

Especially from you, she thinks.

'The important thing is that you are well and will be able to resume your lessons with Jamshid when the time is right.'

'I'll be happy to. Just let me know when.'

'When will you be returning to your villa?'

'Oh? I don't know. When the Embassy kick me out, I suppose.'

'Do not leave it too long, please. Remember, you are here to do a job.'

'Rustram! *You* are the one who phoned *me* telling me not to come in tomorrow, remember?'

'Ah, yes.'

'So as soon as you phone and tell me, I'll be ready.'

That's put you in your place, she thinks.

'I hope it will be soon. This is only a very temporary situation.'

'I'm pleased to hear it.'

'Yes. Well, goodbye, Dr. McPherson. I will be in touch shortly.'

He rings off just as Wendy hears the front door open.

"Paddy, that was Rustram Abdulin on the phone. He told me not to expect to go to work tomorrow.'

'I'm not surprised. From what we are hearing, the whole city is in chaos. Our American friends are telling us that they have monitored a claim from a group calling itself *The Islamic Peoples' Front of Kesheva* claiming responsibility. Sounds credible. The city is still in tight lockdown. All the shops are shut and there is a twenty-four hour curfew.'

'But how are people going to buy food?'

'For the time being, it seems, they are not.'

'And who will the people blame for going hungry?'

'The Government, of course.'

'So the terrorists win.'

'Good girl.'

'I'm not just a pretty face,' she snaps. 'I *do* have a PhD.'

'And a *very* pretty face,' says Paddy, taking it in his hands and kissing it.

Wendy melts to the moment.

'How long must I stay here?' she asks.

'Bored of me already?'

'No,' she laughs, and kisses him back. 'It just that Rustram was asking. I'm more than happy to stay. You must know that, Paddy Winterslow.'

'And I am more than happy to have you. In all senses of the word.' He leers at her, a parody of lust. 'This emergency has given me the perfect excuse to keep you here, all to myself!'

'But sooner or later I will have to go back to the villa and back to work.'

'We'll cross that bridge when we come to it,' he says as he slides his hands into her bathrobe.

21

On Monday the curfew is lifted for three hours in the middle of the day to allow the people of the city to buy the necessities of life. Paddy and Wendy agree that she should remain living in the Embassy flat until she resumes her work in the Ministerial Compound and the situation in Kesheva is deemed safe. They are not yet ready to explore where their relationship is going in the future, whether Wendy will, for example, live with Paddy at the weekends. For the moment, they are happy to let things continue, using the excuse of the state of emergency and the uncertainty of the times.

Paddy drives Wendy back to her villa to pick up clean clothes and her laptop so she can check her emails and send reassurances to anyone who might be concerned for her welfare. The attack in Kesheva has made the international news but interest is dying off with no new developments.

Oybek is in the villa and seems pleased to find Wendy safe. He explains that Ruthinna has gone out shopping and is disappointed when Wendy tells him that she will be returning to the Embassy.

'Is safe now. You can stay here. Ruthinna will make big food for you tonight.'

'Major Abdulin told me not to go to the Compound until he calls me,' she says. 'Until then I think I had better stay in the Embassy. It's not that I don't feel safe here, with you and

Ruthinna. I do, of course. It's just that I...' She leaves the sentence open.

Oybek looks at Wendy and then at Paddy, sitting in the little Mazda. A smile creeps over his face and he winks at Wendy.

'I understand. Is better in Embassy.'

She finds she is actually blushing, a thing she has not done since she was a young girl being teased by her brother over some boy she has a crush on.

'No, it's just that...'

'I understand. Ruthinna will be happy for you. Is good that a good thing has come from a bad thing.'

Wendy hurries into the villa and throws a few things into her carry-on bag, grabs her laptop and tumbles downstairs.

Paddy and Oybek are chatting away in Keshevan, which she had not realised that Paddy spoke.

'All ready and packed?' asks Paddy brightly.

'Yes.'

'Then off we go. *Ma es salaam, Oybek.*'

'*Wa alakum salaam.*'

'I didn't know you spoke Keshevan,' says Wendy, getting into the car and closing the door.

'That was Arabic, actually. It just means "goodbye". More or less. Anyway, my Keshevan is far from fluent. I did a crash course at SOAS in London before coming out here.'

'What else don't I know about you, Paddy Winterslow? Is there a missus Winterslow waiting for you back in England?' She tried to sound arch but to her own ears only manages desperate.

'No, I'm afraid to disappoint you. You're stuck with me. If you want to be?'

'I think I might like that. Very much!'

'I think I would, too.'

'Oh, Paddy,' she says, feeling warm and safe.

'I was asking Oybek about what reaction has been to the bombing,' says Paddy, veering away from the mood. 'He is in the pay of the security services, of course, otherwise he would not be trusted to come into close contact with a foreigner, but he is a useful sounding board.'

'What did he say?' asks Wendy, curious despite Paddy's shift away from romance.

'There has been very little on the state television, but we knew that. We, and the other diplomatic missions have been monitoring that. But despite that and the curfew, people talk, rumours spread. He has heard that up to a hundred people died and many, many more were injured. People are scared, although he stressed that you would be safe.'

'How can he know that?'

'What?'

'That I would be safe?'

'There will be a guard on the villa as soon as you return and a bodyguard with you when you go out. It means the end of your secret messages, of course. But no matter, you can tell me in person now that we have established a suitable cover to explain your visits to the Embassy.'

'What!' she is shocked and deeply hurt by his words. 'So that's it? Our meetings are just to be a convenient cover for me to report back to you with sex thrown in as a perk. You manipulating bastard!'

'No, Wendy. No. That came out all wrong. Seeing you *is* important to me. Your reporting back is the perk. No more creeping around dead letter drops. I genuinely want to be with you, to spend time with you.'

She is less than convinced. She folds her arms across her chest and lapses into a sulky silence. Paddy squeezes her knee and she shifts her legs away.

'Look, Wendy. I'm sorry. I didn't mean to give you the wrong idea. These past couple of days with you have been wonderful.'

'Took a car bomb to convince you,' she mutters, starting to thaw.

'Forgive me?'

'Just this once. Don't let it happen again!'

They drive back through the city. There are people on the streets hurrying home with laden shopping bags. Police and soldiers are everywhere, performing random checks, poking and prodding at bags. Young men are being spread-eagled against walls while policemen frisk them for weapons. Wendy sees a man being beaten and dragged off to a waiting van in handcuffs, blood pouring from his head.

Suddenly a group of men, their faces covered in scarves, erupt from a side street and make a dash for the van. Before the police snatch squad can react, the bleeding man is wrestled away from them and carried off. Fists fly and then some of the men produce clubs and rain blows on the police. One policeman is on the ground. Two men are kicking him in the head and body. The police van is blocking the road and Paddy cannot drive around it and the melée.

'Wendy! Duck down,' he shouts.

For a moment, she is frozen and then instinct kicks in and she sinks beneath the dashboard.

A masked man presses up against the car, sees the two westerners and shouts something at them. Paddy has pressed the central locking. The man rattles the car door, shaking his fist.

One of the policemen manages to un-holster his side arm and fires a shot into the air. The attackers turn on him and he is battered to the floor. Paddy sees a man stoop down to retrieve the pistol. As another man starts to beat the car windows with a club, Paddy makes a decision. He puts the Mazda in reverse and runs the engine, knocking over a rioter standing behind the car and sending him spinning. They have a clear path back down the road and in less than a minute have escaped.

Wendy is crouched in the well of the car, shaking and crying, saying 'fuck, fuck, fuck.'

As they turn down another street, Paddy sees that all the people who were heading home have disappeared; the street is eerily deserted. He points the car in the right direction and heads back to the Embassy.

Safe back inside the Embassy compound, he parks and gives Wendy the key to his flat. She is still badly shaken and clutches on to him, her head buried in his shoulder.

'You're safe now, darling. You're safe,' he says, stroking her hair. 'Go inside and make yourself a stiff drink. I've got to go and report to the Ambassador, tell him I was involved in an incident. Poor old Jim Armstrong, he was hoping for a nice quiet posting to see him into retirement. He won't like this one bit.'

Wendy lets herself into Paddy's flat, pours a far from single measure of a single malt and curls up on the sofa, tucking her legs under her. She is still shaking. Has she just seen a man kicked to death? It is too horrible to contemplate. What the hell is she doing in this madhouse of a country? This is not what she signed up for. But then, she thinks, there is the consolation of Paddy Winterslow. But is he genuine or is he using her? The thoughts rush through her head, confusing her. She sips at her whisky, feeling its warmth and comfort.

The sound of her mobile ringing makes her jump, spilling some of the drink onto the floor.

Her hands are shaking as she accepts the call: she knows who it is from. What the hell does *he* want?

'Dr. McPherson, what must you think of us?' asks Rustram.

'What do you mean?'

'That unfortunate fracas you witnessed.'

'How do you know about that? It's only just happened.'

'A car with diplomatic plates. A car registered to the British Embassy. Driven by the delightful Mr Winterslow. Carrying a most distinguished guest of His Excellency. I am responsible for your safety, so, of course, I was notified immediately. I trust you are safe?'

'I'm a bit shaken up,' she admits.

'Of course you are. But nothing to worry about. A foreign drug dealer was arrested. Members of his criminal gang attempted to rescue him.'

'What happened? I saw a policemen being kicked. They were fighting.'

'Let me set your mind at rest, Dr.McPherson. The police have everything under control. The criminal might have evaded arrest for the moment but he will be apprehended and given a fair trial, as will his criminal associates. There is nothing for you to worry about. I only regret that you had to become inadvertently involved, in however a minor way.'

'When do you want me to goes back to tutoring Jamshid?'

'Not for a little while yet. Have a short holiday. I will be in touch. Give my regards to Mr Winterslow. Goodbye, Dr. McPherson.'

She recounts the telephone call to Paddy when he pops in to check on her.

'If that was a drug bust, then I'm the Queen of Sheba,' he says.

22

Two weeks have elapsed since the bombing in the city; reports have reached the Embassy of riots in the city of Orgush in the far west that was put down with considerable loss of life when the security forces fired into the crowd and also a suicide bomb in Zaamind in the north, but Kesheva itself is quiet under its blanket of heavy security. A night-time curfew from dusk to dawn is still in place but gradually life is returning to a semblance of normality and the bazaar is bustling.

The weather is turning warmer as spring approaches, with clear blue skies and sunshine, a harbinger of the baking summer heat to come. The trees are in bud and early spring flowers appear in the green spaces of the city. The days are beginning to lengthen.

Ordinarily these would be signs of hope after the dark grip of the winter but this year a pall of gloom and doom hangs over Kesheva. While the people are free to go about their legitimate business, gatherings of three or more people have been banned, internet access to social media sites blocked and all public events such as concerts and sporting fixtures suspended for the duration. Friday prayers at the city's numerous mosques are the one event the government dare not ban but the military is omnipresent and the imam's' sermons are vetted in advance for any evidence of sedition. Arrests continue with the people quaking in their beds for fear of a hammering on their doors in the early hours. Things have not been as bad as this since the days of Joseph Stalin's purges in the thirties.

For Wendy McPherson, it has been one of the best fortnights of her life.

She is in love and living with the man she loves.

Paddy has been busy with the communications traffic to and from London, keeping the Foreign and Commonwealth Office abreast of events in Kesheva as the information comes into the Embassy. The Western Embassies share information, pooling the resources of their various assets in the country, building up a picture, as far as possible of the political stability or lack of it in Kesheva.

Aslan Dargan has appeared on state television speaking platitudes of calm but under his make-up and the careful lighting it is possible to detect signs of strain on his features. Since his speech on the day after the bombs, state television has resorted to showing a diet of feel-good soap operas and rousing concerts of folkloric music and dance. The news is of increased oil production and promises of greater prosperity tomorrow.

Wendy's idyll ends with a phone call.

'Dr. McPherson!'

'Hello, Rustram.'

'It is time for you to take up your duties again.'

'OK. I look forward to seeing Jamshid. How is he?'

'He is well and eager to see you.'

'So, what's the plan.'

'I'm afraid you will have to return to your accommodation. Collecting you every day from the Embassy is not practical.'

'Oh.' She feels a stab of disappointment. Her relationship with Paddy is getting stronger; she is sure that it might develop into something lasting. If it came to the crunch, she is prepared to give up her university teaching job to be with him. They have not *exactly* discussed this possibility but she thinks they might have a tacit understanding.

'I can send a car for you,' Rustram suggests.

'You said it was not practical,' says Wendy, confused.

'Now. To take you back to your villa.'

'Now?' The break is too sudden. She needs time to re-adjust her life.

'You start back at the Ministerial Compound in the morning.'

She feels like Faustus begging Mephistopheles for a few more minutes of life before facing damnation. Paddy is off somewhere, probably spying for Queen and Country. Is she leaves now there will be no fond farewell, no goodbye kiss.

'Dr. McPherson? Are you there?'

'Yes.'

'Shall I send the car or will Mr. Winterslow drive you back?'

'Send the car,' she says with a heavy heart and breaks the connection.

Finding a pen and a pad of paper, she writes Paddy a message: *I've been ordered back to work with Jamshid and am being collected. No time to wait. Hope to see you very soon. I will miss you.* She pauses in her writing for a moment and then commits herself: *I love you. Wendy.*

There is a polite knock on the door. Wendy answers it to find the locally employed security guard standing there.

'There is a car for you at the front gate,' he announces.

That bastard Major Abdulin must have had it on the way when he called, she thinks.

'OK. Tell him I'll be right out.'

She scoops her things into her case, closes the door of the flat and walks to the gate of the Embassy.

Rustram Abdulin is sitting next to the driver in his official Mercedes. He gets out and opens the back door for her.

'Did you have a good stay?' he asks her, his face carefully bland. 'I think Ruthinna is making you plov to welcome you home.'

'Oh, goody,' she says, her heart aching.

23

Monday finds Wendy seated in the back of the Mercedes behind Rustram and the driver on the slow drive to the Ministerial Compound. She hardly registers the increased military units stationed along the road, nor the fact that the desert highway is softly turning green. She is feeling disgruntled that the powers-that-be of Kesheva have taken Paddy Winterslow away from her and rudely interrupted her burgeoning romance, and this she cannot forgive. Rustram tries to make small talk but Wendy sulkily ignores him until he gives up and they finish the journey in silence.

Inside the Presidential Palace the guard has been doubled. Wendy nods to the two bearded soldiers who guard the staircase and proceeds to the family quarters on the second floor where she is escorted to Jamshid. She finds him playing a video game that involves much shooting and bloodshed.

'Wendy!' he shouts as she comes in. He rushes to her and hugs her. 'I've missed you!'

'How have you been, Jamshid? Have you kept up with the work I set you?'

'I have. Now, more than ever I want to go to England to study.' He drops his voice and whispers to her: 'I want to get away from here. Trouble is coming. They try to keep it from me, but they can't hide everything. Kamilla and Stas have moved back here. If they don't feel safe, then it must be serious.'

'The city seems quiet enough,' Wendy tells him. 'Lots of extra police and soldiers on the streets but life appears to be returning to normal.'

'My father boiled the Minister of the Interior,' he whispers, his mouth touching her ear.

She laughs at his misuse of the idiom.

'You mean he *roasted* him. That is the correct expression for a good dressing down.'

'You see, two weeks without you and I'm losing my English. Doesn't boil mean to cook in liquid? Like an egg?'

'Yes,' Wendy agrees, wondering where this is going.

'Then I am right. My father had him boiled. Right in front of the Ministry buildings. It was a punishment from the days of the old Khans. They put him in a huge pot filled with cooking oil and lit a fire under it.'

'Oh dear God!' Wendy feels the bile rising up into her throat. She gags and makes a dash for Jamshid's bathroom, vomiting into the loo.

'Are you all right?' Jamshid calls nervously from the doorway.

She rinses away the taste of vomit with water from the tap by the sink and walks shakily back to Jamshid.

'He *boiled* the Minister of the Interior?'

'Yes. Don't the French have an expression: "*to encourage the others*"? Something like that.'

'He boiled him in public!'

'It had to be where the other Ministers could see,' Jamshid says, as if surprised Wendy could not see the logic.

'You have got to get out of here, Jamshid, you really have.'

There is a sharp rap on the door. Before Jamshid can speak, a young man strides into the room. He is dressed in a shiny purple shell-suit and wearing very expensive designer trainers. Wendy blinks; here is a younger incarnation of Aslan Dargan.

'Stas?' says Jamshid.

"I've come to check out my little step-brother's tutor,' Stas announces in English tinged with a slight American accent.

'This is my brother Stas,' Jamshid tells Wendy unnecessarily.

'Hi,' says Stas and gives a little wave of his hand as if acknowledging an audience.

Does he expect me to curtsey? Wendy wonders. She can sense the waves of arrogant self-confidence that Stas gives off. Here is a man to whom no one says No. He is sleek and muscular as befits his role as a footballer, with the easy movements of an athlete who spends time in the gym pampering his body.

'So, what are you teaching my little Bro?'

'We are working on the concept of Human Rights and the rule of Law.' says Wendy a little mischievously. It gets the response she half expects.

'Western bullshit!'

'Why is that?'

'People don't need so-called "Human Rights" if they have a strong leader who knows what is best for his people.'

'Then why are the Western democracies the leaders in stability and innovation, unlike…' She bites back her words before she says Kesheva.

'Are they?' says Stas, wandering around the room, picking up random objects. 'What about China?'

'Fair point,' Wendy concedes.

'Have you read *The Prince* by that Italian guy. A great period of innovation with strong leaders.'

'I see you got *something* from your studies in the States,' says

Wendy impishly. 'Either that or you watched *The Third Man*.'

'What?'

'Switzerland and cuckoo clocks.'

'I don't know what you are talking about. It's not important.' He metaphorically brushes her aside with another little wave of his hand.

No, Wendy realises, if you don't know it, it cannot be important. You are an arrogant little sod, aren't you?

'You won't like the West, little Bro.'

'Why is that?' Wendy asks before Jamshid can speak.

'Petty restrictions.'

Like laws against forcing yourself on women without their consent Wendy thinks but knows better than to say this out loud.

'I think Jamshid can learn a lot if he broadens his horizons.'

'I will become President after my father. Jamshid will become a Minister. He does not need to go to the West.'

'If that is the will of the people.'

'Screw the people!'

'From what I've heard, you've already screwed quite a few!' says Jamshid but softens his remark with a grin.

'And that is what you should be doing, little Bro. Get out and put it about!' Stas is not offended. He is obviously proud of his philandering and macho image.

'You know father keeps me cooped up here. Ever since you came back from America.'

Ah, so that is the elephant in the room. Stas was expelled from the States under a cloud and resents it.

'You've got to be a man, little Bro. Stand up for yourself. Be strong. Tell the Old Man you want a life. You live here like a little mouse. Yes Father, no Father, three bags full Father.'

'Stas,' Jamshid pleads.

'So,' says Wendy, 'why have you come back to live in the Palace?'

She has touched a nerve. A wave of red flashes over Stas's face and he turns on her.

'I'm here to support my father. It is what a son does. Do what is expected of me. These are Keshevan values. Real values. Strong values. Not like the weak values of your Western democracies.'

'Like boiling people?'

Jamshid shoots her a worried look; he's told her this *in confidence*. Stas does not appear to notice.

'Yes. Exactly. You must kill the weak to make the others strong. Like your Darwin said – 'survival of the fittest.''

'So Western thought has *some* uses, then.'

'You think you are clever,' Stas shouts, 'but you are filling my brother's head with garbage. I'll speak to my father about sending you back to where you belong.'

You'd be doing me a favour, she thinks, but keeps her face straight.

'Whatever your father thinks is best for Jamshid is fine by me.'

'Stupid bitch!' Stas shouts and storms out of the room, slamming the door.

Temper, temper, Wendy chides silently.

'I'm so sorry,' says Jamshid, almost in tears. 'He doesn't mean it personally. He hates everything to do with the West after he was kicked out of America.'

'Except for expensive Western designer trainers!' says Wendy, laughing to lighten the moment.

'And cars!' Jamshid joins in with a grin.

'Don't let him put you off,' Wendy tells him. 'You really do have to broaden your horizons, as I said.'

'I know. Kesheva cannot go on like this. I cannot imagine what it would be like when Stas comes to power. If I am there by his side, perhaps I can moderate his actions. He will be another Khan, like in the old days. We cannot go back to those times. The world has moved on. Look what happened to Gaddafi.'

Wendy feels a sudden surge of pride; her teaching has had an effect on her pupil. Five years in the West will make something of this receptive young man. He represents hope for his country, unlike the uncertain future embodied by his brother.

'OK. Well, let's get back to work,' she says.

And won't Paddy be interested in this conversation, she thinks.

24

At the end of the afternoon's session (academic referencing and citation), Wendy sets Jamshid some homework to do online, packs up her papers and heads off to leave. She finds Rustram waiting on the first floor, chatting to a couple of the guards. Usually, he waits for her in the car outside the Presidential Palace. As he sees her come out of the door leading to the family floor, he breaks off his conversation with the soldiers and goes over to her.

'His Excellency would like to speak with you,' he tells her. She still cannot shake off the image of the Minister of the Interior being boiled alive on Dargan's orders and does not know how she will react to seeing him, but she has little choice in the matter. She manages to swallow her repugnance as she is shown into the President's office.

'Thank you for coming,' says Dargan, ever the urbane, cultured elder statesman. 'Thank you, Major Abdulin. You may leave us.'

'Your Excellency,' says Wendy.

Dargan indicates a chair for her and she sits, her hands folded in her lap, her face neutral. Dargan looks worn and surely those are new worry lines in his face since she last saw him?

'Would you like some tea, Dr. McPherson?'

'Yes. Please. That would be lovely.' What the hell does he

want with me? she thinks.

Again, as if by magic, a young lady appears bringing the teapot and bowls, fills the pot from the samovar and places the tea on a table before gliding out of the office.

'As you say in England, shall I be mother?' Dargan pours the tea before she can reply. Wendy is aware of the tension building up inside her. What does he want?

'I am sorry you have to witness these events in my country over the last weeks,' he says. 'We are normally a peaceful country. These are difficult times. Not only for us, but for the whole world.'

'There have been terrorist incidents in my own country, Your Excellency,' Wendy says.

'Yes. That is why I feel I can talk to you. That you will understand.'

Wendy is at a loss what to say; does Dargan want to unburden himself to her?

'You probably think I am a dictator,' he says. 'An enemy of democracy.'

'Well, Kesheva *is* a little different from the West,' says Wendy, trying her best to be diplomatic. She has no wish to be the next course on the menu. Spit-roasted academic, anyone?

'I took over the rule of Kesheva from the Soviets, who could never have been identified as democrats. I had the lesson of rampant corruption and gangsterism of the Yeltsin years to contend with. Before the Tsarists annexed Kesheva, we had the rule of autocratic Khans. This is all we have known for hundreds of years. I cannot change Kesheva overnight.'

'With respect, Sir, why are you telling me this?'

'I want you to understand, to *really* understand the full

importance of what you are doing with my son, Jamshid.'

'I'm doing my best to ready him for university study in Britain.'

'You are doing more than that. You are preparing him for a liberal education. I cannot see Kesheva becoming a democratic state as you understand the concept in the West in my lifetime. I expect to hand over rule of this country to the next generation of my family. In that, we are no different from the old Khans. I admit it. But if and when Jamshid becomes President, he can introduce changes. Slowly, gradually.'

'What about your son, Stas? Surely he is next in line?'

'I am not bound to the idea of primogeniture, necessarily. Stas would follow the old Ottoman practice of eliminating his rivals, by which I mean Jamshid. Stas, much as I love him, will not be good for Kesheva. I might be a dictator, but he will be a tyrant!'

From her meeting with Stas that morning, Wendy is in full agreement with Dargan's analysis but prudently decides to hold her peace. She sips at her tea to cover her silence.

'And then there are the Islamists.'

'The Islamists?'

'The criminals who killed and maimed innocent people, their fellow religionists, in the recent outrages. I cannot allow them to have a voice. In the field of religion, I have tried to practise toleration. The Soviets set out to make us atheists. They closed the madrassas and made some of the mosques into museums but the people kept the faith of their ancestors. I do not wish to change that. I am a Believer but these fanatics want to recreate the world in their vision and they do not understand that this can never happen. It is a dream that makes a nightmare for the rest of the world. That is why I imprison the radical imams who spread sedition and discontent. I am like a doctor who lances a boil lest the pus infects the rest of the body.'

'But do they have popular support?' Wendy asks.

Dargan does not immediately reply. Like Wendy, he resorts to drinking his tea while he mulls over his answer.

'In some quarters,' he admits. And then to Wendy's surprise asks: 'What would you suggest I do?'

Wendy is caught in the age-old dilemma of anyone asked for advice by an autocrat: does he want me to tell him to carry on as he is going or to tell him what I really think, even if he doesn't want to hear it? She decides on the truth.

'My impression of Kesheva, and I haven't seen anything of the country apart from the capital, is that the people *seem* happy enough on a day-to-day basis. The oil wealth is trickling down and I've seen no evidence of poverty. The shops and the bazaars are stocked with plenty of food and consumer goods, which people seem to be able to afford to buy. There is no material lack. But there is no sense of freedom. There are police and security men everywhere. Even before the bombings. I know this is reflected in many of the cities of the West, sadly. The days of the unarmed bobby on the beat in London are long gone and people moan about CCTV surveillance and GCHQ monitoring their Facebook posts but these are trivial. People can, and do, protest freely on the streets. I can't see that happening here.'

Dargan is silent. *Oh God, I'm kebab!* Wendy thinks.

'You are, of course, right,' Dargan says at last and Wendy realises that she has been holding her breath. 'But right now, there is no way I can loosen control. Thank you for being honest with me, Dr. McPherson. It is a pleasant change. More tea?'

She suddenly finds her throat is very dry. 'Yes, please,' she says.

'And I will be honest with you. The situation here is critical. There have been incidents in other parts of the country. The Islamists have attacked a small army post on the western border. That, in itself, is a minor irritation but the post was also a regional arsenal and I fear they now have access to some heavy weaponry. I do not want another Syria in Kesheva, with all that that entails, the Russians and Americans fighting a proxy war in my country. And by the way, please pass this message on to Mr. Winterslow to pass on to his masters.' This last delivered with a mischievous glint in his eye. Wendy feels herself blush. Has he known about her clandestine activities all along? 'Do you think I don't know the value of pillow talk?' he laughs. 'MI6 would be mad not to take advantage of a well-placed source in the Presidential Palace.'

'I…'

'Do not fear, Dr. McPherson. I would do exactly the same in their position. I'm not about to have you shot. You are too useful to my son and the future of my country. Besides, it might cause a diplomatic incident and I fear we might need all the friends we can get. I *want* Jamshid to study in the United Kingdom. I want him to go to *your* university where you can keep an eye on him.'

'I'm flattered,' says Wendy honestly.

'Don't be. I mean it and I have enjoyed our little chat. I will try to loosen the reins but just for the moment, that is not possible. Remember, when you see the police on the streets, they are there for your protection.'

'I will, of course. And I *do* understand the current necessity for all the security. But, please, don't let it last longer that you have to.'

'Thank you again, Dr. McPherson,' he says, dismissing her.

Rustram is waiting outside for her and escorts her down the staircase to the waiting Mercedes.

'What did His Excellency want?' he asks, casually.

'Oh,' says Wendy, 'just an update on Jamshid's progress. Will he be ready to sit for his IELTS exam soon? How does the application process work? Will I write a reference for him? That sort of thing.' Something is telling her not to place too much trust in Rustram Abdulin. She cannot put her finger on it, but the fact that Dargan wanted a private interview makes her cautious. That, and the impression she has that Rustram is jealous of her relationship with Paddy Winterslow.

Whom she now has *lots* to tell.

25

Although Wendy is bursting to tell Paddy her news, she does not trust the telephone with the information, restricting her calls to Paddy to lovers' chitchat and a promise to spend the weekend with him at the Embassy. The working week passes with no further interactions with Aslan Dargan or any of his children, with the exception of Jamshid. At last it is Friday, when Paddy has arranged to collect her. As soon as she is safe in the little Mazda, she tells Paddy of her conversation with Dargan.

Paddy is a *very* happy bunny indeed; British Intelligence now has an asset at the highest level possible in Kesheva. He will have bragging rights over his opposite numbers in the much larger and better-resourced US Embassy. YES! The news of the insurgent attack on the arsenal on the western border comes as a surprise and must be reported back to London asap. He drops Wendy at his flat and heads to the Secure Room in the Embassy to file his report and discuss the situation with the Ambassador.

In the flat, Wendy finds Paddy has made an effort and stocked the fridge with food. She starts to make a meal, humming to herself as she enjoys the sensation of domesticity shared with the man she loves. If life could go on just like this, then the situation in Kesheva might not be so bad. She does not allow herself to think about what will happen when her contract to teach Jamshid comes to its end in a few short months and she has to return to her life in London. Let the future take care of itself.

An hour later, Paddy returns to the flat. Wendy has made a shepherd's pie, a homely reminder of England and something that can happily sit in the oven on a low heat until they are ready to eat. Paddy is too hyper with Wendy's news to want to eat. He sweeps her off her feet and carries her into the bedroom where they make frenzied love.

Later, when they are sitting at the breakfast bar eating their meal and drinking a glass of wine and the glow of sex slowly fades, they talk about the situation in Kesheva.

'How bad is it?' Wendy asks.

'As long as the Army supports Dargan, I think he can contain it. If he loses their support, then he is in trouble. The generals have tribal and ethnic links to the Dargans. Think Syria and the Assad family. The generals have as much to lose as he does. Most of them have commercial interests in the country. They would not want to jeopardize those. If the country were to fall to Islamic fundamentalists, the generals and their families would be the first up against the wall to be shot. The people accept the rule of Dargan but have little love for the military. The young men are forced to do two years' military service for next to no pay and resent it bitterly. And to make matters worse, the generals flaunt their wealth and hardly live strict Islamic lives. They drink and whore around openly and don't care who knows. Their wives drive expensive cars and would not know a hijab if it bit them. I can't see them taking to wearing a burka in a hurry.'

'But in Syria it *was* parts of the Army that defected.'

'The Assad government were too heavy handed. They over-reacted against peaceful demonstrations. They should have pretended to give in and offer reforms like the Egyptians did. Two years of rule by the Muslim Brotherhood and then the Army took over again and started banging up the reformers in jail.'

'You are a terrible cynic, my love.'

'No. I'm a realist. That's my job. Syria descended into a bloodbath, sucked in the Russians and Americans and swamped Europe in refugees, giving fuel to the right-wing nationalist parties all over Europe.'

'And you think that might happen here?'

'As I said, as long as Dargan can keep the lid on it, Kesheva might, *might* escape.'

'He thinks he can. I got the impression he is taking the long view; sending Jamshid to the West before shoe-horning him in as his successor.'

'He needs time, at least five years if not longer. And I somehow doubt that Stas Dargan will roll over quietly and give way to his little brother. He moves in the same circles as the sons of the generals and will be building up a power base of his own.'

'Stas Dargan is a really nasty piece of work,' says Wendy. 'Much like Uday Hussein in Iraq, I should imagine.'

'Very much like Uday Hussein. Born to a life of privilege where nothing was refused to him and everyone feared him.'

'I can't get over Aslan Dargan *boiling* the Minister of the Interior. He always seems such a reasonable man whenever I've spoken to him.'

'Yes. London was very interested in that little snippet when I told them. Beneath the veneer lurks a monster, whatever his protestations of wanting to liberalise the country. Dargan is driven by family. He will do anything to keep the Dargan dynasty in power. If he sees Jamshid as having to slacken off the reins, then so be it, as long as it is a Dargan that still holds the reins. He is a man of his culture, where family is the be-all and end-all. He has come to realise that if Stas takes power, there *will* be a popular uprising, so Jamshid is the better option for stability. More wine?'

'Yes, please. I think I need it.' She pushes her glass over to be refilled. Paddy pours the last of the wine into her glass.

'I think we might need another bottle,' he says. 'If we are to set the world to rights.'

'How are we going to do that? Paddy, I'm frightened.'

'You are safe enough here,' he reassures her. 'And while you have Dargan's protection, I can't see anything happening to you.'

'And what about you? I don't want anything to happen to you.'

'Nor do I, not now that I've found you,' he says softly, kissing her.

Wendy decides that it is time to talk about the elephant in the room.

'What about the future, Paddy? Do we have a future? Together, I mean.'

He is silent. Wendy curses herself for bringing up what might be a taboo subject. She does not want to push him into saying something she dreads to hear; that there *is* no future for them. He takes a drink from his glass and then takes her hand in his and gazes into her eyes.

'Wendy McPherson. I want a future with you more than I

have ever wanted anything. I have applied for a transfer back to London. I have done my stint in the field. I can still do good work as an analyst behind a desk, if that is what they want from me. If not, there are plenty of think-tanks or security firms that would be glad of my expertise. Kesheva is my last foreign posting.'

'Oh, Paddy.' Her eyes are shining with tears and she is actually afraid that her chest will burst with happiness. 'Oh, Paddy,' she says again as she hugs him close, 'I would like that so much. I love you.'

And there it is, out in the open.

'I love you, too, Wendy. Let's forget the new bottle and go back to bed.'

'Can you manage it again?'

'I'll do my best,' he laughs.

And that is good enough for Wendy.

26

Wendy is ripped out of sleep by the sound of a huge explosion close at hand. She is not sure whether she dreamt it but the sight of Paddy leaping out of bed and pulling on his clothes tells her it is real.

'Stay put!' he shouts as he sprints out of the room. A moment later, she hears the front door slam and he is gone.

'Dear God,' she prays to a god she does not believe in, 'don't let anything happen to him.' She gets out of bed and inches to the window in the living room. Outside, she sees a column of black smoke drifting up into the clear spring sky. Members of the Embassy staff are milling around in the courtyard but everyone seems to be moving in slow motion and there is a deafening silence.

Ignoring his order, she stumbles into her clothes and opens the front door. The sound of shouting crashes over her in a wave of confusion. She creeps out and makes her way to the front of the Embassy building that faces onto the street and notices that all the windows have shattered but apart from that, the building appears to be unscathed. She sees Jim Armstrong, the Ambassador, dressed in a checked flannel dressing gown, his pyjamas peeping underneath with a pair of carpet slippers on his feet, looking dazed, his wife with her hair in curlers and clad in a floral pattern housecoat behind him.

'They've hit the American Embassy!' someone shouts.

'How bad?' Armstrong shouts back.

'Can't tell yet, Sir. Paddy Winterslow has gone to have a reccie.'

Paddy! You idiot! Wendy thinks, fear rising in her throat. She heads towards the gates but is shooed back into the compound. A feeling of utter helplessness engulfs her. What if there is a second bomb? She cannot lose Paddy now. Not when they are planning a life together in London, away from this madness.

Armstrong brusquely tells his wife to go back into the Embassy and when he notices Wendy, tells her to do the same. She obediently follows Phoebe Armstrong into the Embassy.

'I think we need a strong cup of tea, my dear,' Phoebe suggests in a voice that will brook no argument. She leads Wendy up a staircase to the surprisingly small apartment that the Ambassador and his wife occupy at the top of the Embassy. It is much more homely and cluttered than Paddy's spartan flat with large, worn and comfortable leather armchairs and glass-fronted cabinets displaying the collected trophies of a life spent in the diplomatic service of the United Kingdom. A small television crouches in a corner. Fresh spring flowers in a vase adorn a battered old coffee table.

'I won't be a minute,' says Phoebe as she disappears in the direction of the kitchen. 'Make yourself at home and try not to worry.'

Wendy flops into the embrace of an armchair and immediately starts to worry about Paddy.

Moments later Phoebe reappears carrying two mugs of tea.

'I've put some sugar in your tea; it helps with shock. I expect you need it.' She does not give the impression that anything is out of the ordinary. She has been the wife of a career diplomat for over thirty years and has learnt the art of *sang froid* to perfection. She gives off the impression that nothing can faze her and that there is nothing that cannot be remedied by a hot cup of strong tea.

Wendy sips scalding tea that could happily support a vertical teaspoon and starts to feel better as the sugar kicks in.

'Well, it may be disloyal of me to say so, but I'm glad that we weren't the target. Goes to show how our position in the world has eroded!'

Despite herself, Wendy cannot help laughing.

'That's better, dear. I'm sure your young man will be all right.'

Does *everyone* in Kesheva know about me and Paddy? Wendy wonders. But in the tight-knit community of the Embassy, *of course* everyone does.

'Now,' Phoebe continues, a picture of unruffled calm, 'if you'll excuse me, I must go and get dressed. See if Jim needs me. Would you like to watch the television? We get all the UK channels. One of the perks of having satellite communications.'

Wendy is beginning to think that reality is slipping away. Here she is sitting in the Ambassador's flat after a bomb has gone off in the immediate vicinity, sipping tea and being asked if she might want to catch an episode of *Eastenders* while the man she loves is poking about a bombsite. Surreal or what?

Once again, she can hear the howl of sirens in the street as the emergency services converge on the Embassy Quarter. She is desperate to know what has happened. Have there been casualties? What happened to the police guards around the Embassy compounds? Why didn't they stop the bombers? And, no, she does NOT want to watch television. She wants no reminders of the normal world thousands of miles away when her world in the here and now might be about to shatter into pieces like the glass from the Embassy windows.

'I'll give the TV a miss, thank you,' she tells Phoebe.

'Can't say I blame you, dear. It's just full of reality shows. I rather like watching a good episode of *Midsomer Murders* myself.'

Wendy suppresses an urge to throttle Phoebe. How can the woman be so calm when some lunatics have just set off a bomb on her doorstep? She supposes it must be some sort of job description from the FCO. "Now, Missus Armstrong, what would you do if someone planted an explosive device outside the Embassy? A: panic; B: tend to the wounded; C: make a nice cup of tea, keep calm and carry on?"

Wendy is positive that Phoebe Armstrong answered C in the great tradition of the wives at the siege of Lucknow. She knows that she herself would always answer A.

Wendy is finishing her tea when Phoebe reappears dressed in a pair of jeans, an old rugby shirt that probably belonged to her husband and what Wendy's mother called "sensible shoes".

'Shall we see if we can be of any assistance, dear?'

Wendy dreads what they might find outside but anything is better than sitting here no knowing and readily agrees to the suggestion.

The Embassy compound is almost deserted. The pall of black smoke still hangs in the air but is rapidly dispersing. The sirens are still blasting the air as the two women venture out of the Embassy gates. Two hundred yards down the road, off to the left, there is a cluster of assorted vehicles, blue lights flashing. Men with guns are fanning out to form a cordon in the road. Wendy can see ambulances with their Red Crescent symbols with open doors; stretchers are being loaded into them.

A young soldier tries to halt their passage but Phoebe politely but firmly brushes him aside.

'I'm the wife of the British Ambassador,' she tells him but Wendy is not sure he can understand English. Phoebe steams on like a battleship, intent on her way. Wendy, like a little frigate, steams in her wake.

Stuck in the imposing gateway of the American Embassy is the burnt- out wreck of a car. The guardhouse and the barrier to the Embassy are shattered shards of wood, smouldering from the blast. The Marines who habitually guard the approach must, Wendy realized with deep sympathy and upset, have been vaporised instantly. The front façade of the once imposing building has taken the force of the explosion and has collapsed, the upper floors concertinaed onto the lower, exposing the naked insides of the rooms behind. Wendy is reminded of pictures she has seen on the news of the aftermath of an earthquake. Men are scrabbling over the debris, hauling at chunks of stone and concrete with their bare hands. A file of walking wounded, bloodied with their clothes in tatters are waiting to be treated by the medics from the ambulances. She sees men and women covered in dust from the collapsed building wandering aimlessly in shock. A shoe sits in a pool of blood. On closer inspection Wendy is horrified to see there is a foot in the shoe. She gags.

Of Paddy, there is no sign amidst the carnage.

'We must get these poor people into the Embassy,' says Phoebe, snapping Wendy out of her fugue state. 'Now. Give me a hand!'

Together, Wendy and Phoebe muster the shocked and dazed survivors into a line and lead them back towards the British Embassy. Wendy is reminded of pictures of gassed and blinded soldiers from the First World War, walking in single file, their hands on the shoulder of the man in front. Keshevan soldiers watch them go impassively, secure in the knowledge that this time it was not their turn to fall victims to terrorist bombs.

27

Back in the Embassy, Phoebe rustles up some of the domestic staff and orders up tea and hot water. The survivors are settled on the floor of the large reception room that Wendy remembers from the New Year's Eve party and she and Phoebe start the process of cleaning up the grime from people's faces and checking for injuries. It is midday before Wendy knows it; she is exhausted from the emotional strain but their ministrations have borne fruit. Many of the survivors are stretched out on the floor asleep while others are beginning to come to terms with what has happened to them and are talking in hushed voices.

Jim Armstrong has returned with the American Ambassador, his broken arm in a sling and has given him free rein of the British Embassy's communications net. At last, Paddy also returns. He is filthy and his hands are torn and bleeding from where he has been shifting rubble. His face is drawn and grey. Wendy runs to him and hugs him, her sense of relief over-whelming.

'Those fuckers!' he says.

'How bad is it?'

'Bad.' His eyes are haunted with the thousand-yard stare of soldiers who have been in bloody action. 'It could have been us.'

'I've been helping with the survivors,' Wendy tells him.

'I love you,' he says and clings to her in a tight embrace. 'That could have been you.'

'But it wasn't. I love you, too. I love you so much.'

For a long moment, they just cling to each other without speaking.

'At least twenty-five dead,' says Paddy. 'Lots injured. The Embassy will be out of commission for some time. The Americans will go ape-shit but there is nothing they can do. Nothing. There are no obvious targets they can strike back at. Nothing.'

'Jim Armstrong has brought the American Ambassador back here.'

'All the Embassies are trying to help. Even the ones the Americans are not exactly on the best of terms with. It's times like this when you forget your differences.'

'Aslan Dargan will be going frantic.'

'What'll he do next?' says Paddy bitterly, 'impale the new Minister of the Interior?'

'What can he do? The city was closed down tight and still they got through.'

'There has to be some sort of collusion between the security forces and the terrorists.'

'But who? You said the generals were all on side with Dargan.'

'There must be plenty of middle-ranking officers who are sympathetic. Those whose family connections are not influential enough to ensure they rise to high rank. Ghaddafi was only a captain when he overthrew the Libyan government.'

'Wendy, I need you here,' Phoebe calls.

'I've got to go, Paddy. Duty calls.'

The Embassy is filling up as more of the lightly-injured

arrive. Phoebe has taken on the role of Matron and is directing members of her staff in nursing the wounded. Diplomats from other embassies are conferring together in small clusters. The resources of the British Embassy are becoming stretched. Jim Armstrong comes down to appraise himself on what is going on and passes from group to group, pausing for a word here and a word there. Some time in the morning, he has managed to change out of his pyjamas into a more Ambassadorial lounge suit.

'You look like you've been in the wars,' he says to Wendy as she is winding a bandage round the head of a young secretary from the American Embassy. Wendy takes stock of herself; she is smeared with blood and her long red hair is as tangled as her nerves. Her clothes are fit only for the bin and as she straightens up to talk to Jim she feels a wave of exhaustion hit her. She realises that she has not eaten anything today apart from a cup of sweet tea. She experiences a moment of giddiness and sways on her feet. Jim catches her and steadies her.

'Whoa, you need a break. The kitchen staff are rustling up sandwiches but God knows we haven't got the wherewithal to feed all these people. Get something inside you while you can.'

Gratefully, she goes off in search of sustenance and finds a member of the kitchen staff with a pile of sandwiches on a plate. She grabs a couple and wolfs them down. Afterwards, she has no recollection whatsoever of the fillings.

Gradually supplies and extra help trickles in from other Embassies: blankets, food and medical supplies. A woman called Roz from the Australian Embassy tells Wendy 'You look fair tuckered, let me take over.' To which Wendy gratefully acquiesces and slumps against a wall with a cup of black coffee in her hand. The Embassy reminds her of Waterloo Station in the rush hour with people swarming everywhere in semi-organised chaos.

Her coffee finished, she wanders outside in a daze. She is amazed to find that the daylight is fading as the sun sets and the sky turns red as blood but the air retains the heat of the day, with the promise of summer to come. The ambulances are long gone but the army are out in force, shutting the stable door after the horse has bolted. They were supposed to protect us, Wendy thinks. Where were they?

She hears sirens approaching and sees a motorcade led by an armoured car draw up. Soldiers spill from the vehicles and form a cordon around the British Embassy, weapons at the ready. Aslan Dargan steps out of a limousine, followed by two men in plain clothes. Somehow, Wendy is not surprised to recognise Rustram Abdulin as one of them.

Dargan strides swiftly through the Embassy gates and stops when he sees Wendy.

'Dr. McPherson? Are you hurt?'

'No, Your Excellency.'

'You are covered in blood. You look terrible!'

'I've been helping with the wounded.'

'A tragedy. Truly, a tragedy. What is my country coming to?'

Wendy cannot think of anything to say in reply. That it is a tragedy is self-evident.

'I believe the American Ambassador is here. Praise God he was not killed.'

'Yes. He is. I saw him this morning.'

'I must speak with him urgently,' Dargan says. 'If there is anything I can do for you, please let me know,'

'There's nothing, thank you. I'm all right. Just very tired.'

'Take some time off before you come back to work. It is the least we can do to show our gratitude. Be assured, we will offer any assistance we can to these poor people. Now, if you will forgive me, I must speak to the Ambassador.'

'Are you sure you are OK? You look terrible.' asks Abdulin.

'I'm fine.' Wendy is getting a little hacked off with people telling her how terrible she looks. What do they expect? Her to be in a ball gown with her hair perfectly coiffured?

'If I can do anything, you have my number,' says Abdulin and quickly follows his master into the Embassy building.

Wearily, Wendy trudges back into the mayhem of the Embassy. Phoebe Armstrong, looking as full of energy as ever and still directing operations, catches sight of her.

'I've got plenty of help here now,' she says. 'Go back to the flat and get yourself into a hot shower. Get out of those filthy clothes. Have a stiff drink. You have done more than enough today. For which I thank you most sincerely.'

Wendy needs no second bidding. Thirty minutes later, she is fresh, clean and scrubbed wearing a tee shirt and a pair of baggy jogging pants, curled up on the sofa in Paddy's flat with a large brandy. She puts the glass down on the floor for a moment and before she knows it is fast asleep.

28

Just like Sleeping Beauty, Wendy is woken by a kiss from her Prince Charming. For a moment she is disorientated and still befuddled with sleep.

'Paddy?'

The events of the day flood back. The memory of the bloodied shoe, the shattered bodies, the terrible noise of the explosion.

'Oh God!'

'It's all right, it's all right,' says Paddy, cradling her in his arms. She is shaking and starts to weep silently, tears rolling down her face. Paddy picks up the glass of brandy from the floor.

'Drink this. It might help.'

She drinks the brandy down in a single gulp, her hand trembling as she holds the snifter. Paddy watches her as the colour returns to her face.

'Better?' he asks.

She nods, wiping the tears off her face with the back of her hand.

'That was so awful. All those poor people. This bloody country. Can we just get out?'

'You know we can't.' He pauses. 'Well, perhaps you can, but right now there is no way I can leave. The situation here is critical and HMG and my bosses are desperate for site reps.'

'I'm not leaving without you,' she says firmly.

'That's my girl. I do love you.'

'How long have I been asleep?' she asks. Outside, through the window, she sees that it is now dark.

'It's about one o'clock,' Paddy tells her. 'Things have been moving quickly. Dargan has decreed that the Embassy area is a no-go zone under any circumstances and has ordered the soldiers to shoot to kill anyone trying to get in. This is going to make life very difficult for those of us trapped inside.'

'How am I going to get out? I've got my work with Jamshid.'

'That's the least of your worries. If Dargan wants you to continue teaching his son, then he will have to make arrangements. I'm sure the estimable Major Abdulin will work something out. But for the moment, you just stay here where I can keep you safe.'

Paddy finds the remote control for the television and switches on the BBC World Service. The bombing of the American Embassy is the lead story but, as yet, there is no picture footage from Kesheva. Paddy flicks through the English language channels; CNN, al-Jazeera, CCTV, Sky News, Fox News, France 24, but none of them have anything much to add. All have a similar tone of shock and outrage and speculation as to who the perpetrators might be. A number of radical organizations have claimed responsibility, including Boko Haram from West Africa.

The state-run Kesheva television station is broadcasting a concert of patriotic folkloric songs and dances. Nothing to panic about is the message Dargan wants to project.

'So, nothing new there then,' says Paddy, switching the television off. 'Everyone and his dog trying to get in on the act and claim the kudos. Bunch of losers!'

'Do *you* have any idea who was behind it?'

'Most likely The Islamic Peoples' Front of Kesheva. They seem to be the best organised bunch of nutters.'

'Are they the ones who attacked the army base that Aslan Dargan told me about?'

'We think so.'

'We?'

'Us and the Americans. The Keshevans are keeping tight lipped and not sharing. Perhaps after this they might open up a bit more. It's got to be in their interest to do so. Maybe Dargan will have a little chat to you if and when you go back to the Presidential Palace. A back-channel, so to speak.'

'Paddy Winterslow! You just want me to spy for you!'

'I'm quite interested in your body as well!'

'I'm not sure I should give in to your wicked lust,' she laughs, hitting him over the head with a cushion.

'You know you can't resist me, my little Mata Hari,' he says, grabbing her and planting a theatrical kiss on her mouth. She pretends to push him away.

'Away with you, Sir! I am but a poor innocent girl up from the country and looking for honest work.'

'And I will find you a suitable position,' he replies, entering into the game.

'And what position might that be, Sir?'

'I was thinking of missionary work. Or perhaps employment as a cowboy on my ranch.'

'A ranch, Sir? Is that what you call it?' she says. 'And is it a big ranch?'

'Let me show you,' he says with a leer, twirling an imaginary moustache.

'Oooh, Sir.' Wendy has stopped shaking and her black mood has lifted, as Paddy knew it would.

'Another brandy?' he asks.

'I think I might like to see the ranch now,' she says.

29

Sunday. The Day After the Bomb. Paddy rises early and is soon locked in the Embassy Secure Communications Room with the British and American Ambassadors and the ranking members of the CIA who have survived the blast.

Wendy wakes some time later, brews herself a cup of coffee and takes stock. Her first task is to gather up her soiled and bloodied clothes from yesterday and put them in the washing machine. She gets dressed in clean clothes and goes to the main Embassy building to see what help she can give.

She finds the situation much improved since yesterday; other embassies have pitched in and taken in many of the victims to ease the overcrowding. Phoebe bustles about organizing hot food and directing her staff. She looks fresh but Wendy has a sneaking suspicion that she has had little sleep.

'Wendy!' says Phoebe, 'how are you today?'

'I'm fine. How about you?'

'We're coping. As you can see, the pressure is off us a bit, thank God.'

'What can I do?' Wendy asks.

'There's not a lot you can do. The worst of the wounded have been taken into the Zayed Ali private hospital and are being guarded by what seems to be an entire Keshevan army regiment and the rest of the army are camped around the Embassy Quarter. Bit late, if you ask me!'

'Is there any news?'

'Poor Jim has had a hell of a night of it. He hasn't had a wink of sleep, poor lamb. He and Frank Pinchetta have been communicating with Washington non-stop.'

'Who is Frank Pinchetta?'

'The American Ambassador.'

'Oh.'

'The Americans are sending a plane to evacuate non-essential staff and another kitted out as a flying ambulance for the wounded who are able to travel. Another four poor souls died in the night. I believe the Americans are also sending a company of Marines to guard the Embassy compound. Lots of sensitive stuff buried in the debris.'

'What about us?'

'Us?'

'Our Government. What are they going to do?'

'HMG, in their wisdom, are sending out a small detachment of Special Air Service troopers. We call them the Hereford Hooligans in diplomatic circles. But, to be honest, I don't see what a dozen soldiers can do against madmen driving cars full of explosives who are convinced that if they die killing non-believers, they have an express ticket to paradise.'

'Well, that's a relief, then. We can all sleep secure in our beds.'

'Yes, indeed,' Phoebe says with heavy irony.

'And talking of beds, when did you last see yours?'

'The night before last. In another lifetime.'

'Why don't you get your head down? Everything seems to be running smoothly, as far as it can be. I'll be here if I am needed. Go to bed.'

Phoebe sags visibly and suddenly looks her age.

'I *could* just have forty winks,' she agrees. 'And a nice hot cup of tea.'

The morning passes. At midday, a fleet of buses arrive in the Embassy Quarter and the evacuation of survivors begins. The staff of the British Embassy begin the task of clearing up and putting the Embassy to rights. By the end of the afternoon, it is as if nothing out of the ordinary ever happened. Wendy supposes this is a human survival instinct: push the horror away until it becomes a distant memory and can be lived with. She is not sure whether she will be able to sublimate it entirely and suspects that she will resurrect the experience at dinner parties and social gatherings to enthrall her listeners.

'The worst part of my stay in Kesheva was the bombing of the American Embassy...' she fantasies herself saying to a rapt audience. 'I was there at the time. You can't begin to imagine...'

Oh God, she thinks, am I *really* that shallow?

Sitting back in Paddy's flat, she watches the World Service news. The bombing in Kesheva is still the lead story. The American President has made a statement condemning the bombing and promising to hunt down the guilty parties. He assures the American people that the government of Kesheva is co-operating fully with the State Department and American intelligence agencies and has the situation in the country fully in control. However, he advises against all unnecessary travel to Kesheva, advice, the BBC tells her, that is echoed by the British government.

'Goody,' Wendy says to the television, 'but what about us poor sods who are stuck here?'

The television has no answer for her.

But Rustram Abdulin does.

He phones her at eight o'clock just as she is making dinner for Paddy and herself.

Paddy came home an hour earlier, looking drawn and drained.

'I'm wacked,' he says as he flops onto the sofa.

'Nice one!' says Wendy brightly.

'What "nice one"?' he says, shaking his head. Has the woman lost her wits?

'"Paddy wacked"' she laughs.

'You're a nut job, you know that?'

'But I'm your nut job. Paddy Winterslow. For better or worse you are stuck with me.'

'Any chance of a strong drink?'

'You've been out here too long. You must be mistaking me for a harem slave.'

'Wendy, I've had one fucker of a day.'

'I'm only teasing, O Lord and Master. Your every wish is my command.' She makes a mock curtsey and pour him a large single malt.

'Paddy!' she calls, 'keep an eye on the omelettes. That's my phone.'

'Dr. McPherson, are you well?'

'Rustram. What can I do for you?'

'The President is most insistent that you return to work as soon as possible. Tomorrow?'

'What about the lock-down around the Embassy Quarter?'

'Let me worry about that. I will personally collect you in an hour's time and escort you through the cordon to your villa.

You will be able to prepare your lessons tonight. I have arranged for extra security for your safety.'

'In an hour?' says Wendy.

'Yes. Is that convenient?' His tone implies that she has little choice in the matter.

'I suppose so,' she says reluctantly.

'Excellent. I will see you shortly. Goodbye.'

'Who was it?' Paddy asks.

'Major Abdulin. He's coming to collect me in an hour. Dargan wants me back at work tomorrow.'

'Does he think it's safe?'

'Apparently.'

'Well, if you've gotta go, you've gotta go.'

'Say it like you'll actually miss me.'

'You know I will. Now, eat your omelette. I made it especially for you!'

'Yeah, right! I keep you barefoot naked tied to the kitchen.'

'Now, there's a thought!'

At eight o'clock Wendy is lurking by the Embassy gates. A small knot of soldiers are eying her up in speculation.

Don't ogle me, she thinks, keep your eyes on the street. But when they hear the sound of an approaching vehicle, they spread out and ready their weapons. Rustram's Mercedes coasts gently to a stop and he jumps out. He is wearing a uniform that Wendy does not recognise but the soldiers certainly do. They snap to attention and salute.

An engineer officer my foot, thinks Wendy. Now, my lad, we see you in your true colours.

He opens the back door of the car for her.

'A terrible business. We will catch them and they will regret the day they were born.'

I can well believe that, she thinks. *I bet you can be a mean bastard if you want to.*

'Shall we go? The streets are empty and the journey will not take long.'

And the streets are indeed deserted. Kesheva has the air of an abandoned city: a city in the grip of fear or plague.

'This is so sad,' Wendy observes.

'It is the price we pay. But we will win in the end and life will return to normal. The summer is coming.'

What difference will that make? she wonders. Terrorism is not a seasonal event like Christmas. More like year-round Hallow'en with the monsters out and about.

When they arrive at her villa, she finds a picket of four soldiers camped outside. Oybek and Ruthinna rush out when they hear the car. Ruthinna embraces Wendy in a big motherly hug.

'I so glad you are safe,' she says, tears in her eyes. Oybek, too, is looking tearful.

'They bad, bad men. Reputation of Kesheva now bad. I, too, glad you safe.'

'I've missed you,' says Wendy, welling up herself.

'I will return to collect you at ten o'clock,' says Rustram, curtly. 'Please be ready.'

'I always am,' is Wendy's frosty reply as Oybek and Ruthinna usher her in to the safety of the villa.

30

And so life begins to return to what is now normal in Kesheva for Wendy. She is driven to the Presidential Palace every weekday, only now her car is driven in a convoy with an armoured personnel carrier and another car with armed police inside and Rustram Abdulin rarely accompanies her now. She suspects that he is employed on more important duties than babysitting her.

The temperature is climbing into the 30s Celsius as March becomes April. Wendy's work with Jamshid progresses well and she feels he is ready to take his entrance exam. She has negotiated a place for him at her university with George Rhys, her Head of Unit, who is keen for an injection of money from Aslan Dargan into the university's coffers.

She is now halfway through her contract and can see an end in sight; she will not be unhappy to return to London but she has become fond of Oybek and Ruthinna and will most certainly miss them. Maybe they will be able to stay in touch, but in her heart of hearts, she feels that it is unlikely.

Wendy spends the weekends at Paddy's flat, although he is often too busy chasing up reports of incidents of insurrection in the various outlying regions of Kesheva to devote all of his time to her. However, he has received assurances from his masters in London that he is due a home posting and they have made tentative plans for a life together after Kesheva.

Aslan Dargan has only spoken to her briefly about Jamshid, about where he will live in London, what courses he might take and whether Wendy is prepared to send regular reports on his progress back to Kesheva. Which she agrees to do. Of the political situation in Kesheva he is reticent to comment, so she has nothing of importance to offer Paddy.

There have been a number of small demonstrations in the city, but these have been ruthlessly dispersed by the police and army. The mood in the city is brooding and sullen. The former hubbub of life in the streets and the bazaars and the mosques is muted and people are closed and suspicious of strangers. There have been a wave of arrests in the early hours of the night and fear of government spies is rampant. Paddy tells her of reports the Western intelligence agencies have received of other bombings and attacks on army and police posts in small towns and villages across the country. The agencies describe Kesheva as 'volatile'.

The work of clearing the damage to the American Embassy is nearly finished and the skeleton staff have returned to the undamaged section, while still making use of the facilities of the British Embassy, doing the Special Relationship no end of good. The Marine Company have turned the site into a fortress, with concrete dragon's teeth littering the approach and machine gun nests covering the road. The small detachment of Special Air Service troopers based in the British Embassy seem insignificant by comparison. They appear to spend much of their time stripped down to their shorts and working on their suntans but always with their weapons close to hand. Phoebe Armstrong make sure they are regularly supplied with mugs of tea.

'Got to keep the troops happy,' she tells Wendy. 'You never know what will happen.'

The terrible events of the bombing are beginning to take on a sense of unreality for Wendy as she focuses on the future but she wakes up some nights to find herself sweating and overcome by feelings of vague dread. She knows that the aftermath of the death and destruction will never really leave her but that she must try and put it behind her. To dwell too much on the horror can only lead to black depression and wreck the life of domestic normality that is only weeks away.

Wendy will not let that happen, come what may, on that she is resolute.

She holds on to the thought that she has not long to go before she is on a plane back home.

31

Wendy has arranged for a registered IELTS examiner to fly out to Kesheva at Aslan Dargan's expense to administer the examination to Jamshid. To her great joy, she learns that the examiner will be her friend and colleague, Mary Bowyer, who will fly out on the BA scheduled flight to arrive on the last Thursday in April, administer the test on the Friday and fly back to London the following Monday. Wendy's only regret is that she cannot show Mary the bustling, vibrant city that she first encountered in January.

Wendy is given the day off to meet Mary at the airport and is driven there in the Mercedes, followed by her bodyguards. She wonders what Mary will make of all the security, although she suspects Mary will have been given a full briefing before she left London; the FCO are still advising travellers against going to Kesheva.

She watches the plane land and a trickle of passengers disembarking. She spots Mary coming off the plane and fanning herself. The heat is in the 40's C. Wendy has become acclimatized but can imagine the effect the blast of hot air is having on Mary, who quickly disappears into the Terminal building. Ten minutes later, she is escorted out by a small gaggle of security men. Wendy rushes to her and embraces her.

'Mary! Oh, it's so great to see you!'

'Is it always this bloody hot? It's like stepping into a furnace.'

'It was bloody freezing when I got here,' Wendy laughs. 'Brass monkeys.'

'So, how have you been? This place sounds like a bundle of laughs.'

'Let's get you into the car. It's got air con.'

A security man loads Mary's small carry-on case into the boot of the Mercedes as the two women climb inside.

'Fuckin' hell,' says Mary, 'do you always travel with a small army?'

'Things *are* a bit fraught here at the moment. Lots of paranoia. But the city is mostly safe. You'll be staying with me. I expect Ruthinna will be making a plov for you tonight.'

'Plov?'

'Wait and see. I hope you like carrots.'

'And when do I get to meet the lovely Paddy?' Mary says archly.

Wendy has been in email contact with her friends and admitted to the existence of the dashing man from the Embassy, while being circumspect about his actual duties.

'Maybe tomorrow. Jamshid is taking the test in the Embassy. So there can be no suspicion of cheating and fakery. I'm to collect him and convey him thither.'

'This is an Islamic country, isn't it? Any chance of a drink?'

'Don't worry about that. Oybek, he's Ruthinna's husband - they are a sweet old couple who look after me - seems to have a never ending supply of booze. But you will have to take it easy tonight if you are examining in the morning.'

'Maybe just a sip of something, then. Bloody hell! What's that?'

'What's what?"

'That bloody great armoured monstrosity.'

'Oh. That's just a tank. We're getting near the city.'

'And you are not fazed by this?"

'Not really. As I said, things are a bit fraught just now. It's changed, Mary. It always has been a police state, but it was much livelier when I first got here. Colder, but livelier. People thronging in the bazaar, chatting and joking. The terrorists have a lot to answer for.'

'What about the bomb at the American Embassy? Did you see it?'

Wendy has not confided her part in the aftermath of the bombing to her friends back in England. Like a soldier who has seen death and destruction on the battlefield, she finds it hard to talk about her experience with those who were not there. It is something she wants to forget and she knows that her friends can never understand what it was like in the smoke and the dust with the dead and the wounded staggering like zombies.

'It was pretty bad, I guess,' she says vaguely.

'But you've not been caught up in anything?"

'Nothing much. How is everything back at the University? Students still playing up?'

Mary senses that her friend wants to talk about safer, more mundane things and launches into the tittle-tattle of university life, of strikes and feuds, of chaos on commuter trains and what a lousy spring it has been.

'Here we are,' Wendy announces as the car draws up at the villa. 'There are Oybek and Ruthinna, waiting to say hello. Their English is not perfect, but it's improved since I've been here. A little extra-curricular teaching on my part.'

'There are soldiers in the garden!'

'Just a precaution. People know I work for the President.'

'You *are* joking?'

'As I said, just a precaution.' Wendy laughs to make light of the situation. 'Come and meet my surrogate parents. They're dying to meet you.'

Ruthinna embraces Mary and kisses her on both cheeks; although it is not yet quite midday, Oybek insists on a toast to welcome Mary to Kesheva. A smell of grilled meat permeates the house.

'One thing, you won't starve while you are here,' Wendy tells Mary. 'Ruthinna lives to cook. It's her main purpose in life. I put on pounds in my first few weeks until I could convince her that she was not cooking for the Golden Horde and its brother.'

Later, seated at the table and replete, Mary suggests she could get used to living like this. She and Oybek have made inroads into a bottle of brandy, despite Wendy's advice to be abstemious.

'I'll be fine. Apart from the interview section all I have to do is sit there and make sure your student isn't getting the answers off his smartphone,' says Mary. 'Piece of cake. Talking of which…' She reaches for another slice of apricot pastry.

'You like?' asks a beaming Ruthinna.

'I like,' says Mary with undisguised enthusiasm. 'You really are living the life of Reilly, Wendy. You'd be mad to come back to London.'

'Come on. If you have finished stuffing your face, I'll show you something of the city. The Old City is close and you've never seen anything like it. It's like something out of the Middle Ages or the Thousand and One Nights. You expect to see people zipping about on flying carpets and rubbing oil lamps for all they are worth.' She stops in mid-flow. That was what it used to be, only a few short months ago. Not so much now. 'It's a bit quieter these days. A lot more security but you'll still love it.'

'Come on, then, Scheherazade, show me.'

As they leave the house, two soldiers fall in behind them. Wendy, with Oybek and Ruthinna's help, has picked up enough Keshevan to tell the soldiers what the plan is. The soldiers nod and bracket them, one in front and the other just behind.

'Do you always go out with an armed guard?' asks Mary with a touch of alarm in her voice.

'Since the bombing at the American Embassy. Foreigners are few and far between in the Old Town now. It's just a precaution. Don't worry.'

'No, of course not. Why should I worry? I've only landed in the middle of a terrorist hotbed.'

'You're only here for a couple of days. Nothing is going to happen. The city is locked down pretty tight.'

Mary is blown away by the architecture of the Old City; Wendy notices some people looking at them with naked hostility in their eyes, something she has not seen before. She catches snatches of muttered curses and is glad of the presence of their guards. Or perhaps it is the guards that the people resent, but she feels sure it is them, two western women with their heads uncovered, generating resentment. Such tourists that used to visit Kesheva have not been seen in weeks and the owners of the tourist trap shops are suffering.

'It's not *my* fault!' she wants to shout but bites back the words. 'What happened to you?'

But she knows what happened: terrorism and repression; printed sermons by extremist imams printed off and clandestinely circulated like samizdat from hand to hand; young men arrested and interned without trial; young girls assaulted and beaten for wearing immodest dress. How swiftly a place and a people can change, she thinks. I need to get out!

'This is *fabulous!*' says Mary, who notices nothing and knows no better.

'Yes,' Wendy agrees. 'Fabulous.'

'But bloody hot.'

'Let's get a cold drink. I want to show you my favourite café.' And get off the streets.

They sit in the cool gloom of the café that Rustram first took her to on her first day in Kesheva and drink iced tea. The soldiers sit by the doorway, but not too close, and drink coca cola, keeping wary eyes on the street, their guns resting on the table, close at hand.

'So? When am I going to meet him?'

'I expect you'll meet him tomorrow, at the Embassy. When I bring Jamshid for his exam.'

'Is he ready?'

For a moment, Wendy is confused: 'Is who ready?'

'Jamshid.'

Wendy laughs, 'I thought you meant Paddy. I have warned him about you.'

'A beautiful divorced woman ready for love?'

'An old harpy out on the pull. Look what happened to us last year.'

'Don't remind me. I haven't lived that down. You did well to scarper over here. The girls don't miss a chance to take the piss. Seriously though, is he the one? You've been alone ever since That Bastard Tony.'

'I think it might be,' Wendy admits softly, not wanting to jinx it by being too positive. 'I hope you like him.'

'What does he do?'

'He's the Cultural Attaché.'

'Does that mean he's a spy?' asks Mary, who has read her share of spy thrillers.

'Of course not!'

'Humph!'

'He's *not*!'

'And are you his beautiful Mata Hari?'

'He's just a bloke who works at the Embassy. He co-ordinated my secondment.'

'I bet that's not all he organised.'

'Mary Bowyer, you've got a mucky mind.'

They hear the sound of shouting in the street outside. The two bodyguards spring to their feet, their weapons raised. A stone shatters the window. The guards are in the doorway, crouched, scanning for a target. Other people in the café drop to the floor or duck under tables. Mary screams as Wendy pulls her down. The guards are outside, scouring the now deserted street. For a moment, everything is frozen. Then one of the guards beckons; the danger has passed.

'Time to go home, I think,' Wendy say nonchalantly.

'Bit like the last student occupation of the University Senate Chamber,' says Mary. But her voice is not as steady as Wendy's.

32

Friday morning. Two little convoys converge on Wendy's villa. One takes Wendy on the familiar route to the Ministerial Compound to collect Jamshid for his exam and the other takes Mary to the British Embassy to set up and conduct the exam.

Mary is met at the Embassy by Jim Armstrong and Paddy Winterslow.

'Dr. Bowyer, pleased to meet you,' Jim greets her. 'All ready to meet the Hope of Kesheva?'

'Sorry?'

'The young hopeful that Wendy has been grooming.'

'Ah, yes. I'll need a room.'

'Let me introduce you to our cultural chap. Paddy Winterslow. He will sort you out.'

'I've heard *all* about you,' Mary says and winks at him.

'Ah, yes,' says Paddy, nonplussed.

'All good, of course.'

'I'll leave you two to get on. No rest for the wicked. I'm rushed off my feet. People to do, things to see. I'm sure my wife will want to have a chat with you later. Catch up with things at home.' Jim heads off back into the Embassy.

So, thinks Mary, this is the famous Paddy Winterslow who has captured the heart of my friend. I can certainly see the attraction. I just hope to God that he doesn't let her down.

'So, Dr. Bowyer,' Paddy is saying, 'let me show you what I've set up for you. If you'd like to follow me? It's much cooler inside and you can tell me if there is anything more you need. I'll arrange for some refreshments while we wait for Wendy and her protégé to arrive.'

He leads the way into the Embassy.

Wendy and Jamshid arrive in the Mercedes limousine accompanied by a company of soldiers in armoured personnel carriers. The SAS troopers in the Embassy compound run professional eyes over the young conscripts and are less than impressed. The Keshevan soldiers radiate nervousness and tension. These are men who might well shoot at the drop of a hat or break and run if they themselves come under fire. They do not inspire confidence in the highly trained and utterly professional British soldiers, who resolve to make themselves scarce if the shit hits the fan with these guys. Blue on blue is *not* a scenario the SAS are keen on.

Paddy takes Wendy and Jamshid under his wing and into the Embassy where Mary is waiting in an office room to conduct the examination. Wendy introduces Mary to Jamshid and leaves them to it.

'I expect Wendy has prepared you for this? But I'll just run through it again. The exam is in four parts; reading, writing, listening and an interview and takes about three hours altogether.'

'Dr. McPherson and I have done several practice tests so I know what to expect, thank you.'

'We will take some breaks, don't worry. Mr Winterslow has told me the Embassy staff will provide us with some lunch somewhere in the middle of it. The important thing, as I am sure Wendy has told you is to relax and read the questions carefully.'

'I'm a bit nervous,' Jamshid admits.

'Don't be. I am sure you will be fine. Now, if you are ready?'

Four-thirty and the test is over; Jamshid has done well and will be guaranteed a place in October. Mary cannot divulge the result officially but has let Jamshid know that she thinks he should be pleased with himself. The young man is over the moon and cannot wait to tell his father the news. He keeps thanking Wendy for all her hard work and tells her how happy his father will be.

In the car back to the Presidential Palace, they discuss what he will do in London and what courses he should take. Wendy is pleased for him but also relieved that her work in Kesheva is coming to an end and that she can go home a little early. Mary's visit to Kesheva has brought on a mild case of homesickness and she realises how much she misses her day-to-day routine at the university and all her friends and colleagues. The atmosphere in Kesheva is oppressive and Wendy has had enough. She dreams of a life with Paddy away from the heat and the dust - a life of suburban mundanity. She has had enough adventure, of spying and riots, of living in a police state and having armed soldiers at her back. The morning commute on the District Line is suddenly quite appealing, for all that she used to find it a chore to be endured with gritted teeth and a crumpled copy of the *Metro* and the enforced close proximity of strangers. Happy days! She thinks in retrospect.

She is lost in her thoughts when Jamshid suddenly says

that something is wrong. She looks out of the windscreen and sees black smoke in the distance coming from the Ministerial Compound.

'What is it?' she asks.

'Trouble,' says Jamshid. 'Something bad.'

The car slows and is overtaken by an armoured personnel carrier, a soldier now manning the turret behind a machinegun. Another APC closes in tight behind them.

A car coming from the Compound hurtles towards them only slowing down when the soldier in the lead APC aims his weapon at it. The car stops as it reaches the small convoy and a man tumbles out waving his arms.

'It is the Minister of Agriculture,' says Jamshid as he recognises the dishevelled figure. 'What the hell is going on?'

The man runs past the APC as Jamshid winds down the window. He is shouting something but his words are a garble. He leans his arms on the roof of the car as he catches his breath. Gradually his panting stops and he is able to speak coherently.

'A coup. In the Palace. A coup!'

'What do you mean? A coup? What coup?'

'The soldiers! There is fighting. Shelling.'

The man is speaking rapidly in Keshevan and Wendy is unsure if she had understood correctly. Obviously, something awful has happened in the Ministerial Compound.

'Is my father safe?' Jamshid demands.

'I don't know. There was shooting around the Presidential Palace. But a tank was shelling it and I don't know if the defenders can hold out. I think some of the Presidential Guard have defected to the rebels. It's chaos!'

'Jamshid! Jamshid! What is going on?' Wendy is frightened.

'There is fighting around the Palace,' he tells her in English. 'I must go to my father.'

'No!' says Wendy, taking charge. 'You will not be safe. We must go back to the Embassy. You will be safe there. If anything has happened to your father, you are in danger. If he is safe, then you can go to him when we are sure. You've got to get away.'

For a moment, she thinks he is going to overrule her but then the defiance drains out of him.

'You are right,' he says, almost in a whisper.

Their escorting soldiers pour out of their vehicles and talk together in loud, excited voices, hands waving and fights threatening to break out. A young officer, hardly older than Jamshid climbs up behind a machinegun and loudly cocks the weapon, covering the groups of soldiers.

Before she can stop him, Jamshid gets out of the Mercedes and stands with his arms extended to the soldiers. He speaks to them in Keshevan.

'We must return to the city until the situation becomes clear. You are loyal soldiers of Kesheva and the appointed and legal government of the country and I ask for your loyalty now. We do not know exactly what is happening. I suspect a disaffected group of soldiers have tried to overthrow the government and are being rounded up as I speak. I know my father considers your duty at this time is to me. You will be well rewarded for your loyalty and trust, believe me. Now, take me back to the city and await further instructions.'

He stands there, facing them down, a young boy who has become a man.

The soldiers mutter but re-embark into their vehicles and

the young officer with the machinegun breaths an audible sigh of relief. The convoy turns and speeds back to the city, leaving the smoke from the Ministerial Compound in their wake.

In the car, Wendy hugs Jamshid; she has not understood all he said but has understood the gist.

'Jamshid! I'm so proud of you. That took real guts.'

'I fear for my father and family. They are all in the Palace. Stas, Kamilla, my mother and Denza, my stepmother. Am I going to see them again?'

He starts to sob quietly. Wendy holds him, stroking his head.

'There, there,' she says. 'There, there.'

33

They reach the British Embassy and the soldiers are dismissed back to their barracks. News of the coup has not yet reached the city and all is quiet.

Wendy and Jamshid run into the Embassy and call for Jim Armstrong who comes running down from his office on the first floor.

'What is it?' he asks. He can see that something is obviously wrong.

'There's been a coup at the Palace. There is fighting. We couldn't go on so I've brought Jamshid back here. It's the safest place I could think of.'

Armstrong runs back to his office to contact the American Ambassador and to start phoning around to other diplomatic missions. He shouts for Paddy who immediately comes to debrief Wendy and Jamshid.

'We met the Minister of Agriculture fleeing the Ministerial Compound,' Jamshid tells him. 'He told us there had been a coup. There is fighting going on. He did not know whether my father was still alive. I fear the worst. Can you find out what is happening? I must know.'

'I'll do what I can,' Paddy promises. 'In the meantime, Wendy, take Jamshid to my flat and lie low.'

'Where's Mary?'

'She went back to the villa. I will phone Oybek and tell him not to let her out under any circumstances.'

'Poor Mary. She thought she was coming out here on a jolly for a few days.'

'Well, she'll have a story to tell when she gets home,' Paddy snapped, greater issues on his mind. 'Now, for God's sake get to the flat and stay there. I'm going to be busy.'

Wendy takes Jamshid's hand and runs around the Embassy building to the apartments behind. She opens the door with her key and ushers him inside. He looks around and notices some of her things that he recognises scattered here and there in the living-room. Understanding dawns.

'Do you *live* here?' he asks. 'I thought…'

'Some of the time,' Wendy replies quickly. She does not want to go into the ins and outs of her love life.

'Ah.' He gives a knowing smile. Wendy can feel herself blush. I'm a big girl, she thinks. I don't have to explain myself to anyone.

Jamshid asks permission to switch on the television. Usually at this time in the early evening the state-run channel feeds its viewers with dubbed South American *telenovelas*. This evening, however, the station is showing stock footage of scenes of Keshevan life with a soundtrack of folkloric music.

'This is not good.'

'Why? What does it mean?'

'It means there is a national emergency. The TV station played much the same stuff after the bombing in the city,' Jamshid explains.

They sit together watching the television in silence for want of anything better to do. Jamshid gets to his feet and paces around the room. Wendy feels helpless; what can she do to comfort Jamshid? How must *he* be feeling, not knowing if his family are safe?

'Can I get you something? A beer? Tea? Coffee?'

'No, nothing, thank you.'

'I'm sure it will be OK,' says Wendy, realising just how lame that sounds.

Jamshid stops his pacing and sits back down but within a minute is up on his feet again. His tension is palpable, a malign presence in the room.

'Paddy will tell us as soon as there is any news.'

'I thought he was the Cultural Attaché. But he is really a spy, right?'

Wendy does not answer. Whatever cover Paddy Winterslow might have had in Kesheva has been well and truly blown by now. Just as well that London have promised to recall him.

The folkloric music on the television comes to an abrupt halt mid bar. The pictures of happy peasants bringing in the harvest die.

The face of Rustram Abdulin appears on the screen.

Oh thank God, Wendy thinks, Aslan Dargan has survived and the insurrection is over. Abdulin starts to speak.

'My fellow citizens of Kesheva, today a new dawn is breaking for our country. The ungodly and tyrannical regime of the dictator Dargan is over.'

Jamshid gives a cry of horror; Wendy clutches him. Although Abdulin is speaking in Keshevan, she has understood his words.

'From this day forward Kesheva will become an Islamic republic ruled by the divine laws of God as revealed to His Holy Messenger. For the interim, an Army Council will oversee the transition to a glorious future for our beloved country. It is my great honour to head this Council.'

'You treacherous bastard,' Jamshid shouts at the television. Wendy is stunned. Rustram has never struck her as a religious man.

'The tyrant and stooge of the Ungodly, Dargan, has been killed before he could be brought to trial to answer for his crimes against the Keshevan people.'

'Father!' Jamshid collapses to the floor, sobbing.

'Members of the former Government are being arrested as I speak to you and will be replaced by members of the New Islamic Revolutionary Council. My fellow countrymen and women, do not be alarmed. Order is being restored but for the present time, for your own good and safety, a curfew is in force for the next twenty-four hours. Please, I ask you, stay in your homes and stay tuned to the television. Further announcements and instructions will follow.

God bless the revolution, and God bless you, my dear fellow countrymen.'

Abdulin's face fades and is replaced by an image of the Keshevan flag and the national anthem.

'Jamshid, I'm so sorry.'

'This will destroy the country,' says Jamshid, his voice raw. 'Abdulin is ambitious. He always has been. He is not a religious man; he is using them to consolidate power into his own hands. Kesheva is in for a bad time of blood. My father *was* an autocrat in many ways but he was trying to keep the lid on a boiling pot. Abdulin's solution will be to pour out the water.'

'Jamshid, I must find Paddy and the Ambassador to see if they have heard the news. Stay here, you will be safe.'

'Abdulin will be looking for me. You heard what he said.

Wendy, what can I do?'

Jamshid stands before her, a frightened teenager who has just heard that his father has been murdered and knows that he, himself, is in imminent danger.

'Do nothing,' she councils him. 'You are on British soil; you are safe. They cannot touch you here.'

'I'm sure that is what the American hostages thought in Tehran,' he says bitterly.

'There are British soldiers here.'

'There are a lot more Keshevan soldiers out there,' he points out.

'I've got to go.' She has no response to his logic. The SAS soldiers may be very good at their jobs but they are ridiculously outnumbered and not equipped with heavy weapons. It is an unequal contest. Her only hope is that Abdulin will respect the international conventions on the inviolability of diplomatic missions. In her heart of hearts, she doubts it but knows that she must give Jamshid some kind of hope.

She leaves him staring at the television screen and hurries to the main Embassy building.

34

Inside the Embassy, Jim Armstrong is calling a meeting. The staff are assembling in the main reception room. There is a hubbub of voices. The news is not yet generally known and people are speculating as to the reason for the assembly; this is not the way things are normally done. There are channels of information to be gone through, even in a relatively small mission like this one, so something big must be afoot.

Jim mounts the raised platform, flanked by Paddy. This was where the band played, Wendy thinks. *In a lifetime ago at the dawning of the New Year, when all was bright and new and hope was in the air and my adventure was just beginning.*

'Ladies and gentlemen, I can see you are all wondering why I have broken with protocol and called you all here.'

There is a buzz of acknowledgement from the audience. Most of the people in the room are the British embassy staff but there is also a scattering of locally employed staff, consular officials, driver, cooks and cleaners – people with families in Kesheva. They look worried.

Armstrong's face is grave. Phoebe Armstrong stands next to Wendy and grips her upper arm. For once, her normally serene manner is slipping. Wendy pats her hand in a gesture of comfort.

'We have just heard that the government of Aslan Dargan has been overthrown,' Armstrong announces. There is a collective gasp from his listeners and then a burst of voices.

Armstrong holds up his hand for silence and the noise gradually subsides.

'To be honest, at this time we do not have more concrete information. It appears that there has been a coup led by middle-ranking officers of the army. An officer called Rustram Abdulin seems to be the leader of the plotters and has made an announcement on Keshevan television to that effect. He is proclaiming an Islamic Army Council. Just what exactly that means is unclear. As are the implications for all foreign diplomatic missions in Kesheva. I am awaiting instructions from HMG as to how we proceed. The Army Council have announced a twenty-four-hour curfew with immediate effect, so if any Keshevan staff members wish to return to their homes, I urge you to leave immediately.'

A few of the Keshevan staff head for the door as the SAS captain enters, approaches Armstrong and whispers in his ear.

'Wait,' Armstrong calls to the departing Keshevans. They turn back, worry on their faces.

'Captain McMahon has just informed me that members of the Keshevan army have blocked the entrance to the Embassy and are refusing to allow ingress or exit. I will be making a strong protest about this in due course when we establish just *who* to talk to. This means, I'm afraid, that we are stuck here for the moment. I sincerely hope good sense will prevail and law and order is swiftly resumed. I'm sorry.'

'I hope we are not in for a long siege,' Phoebe whispers to Wendy. 'I don't know how long the kitchen can cope. Might be short rations all round.'

Wendy experiences a gush of affection for this ever-practical, unflappable Englishwoman. Who better to have beside you in a crisis? The Dunkirk Spirit personified.

What Armstrong is not telling his staff is that the Embassy is harbouring the son and heir presumptive of the murdered President and presumably Fugitive Number One on the Army Council's wanted list. This might turn out tricky, but the decision on how to proceed is not his to make; instructions from HMG are awaited.

'For the moment, ladies and gentlemen, there is nothing I can add. Please return to your posts while we try to establish contact with whoever is in authority. I will, of course, be in contact with our fellow diplomats as soon as this meeting concludes. If any members of our Keshevan staff wish to try and contact their families and loved ones, the Embassy telephones are at your disposal if you do not have mobiles. Any useful information that you might glean will be gratefully received. For the moment, that is all. Thank you.'

The meeting breaks up. The mood is sombre and voices are subdued. One or two of the Keshevan staff are in tears; others are whispering into their mobiles, as if fearful of being overheard.

Paddy strides over to Wendy.

'We have a problem,' he says.

'Jamshid?'

'Exactly. Jamshid.'

'We can't give him up!'

'No,' Paddy agrees. 'But that will be what Abdulin will demand.'

'I can't believe that Rustram is behind this. He seemed so loyal to Dargan. He was his right-hand-man.'

'*"Keep your friends close and your enemies closer"*. Who said that? You're an academic. You should know.'

'It's attributed to lots of people. The usual suspects, Machiavelli, Sun Tzu, Mario Puzo.'

'Who's Mario Puzo?'

'He wrote *The Godfather*,' Wendy explains.

'Ah. Wise man.'

'What a bastard!'

'Mario Puzo?'

'No, you idiot!' Wendy says. 'Rustram. He seemed so nice when I first met him.'

'Hitler loved dogs and children.'

'And yet the Nazis blithely murdered children with no second thoughts. What are we going to do?'

'To be honest, my love, at this precise moment, I haven't the slightest idea.'

'We can't give him up. He'll be murdered.'

'That is the likelihood, I agree.'

'So?'

'All we can do is wait and see,' says Paddy. 'The coup is in its infancy. Let see how it plays out over the next few days. We need instructions from HMG. Iran ended up in the international wilderness after the students stormed the American Embassy; is Abdulin prepared to take the same risk? The people here are predominantly Sunni so I can't see the Iranians jumping in, and the Gulf States live in fear of a fundamentalist uprising. If they believe he is genuine in his beliefs, the various radical Islamist factions in Afghanistan and the Middle East will be slaughtering the fatted sheep to celebrate but I don't believe that Abdulin is serious in the long run. I think the situation is going to evolve more like the Egyptian scenario after the overthrown of Mubarak. A brief period of fundamentalist chaos and then another no pretences military dictatorship with our friend Rustram Abdulin calling the shots.'

'So we sit tight and wait and see. Is that it?'

Patrick nods. 'In a nutshell, yes.'

'I'd better get back to the boy. He must be going frantic on his own.'

'Yes, you do that. I'll pop by if I hear anything. Jim is contacting the other embassies and I'd better go and see what our American masters are making of it. At a pinch, see if they can spare us some of their Marines. I'm sure Captain McMahon wouldn't mind his ranks being stiffened a bit.'

'If the Keshevans let them through,' Wendy says.

'I can't see Abdulin risking a shooting war with Uncle Sam or with us. Although to get his hands on Jamshid, perhaps.'

'Do you honestly think it might come to that?'

'Don't worry your pretty little head about it.'

'Paddy Winterslow, if you ever patronise me like that again you'll be cradling your balls for a week.'

'Are you willing to cut off your nose to spite your face?' he laughs.

She grins. 'Just try me!'

'Now I *am* worried. Go back to Jamshid and hold his hand. I'll see you when I have something to tell you. Love you!'

'Smarmy git! But I love you too.'

She kisses him and hurries back to try and comfort her student.

35

Wendy's phone rings. She checks the Caller ID in disbelief and accepts the call.

'Rustram?'

'Dr. McPherson. I trust you are well?'

'This can't be a social call. I saw you on television.'

'I am busy, that is true. I am engaged in the service of my country.'

'Then why the hell are you calling *me*?'

'Just to let you know your colleague, Dr. Bowyer, is safe.'

'That's very kind of you but I'm sure you have more pressing matters to consider.' Wendy cannot fathom what the man is after but knows for sure he wants *something*.

'Sergeant Niyazov has taken her into protective custody. For her own safety.'

'Who the hell is Sergeant Niyazov?'

'You have been living in his house ever since you arrived in Kesheva. When you are not consorting with the British spy Winterslow.'

The penny drops. Paddy had long ago warned her that Oybek and Ruthinna worked for the security services but she had never taken him seriously. Wendy thought the kindly old couple could not possibly be other than they seemed. She curses herself for a trusting fool. In a police state like Kesheva, *of course* they would want to monitor the activities of someone closely connected to the Presidential Family. What a naïve, stupid, trusting idiot!

'Mary Bowyer is a British citizen,' Wendy protests. 'You can't harm her.'

'Who said anything about harm?' Abdulin's voice is silky smooth. Wendy can almost imagine a forked tongue flickering over his dry lips.

'What do you want?' Let's cut to the chase, she thinks.

'I believe you are harbouring the son of the deposed traitor Dargan in the British Embassy…' He leaves the sentence hanging but his meaning is crystal clear.

'He has applied for asylum,' Wendy replies, although, as yet, Jamshid has done no such thing. Wendy resolves that he will do so as soon as she is off the phone.

'Of course. I expected nothing less of the British. But his *late* father is no longer in a position to fund your library extension, or, for that matter, to sell Kesheva to your government. Jamshid Dargan is no longer of any use to you. He must be tried in a Sharia court for crimes against the Keshevan people.'

'That's bullshit, Rustram, and you know it. What crimes has the boy ever committed? He's hardly ever been out of the Ministerial Compound.'

'He is guilty by association. All the Dargan family have raped and murdered and plundered Kesheva. He must pay for these crimes.'

'What? You're going to put the whole family on trial?'

'He is the last of the Dargans,' says Abdulin.

'What do you mean?'

'The rest of the family perished resisting arrest.'

Wendy hears a cry of anguish; Jamshid has been straining

to hear the conversation. He has heard enough. Abdulin picks up on the sound.

'The Dargan boy is with you now?'

Wendy breaks the connection and throws her phone down. She is furious and, at the same time, desperately anxious for the safety of her friend, Mary.

'They are all dead?' Jamshid asks softly.

'That might be a bluff,' she tries to reassure him, knowing her bluff will not be believed.

'And now Abdulin wants to finish the job. He wants me dead as well.'

'You are safe here, Jamshid. Don't worry. Abdulin will not try to enter the Embassy. It is protected by international law. You remember, we studied that.'

'You don't understand. Abdulin is riding on the back of an Islamic fundamentalist wave. When have those people ever cared for international law? The only law they recognise is their own twisted interpretation of Sharia. You are Unbelievers and therefore outside the law.'

'We need to talk to the Ambassador and you need to formally request asylum. Let's go.'

And I need to tell Jim Armstrong that Abdulin is holding Mary Bowyer as a hostage and a bargaining chip for Jamshid, Wendy thinks.

In the Embassy building, Wendy is told that Jim Armstrong is desperately busy but once she has made it clear that she has just received a communication from the new de facto ruler of Kesheva, she is shown into his office. He has a phone to his ear and is talking earnestly to the French Ambassador. He waves her and Jamshid to a seat and winds up the call with a promise to pass on any new information.

'What can I do for you?' he asks, his voice weary.

'I have just spoken to Rustram Abdulin on the phone,' Wendy starts to explain.

'*What!* The weariness leaves his voice and he focuses his full attention on her.

'He is holding Mary Bowyer in "protective custody". He wants Jamshid. I have suggested to Jamshid that he formally apply for asylum.'

'The bastard. Look, I may be the Ambassador, but this is above my pay grade. I need to talk to my masters in the FCO, probably the Foreign Secretary. I imagine this will also go up to the PM. Give me some time. Thank God we still have secure communications with London. I wouldn't put it past Abdulin to have a rent-a-mob howling at the gates in short order. The SAS chaps might deter them for a bit but if Abdulin is mad enough to bring in units of the army, then we are buggered. Leave it with me. Go and find Phoebe. She'll make you a cup of tea. As for you, young man, consider your application officially made. The British government does not give in to blackmail.'

Wendy can think of a number of instances where HMG has done just that, but figuratively bites her tongue.

Seated in the Ambassador's comfortable living room they sip tea and try to make small talk with his wife. They go through the motions as if all is well and that soon they will be back in England watching cricket on the village green, a glass of cold Pimms in hand.

Jamshid has hardly spoken since he learnt of the deaths of his family. Perhaps he is hoping that it is a bluff, that somehow they escaped the coup and the assault on the Palace. But he saw the smoke, heard the shelling, spoke to the terrified Minister of Agriculture. He knows.

Armstrong comes into the room. He puts on a brave face.

'Good news, young man. HMG have provisionally agreed your application and will send a strong request for the release of Dr Bowyer. That's my job. The trouble is, it's still very early. We have no clear idea at this time just *who* to contact. I have tried to get in touch with Rustram Abdulin but have had no joy. I imagine he plans to let us stew, turn the screw as it were. I can't say I ever liked that man, the few times I met him. What's your opinion of him, Wendy? You seem to have had a lot of contact with him.'

'I quite liked him,' she admits. 'He always had a secretive side and this became more obvious the longer I knew him. But I had him pegged as a loyal aide to President Dargan. I had the impression that he was the President's right-hand-man. The go-to guy. He certainly never gave any indication of radical religious beliefs.'

'He is a hypocrite of the worst kind,' says Jamshid. 'He is a married man but has a string of girlfriends and likes to drink and gamble. He and my brother Stas were close at one time. They used to organise private parties in nightclubs. Stas liked to brag about what they got up to. It was disgusting. I am ashamed to admit he did my father's dirty work. I know he killed and tortured people. I am not proud of this side of my father.' Jamshid's eyes blaze with anger, his voice drips with hate. 'He wants power for himself. His rule will be a thousand times more repressive than anything my father's ever was. He will use the Islamists for his own ends and destroy them when he has no further need of them. Poor Kesheva. Poor, poor Kesheva.'

'That tallies with the files we have on him,' Armstrong confirms. 'Paddy Winterslow was concerned about your contacts with him, Wendy. He never trusted Abdulin.'

Perhaps he was also just a teeny bit jealous? Wendy wonders with a touch of glee. I certainly like to think Rustram was jealous over my relationship with Paddy.

'So, what about Mary?' asks Wendy, feeling just a little bit guilty about her speculations of sexual rivalry.

Armstrong spreads his hands in a gesture of helplessness. 'Nothing I can do. As I said, I will be making representations. But there are still a number of other British citizens in country that we are trying to contact. HMG's advice is to get out but it appears that the airport has been shut to all incoming and outgoing flights. As soon as it reopens, HMG will charter planes to evacuate any British citizen wanting to leave. However, for the moment, we are trapped.'

36

Monday, the first of May. In London, the great and the good have met in COBRA to discuss the crisis in Kesheva. Opinions in the Inner Cabinet are divided; should Jamshid Dargan be sacrificed to obtain the release of Mary Bowyer? The implications are vast. On the one hand, Britain has always had a policy of non-negotiations with hostage-takers; on the other HMG has had a request from the *de facto* new government of a sovereign state to hand over someone implicated in human rights violations by the ousted regime. Britain has commercial interests in Kesheva and the FCO are counselling a resumption of normal relations asap. The argument rages while the Cabinet agonises.

Outside the British Embassy in Kesheva, a small but very vocal mob has been broadcasting their demands through loudspeakers since the coup. Making sleep all but impossible. A thin line of Keshevan soldiers stand between them and the Embassy gates, ostensibly to protect the Embassy. The SAS soldiers have been reinforced by a platoon of US Marines sent over by the American Ambassador as a quid pro quo for the help the British gave after the bombing. No-one tried to stop them entering: Rustram Abdulin is not prepared to risk upsetting a super-power, at least, not just yet.

Jim Armstrong is looking haggard. He has not slept properly since the coup and is showing every one of his years. He has tried to reason with Abdulin but is getting nowhere. Abdulin refuses to shift his position: Hand over Jamshid Dargan to face justice.

The Embassy has been working tirelessly to establish the whereabouts of all British citizens in the country. Those who were outside of the capital seem to be safe, for the moment, but those in the city of Kesheva have, like Mary Bowyer, been taken into 'protective custody – for their own safety'.

No-one has been able to leave the British Embassy, but, again, the Americans have come to the rescue, ferrying in food supplies under armed guard. How long they will be able to continue to do this is open to question; since the morning a mob shouting threats against the Great Satan and pledging death to all Unbelievers has started to gather outside the still-shattered gateway of the US Embassy. The Marines have constructed makeshift machine-gun emplacements using the rubble from the bombing and are manning them round the clock. Other Western embassies are reporting similar mobs at their own gates. The airport has re-opened but incoming flights are restricted to traffic from the small number of countries that leapt to recognise the new government, China being one of the first, with the Beijing government sniffing at the commercial advantages to be had.

Wendy has had a fraught three days with Jamshid. He is suffering terrible mood swings, understandable in the circumstances. Grief, anger, guilt that he is the cause of the siege and Mary Bowyer's detention, impotence that he is powerless. Wendy tries to comfort him but there is little she can actually do. His fate hangs on the decision of the British Government. While he is in the Embassy he is safe but he cannot set foot outside and if the mob attempt to storm the Embassy he knows he will be killed.

Paddy can only put in fleeting appearances to try and reassure Wendy. He is working flat out trying to contact his assets and glean what intelligence he can of the fluid situation. It is clear that middle-ranking officers from the armed forces of Kesheva have seized power and that many of the generals who were tied to Aslan Dargan have been purged. How many have been executed is still unclear, although reports have reached him that some managed to flee to the borders with their families. It is also clear that radical clerics have thrown their weight behind the coup. Religious programmes have replaced the telenovelas on the state television and women are urged to adopt a strict dress code if and when they leave their homes; men are being urged to grow their beards. Alcohol has been banned and the television has broadcast images of liquor shops and bars being trashed. Wendy wonders bitterly how Oybek will manage. She finds his complicity in Mary's capture very hard to take as well as the fact that all the time she was living with him and Ruthinna, he was spying on her and reporting her doings to Abdulin.

Jim Armstrong knocks on the door of the flat at midday. Wendy opens the door to him. Jamshid peers over her shoulder. She motions for him to come in and he enters, closing the door behind him. She looks at him in expectation.

'HMG have reached a decision,' he tells her, not giving anything away. Her heart skips a beat.

'What?'

'They have decided that Jamshid can have asylum,'

'Oh, thank God!' Behind her, Jamshid gives an inarticulate cry.

'The PM has personally managed to phone Rustram Abdulin and have a conversation with him. The PM has made it clear that the Embassy and all who are inside it are inviable under international law and that this *must* be respected. The PM also made it clear that all UK citizens presently in Kesheva are not to suffer hindrance in their movements. The offer was also made to evacuate all British citizens as soon as normal flights are resumed. The RAF are standing by to mount evacuation flights as soon as the new government give their permission for them to land.'

'And did he take any notice?'

'Ah,' says Armstrong, 'there's the rub! Abdulin is insisting that young Jamshid is wanted to pay for the alleged crimes against the people of Kesheva committed by his father.'

'I didn't do anything!' Jamshid wails. 'I hardly ever left the Ministerial Compound. How can I have committed any crimes?'

'That's not the point, I'm afraid,' Armstrong tells him sympathetically. 'While you are still alive, if I can put it bluntly, those who supported your father have a symbol to rally around. While you are still in the country, you are a danger to the new regime.'

'Then we must get him out!' says Wendy.

'I agree,' Armstrong replies. 'But how?'

'Smuggle him out somehow. There must be a way.'

'Have you seen the mob outside?' Armstrong drily asks.

'At night. In disguise.' Wendy is clutching at straws.

'Too risky.'

'I am prepared to try,' says Jamshid.

'Too risky,' Armstrong repeats.

'There must be a way,' Wendy insists.

'Give it more time. Let's see what develops. Abdulin might have a change of heart. I'll speak to the other sympathetic diplomatic missions. Get them to put pressure on Abdulin. Sooner or later he is going to need to normalise relations with the outside world. He will need international recognition. Britain still has a veto in the Security Council, don't forget.'

'How long did it take Iran to come in from the cold?'

'Fair point!'

'I will not put your lives in danger,' says Jamshid. 'You have been good to me. If that is what it takes to free Mary and the other British, then I will leave and face them. Let them put me on trial! I will defend myself. I am innocent of any crime.'

Wendy and Jim exchange a look. They both know that Jamshid would never come to trial.

'That's a brave offer, lad,' says Armstrong, 'but don't be hasty. Let's sit tight and see what transpires, eh?'

'Yes,' says Wendy, turning to face him, 'don't do anything rash. There must be a solution to this standoff. We'll find one.' But secretly, she is far from convinced by her words.

At four o'clock, Wendy's phone rings. She checks the caller and then goes into the bedroom, shutting the door behind her. When she is sure that Jamshid cannot hear, she answers the call.

'Dr. McPherson, I trust you are well?'

'Why are you calling me? Speak to the Ambassador.'

'But it is you I wish to speak to, Dr. McPherson,' says Rustram Abdulin.

'Why? Why me.'

'You have influence over the boy. You can persuade him to give himself up.'

'And be killed?'

'He will have a fair trial.'

'And pigs might fly.'

'Pigs are unclean animals, you should know that. They have no place in the new Democratic Islamic Republic of Kesheva.'

'You know exactly what I mean.'

'Dr. McPherson, I thought we were friends.'

'I thought so too. Until you started killing people.'

'I have only acted for the good of the whole people of Kesheva. The people the Dargans oppressed. And now the Dargans must account for their crimes.'

'You know full well that poor Jamshid had nothing to do with any of it.'

'Nevertheless, he must answer. If, and I say, if, he is innocent then he will not be punished.'

'Get real. You can't afford to leave him alive.'

'What a cynic you are, Dr. McPherson.'

'I don't have blood on *my* hands.'

'Nor I on mine.'

'You just gave the orders.'

'These recriminations are getting us nowhere. I have phoned to offer you a deal. An exchange. Your colleague for the Dargan boy. As simple as that. I will make sure the popular protest outside your Embassy disperses and agree to your Prime Minister's request that all the other Britons in the country may leave, should they choose to do so. Although, I can assure you they are in no danger.'

'You want to swap Jamshid for Mary?'

'In essence, yes.'

'And if the Ambassador does not agree?'

There is a pause.

'The Ambassador has a responsibility for the wellbeing of his fellow countrymen. He has no authority or responsibility for the nationals of his receiving country.'

'The British Government has agreed to grant Jamshid asylum.'

'That is unfortunate. Please convey this message to Jim Armstrong.' He rings off abruptly.

'You bastard,' Wendy shouts at the phone. Unnoticed, Jamshid has crept into the room.

'I heard,' he says softly.

'Fuck him. You're not going anywhere.'

'He will kill your friend.'

'He wouldn't dare!'

'Trust me, he would.'

'Look, Jamshid, he is bluffing. You just stay here. Make something to eat. Don't you dare move out of this flat. I've got to tell Jim about this call. Promise me you won't budge. Promise me!'

'I'll stay here,' is the reluctant answer. For now, he thinks.

37

Jim Armstrong explodes with rage. 'No! Absolutely not! I will *not* give in to blackmail.'

'Being realistic,' Paddy says, 'what choice do we have?'

'Paddy,' says Wendy in a shocked voice, 'we can't hand Jamshid over. He'll be killed.'

'I know that, my love. But in *Realpolitik* what options do we have?'

'I won't sanction it, Patrick,' says Armstrong.

'It's not just Dr. Bowyer,' Paddy argues, 'there are other British citizens out there. Abdulin is using Wendy's friendship with Mary Bowyer as emotional blackmail. He knows that Jamshid Dargan will listen to her. Let's be frank, Wendy is the only friend Jamshid has left.'

'Do you think I don't know what Rustram is doing?' Wendy demands.

'Of course you do. I don't doubt that for a minute.'

'I do not think Abdulin will permit a wholesale massacre of British citizens just to lay his hands on the Dargan boy. I'm going to call his bluff.'

Jim Armstrong is very angry and deeply offended that his last diplomatic posting has come to this impasse. Eight more months and a peaceful retirement and a knighthood in recognition of a long life of service to his country would have been his reward. And now this debacle. If the shit hits the fan much more, he'd be lucky to escape with a reduced pension. He calls his secretary over the intercom. 'Get me Rustram Abdulin.'

'Putting you through now, sir,' says the secretary.

'At least the phones are still working. I'll put this on speakerphone.'

The ringing tone sounds for a full minute.

'Playing hard to get,' says Paddy.

'Jumped up little prick,' says Jim, most undiplomatically.

'The office of the Chairman of the Islamic Army Council,' says a disembodied voice on the phone in Keshevan.

'This is Jim Armstrong, the British Ambassador to Kesheva,' Jim announces in English, although Wendy knows he has more than a passing knowledge of Keshevan. 'I wish to speak to Major Abdulin.'

'A moment please,' says the voice, switching to English, 'I will see if His Excellency can speak with you.'

'Not taken him long to pick up the title. Wonder if he's promoted himself to general as well?'

'Ambassador Armstrong! So lovely to hear from you. I imagine Dr. McPherson has relayed our earlier conversation to you.' Rustram Abdulin's sibilant voice snakes out of the speaker.

'She has. She is here with me now. We are listening to you on speakerphone.'

'And is the estimable MI6 agent, Paddy Winterslow, also privy to our conference?'

'I can confirm that Mr Winterslow is here, yes.'

'And what have you decided vis a vis the traitor, Dargan?'

'Your Excellency,' says Jim, swallowing his rage and letting years of training in the arts of diplomacy over-ride his feelings,

'Jamshid Dargan has applied to the British Government for asylum and that request has been granted. I cannot, in all good conscience now expel him from the sanctuary of this Embassy.'

'That is a shame,' says Abdulin. 'Sadly, for my part, I cannot guarantee the safety of all British subjects at present resident in Kesheva. These are troubled times and while the Army and the Islamic Council are in control of the country as a whole, I fear there might be rogue elements waiting to be apprehended. I will, of course, make every effort to ensure the safety and wellbeing of all British nationals but I cannot be everywhere.'

'Is that a threat?' Wendy demands.

'Dr. McPherson. So nice to hear from you again. It is absolutely not a threat. Merely a statement of fact. A revolution brings a certain turmoil in its train, does it not? The situation *shall* stabilise and all will be back to normal. Kesheva treasures its long and profitable association with Great Britain and I sincerely hope nothing untoward happens to jeopardize that relationship.'

'That is also the wish of HMG,' says Armstrong. 'We also fervently hope that nothing will happen to jeopardize our relationship with Kesheva.' His words are heavy with unsaid meaning.

'So, as a symbol of this excellent relationship, I trust you will be delivering the traitor Dargan to face a Keshevan court. He will be given a fair trial, which is more than his father gave his many victims.'

'But Jamshid was not responsible for his father's actions,' Wendy pleads. 'He is only a boy. He hasn't done anything.

For God's sake, Rustram. Leave him alone. I will take him out of the country and into exile.'

'Where he might be a magnet for pro-Dargan factions who might seek to try and overthrow the revolution.'

'Might, might! That's not going to happen!'

'How can you be so sure, Dr. McPherson?'

'Let him go, Rustram. Please, just let him go. He can't hurt you.'

'But he might,' says Abdulin, his voice low and full of menace. 'Please, Mr. Ambassador, contact your superiors again. Explain the situation to them very carefully. Perhaps there will be a change of heart.'

'I doubt it, Your Excellency. The decision has been made.'

'I believe you have an expression in British political circles. A U-turn? I shall contact you tomorrow. I trust there will be good news. For now, good night.'

Jim puts down the phone and slumps his head onto his folded arms. To Paddy he looks like a defeated man.

'So, sir, what are you going to do?'

'Nothing, Paddy. I'm going to call the bastard's bluff. I suggest an early night. We've none of us had much in the way of sleep these past few days. If we can sleep with that infernal racket going on day and night.'

'Good night, sir,' says Paddy and takes Wendy by the arm and propelling her out of the Embassy building and in the direction of their shared flat.

'Paddy, I'm desperately worried about Mary.'

'There is absolutely nothing we can do, my love.'

'There must be *something*?'

'What do you suggest? Get the SAS lads to stage a daring

rescue. We don't even know where she is.'

'She's in the villa. With Oybek and Ruthinna.'

'Highly unlikely. They will be holding her somewhere very secure. She's too important a bargaining chip.'

Wendy sees a ray of hope.

'Then they won't want to hurt her.'

'Not at present.' Paddy's tone is ominous.

'What do you mean? You're frightening me.'

Paddy hugs her close and kisses the top of her head.

'Abdulin is a ruthless snake. He'd kill and skin his own grandmother if it suited his aims. Mary is safe for as long as he needs her alive. Look, I'm sure she is OK. Abdulin needs her to get his hands on Jamshid. If we give him the boy, he'll give us Mary and whoever else his men have managed to round up.'

'Oh Paddy, this is all my fault.' Her face is white, her eyes wide and beginning to brim with tears.

'How is it your fault? Mary came over here in good faith to do a job. Just like you did. None of us expected Aslan Dargan to be overthrown and murdered. I knew the country was unstable. I sent reports back to London to that effect but there were no FCO advisories against travel. Do you think I would have let you stay if I thought you were in any kind of danger? I love you. I would never put you in harm's way.'

'You let me spy for you!' she sniffs through her tears.

'Well, yes, there was that. But that was before I fell in love with you. And you were never in any real danger. I always had people looking out for you. At the slightest suspicion that you were being followed they would have tipped you off.'

'Thanks a million!'

'I love you, Wendy McPherson. Give me a kiss.'

'You don't deserve one, you cold-hearted, manipulating swine!'

But she kisses him anyway.

38

Tuesday, May the second. The heat of summer is really kicking in now with temperatures in the low 40s Celsius. Overnight the external power supply to the Embassy was cut off and the Embassy is now using the emergency generators. To conserve fuel, only essential services are running; the air conditioning units that gobble up power are off and the heat is making people cranky. Outside, the mob has grown and become bolder, with stones being flung over the heads of the Keshevan soldiers, who do nothing to stop it. Captain McMahon braves the hail of missiles to drive the Ambassador's Rolls-Royce across the gateway as a makeshift barricade and two of his men crouch in the shadow of the car. Their weapons are loaded and the safety-catches are off. The Marines have taken up firing positions on the first floor of the Embassy building while the remaining SAS troopers patrol the perimeter of the Embassy grounds.

The situation is grim. The slightest false move on either side could result in a bloodbath.

Paddy and Wendy have spent a miserable night trying to comfort an increasing disconsolate Jamshid. Wendy is afraid that he will attempt to leave the Embassy in an heroic gesture to break the siege, which she is determined he will not do. Her resolve to keep him safe has hardened. She feels an almost maternal responsibility for him. He is frightened and confused, in shock and grieving for the loss of his family, alone in a world that seeks his death. His eyes are ringed with black shadows and his movements are jerky and clumsy. He spends the night on the sofa, hunched in a foetal position, his arms thrust between his legs, his head buried in the cushions, but sleep does not readily come. Thankfully, by the morning however, he falls into an exhausted sleep. Paddy is careful not to wake him as he goes out. Wendy, fortified by black coffee with a dash of brandy, keeps watch.

At midday, Jim Armstrong receives a telephone call from Rustram Abdulin.

'Good day, Ambassador. I trust you are well.'

Armstrong, too, has had a restless night and he is at the end of his tether.

'No, I am not well. I am not a happy man. I insist that you restore the power supply to the Embassy. Now!'

'Has the power supply gone off?' asks Abdulin, feigning ignorance. 'Please accept my sincere apologies. This is the first I have heard of it. I will make sure it is restored as soon as possible. Most regrettable, in this heat. I'm sure it is just a temporary what do you call it? Glitch? Is that the correct word? And have you had any word from your government concerning the status of the traitor Dargan?'

'He stays here,' Jim snaps.

'That is also most regrettable. The popular mood in the country demands that he go on trial to answer for the crimes of the late regime.'

'He is under the protection of HMG. His safety is sacrosanct under international law. You know that.'

'I am genuinely afraid that your position might provoke a

wave of anti-British resentment throughout the country.'

'Stoked and encouraged by your propaganda!'

'Absolutely not, Ambassador. The Islamic Army Council strongly adheres to the rule of law. As of now, Sharia law.'

'With respect, Your Excellency,' Jim points outs, subsuming his anger in the greater interest of finding a diplomatic solution, 'this is getting us nowhere. The position of HMG is clear and unequivocal.'

'And most regrettable.'

'There it is. My hands are tied.'

'Then I can only hope that I can rein in the righteous anger of the people of Kesheva. On your head be it. I wish you a good day.'

I wonder what the bastard will do next, Jim speculates. He picks up his telephone and starts to ring around the friendly embassies.

At two o'clock, a large drone aircraft hovers over the Embassy compound. From it hangs a small pallet loaded with supplies of water. Members of the Embassy staff rush to unload it and it returns to the American Embassy from whence it came. For the next hour, more supplies arrive. While this is happening, Rustram Abdulin is bombarded by phone calls from the various Ambassadors from the Western missions, protesting against the siege of the British Embassy but to no avail; the siege is not lifted. Indeed, the numbers of demonstrators outside the British Embassy swells. A number of vans and cars arrive laden with refreshments for the mob.

The stand-off continues with no end in sight.

At six o'clock, the heat is being to abate and the protesters, who had been subdued during the afternoon, apart from some half-hearted efforts to bring down the drone with flung stones, perk back into noisy life.

A car approaches the Embassy. It is a nondescript blue Toyota. The doors open and three men get out. Two of them reach into the back of the car and drag Mary Bowyer out, holding her by her arms. They push their way to the front of the crowd but halt twenty metres from the Embassy gates. A howl of hatred goes up from the crowd. Mary looks terrified. She has not had a change of clothing since she was detained five days ago and her hair is a mess, tangled and dirty. A number of the protesters try to attack her but are prevented by her guards, who draw their pistols.

Captain McMahon calls Jim Armstrong on his mobile.

'Sir, you need to come and see this.'

Jim comes down from his office and stands in the doorway of the Embassy. He appraises the situation and runs back upstairs to phone Abdulin.

'Are you letting her go?' he demands.

'Who?' asks Abdulin.

'Mary Bowyer. She is here outside the Embassy.'

'She must have escaped her protective custody. She was being held, very comfortably, I must stress, for her own good.'

'Cut the bullshit. She is being held by armed men here outside the Embassy.'

'I am sure that were the traitor Dargan to walk out of the Embassy, Dr. Bowyer would, in turn, be free to walk into the Embassy.'

'That is not going to happen.'

'Then I fear I will not be responsible for the consequences. Goodbye.' He terminates the call.

Armstrong goes back outside where he is joined by Captain McMahon.

'What are your orders, sir?' the soldier asks.

'Do nothing to provoke them. Let's see where this goes. I suspect they will parade her around for a while and then whisk her away. Abdulin is making a point.'

Armstrong is shortly joined by Winterslow.

'Paddy, can you find me a loudhailer?'

'I'll see what I can do,' he replies and hurries back into the building. Five minutes later, he returns and hands the loudhailer to Armstrong.

The mood of the crowd is febrile; they sense blood.

'Dr. Bowyer,' Armstrong calls through the loudhailer, 'are you alright? Nod if you are.'

Mary gives a faint nod. A stone flies out of the crowd and strikes her on the head. A trickle of blood flows down her face and her knees sag. She is held up by the guards on either side of her.

'Do you want my men to shoot over the heads of the crowd?' McMahon asks.

'No. Do nothing to provoke them. Dr. Bowyer's safety is my primary concern. Do nothing to endanger her life. Paddy, you'd better get Wendy. She might be able to help.'

Paddy runs to find her. He bursts into the flat. Wendy quickly puts her finger to her lips to silence him. Jamshid is still asleep. The emotional strain has caught up with him; he has been asleep all day.

'Come quickly,' Paddy whispers, 'they've got Mary Bowyer outside.'

'What about Jamshid?'

'Leave him. Come on! Run.'

They run to the front of the Embassy to join Armstrong and McMahon. Wendy is horrified to see the condition of her friend. She has been hit by more stones and is barely conscious, sagging in the grip of her guards. The third man is talking into his mobile phone. He puts the phone back into his pocket, cups his hands around his mouth and shouts something. He cannot be heard over the baying of the crowd.

'What do you want?' Armstrong calls over the loudhailer.

The man steps forward and approaches the gates. The small group of Brits move closer to him. Stones fly towards them and they duck.

'Give up the traitor, Dargan,' the man shouts.

'NO!' Jim roars back through the loudhailer.

The man steps back until he is standing next to Mary. He points his pistol at her head.

'Sir!' says McMahon urgently. 'Give the order.'

'If you open fire that mob will tear her to pieces. I can't allow that to happen.'

Wendy looks on horrified as a wet patch spreads down Mary's jeans.

'Oh, God! Mary!' she shouts.

There is a shot. Mary Bowyer's head jerks back and a jet of blood flies from her head. The two men holding her release her and her body pitches to the ground. The mob howl and jeer as the three men quickly retreat and are lost in the crowd. Moments later, their car speeds off, leaving Mary's body.

Wendy screams 'NO' and tries to run towards the body of her friend. Paddy grabs her, preventing her from moving and she struggles to break free. She is sobbing and gagging. 'Oh

God, oh God. Mary!' Between them, Paddy and Armstrong drag her back to the Embassy doors. Jim Armstrong is incandescent with rage. Paddy is pressing Wendy's head to his chest.

'Captain McMahon, tell your men to fire over the heads of these animals. We *will* retrieve her body,' Jim orders.

McMahon runs to his troopers crouched behind the Rolls.

'Five rounds, rapid, over their heads.'

The shots crash out. The crowd surges back like a single living organism. At the sound of the shots, Wendy collapses, her whole body shaking with the horror of it all.

On the first floor of the Embassy, the Marines, who have been monitoring the situation but are out of direct communication, fire a two second burst from a heavy machinegun. A small number of protesters fall dead and wounded. McMahon frantically makes cease-fire gestures and the firing stops. Within minutes, the mob has fled, leaving the bodies behind.

'Now the shit really has hit the fan,' Paddy observes.

39

Night falls. The sirens of the ambulances have been and gone, bearing away the dead and wounded. The protesters have not returned and the body of Mary Bowyer has been retrieved by the SAS soldiers and lies in a chest freezer in the Embassy kitchen, an undignified but necessary resting place given the heat. Wendy has been given a mild sedative by the Embassy doctor and is lying on a sofa in the Armstrong's apartment under the care of Phoebe, who regularly plies her with strong tea.

Jim Armstrong reports the events to London, where his news is met with extreme displeasure and concern. Jamshid has not been told of Mary's death, all agreeing that given his fragile mental state it could push him over the edge.

At their post by the gates, the SAS soldiers hear the rumble of tanks. Soon, two metal monsters take up position, their cannons trained on the Embassy building. There is a terrible stillness as the soldiers wait for the guns to fire. With their light weapons, the British and Americans are powerless and can only expect to die bravely in an unequal battle.

Jim Armstrong orders all Embassy staff to evacuate the building and assemble in the grounds behind the staff flats from the rear. Perhaps, if things come to the worst, the loss of life can be kept to a minimum. The grounds behind the flats consist of about an acre of land. There is a swimming pool and tennis court for the use of the Embassy staff and a small flowerbed that Phoebe Armstrong tends lovingly. The area is surrounded by trees and a wall. A small road separates the British Embassy from rear of the German Embassy to the right and the Swedish Embassy to the left. This morning there had been demonstrators in the road but, since the shooting, they have disappeared. Paddy props a small ladder up against the wall and peeks over. He sees a detachment of half a dozen Keshevan troops sitting down drinking tea from thermos flasks, their weapons strewn carelessly on the ground but still close to hand. There is no escape here.

They wait.

The tanks do not shoot.

After fifteen minutes, Captain McMahon finds his way to the assembled Embassy staff to give a sitrep to Jim Armstrong.

'There is no movement, sir. They are just sitting there. The tank commanders are perched on the turrets and smoking cigarettes. They seem to be waiting for orders.'

'I'll come and see. Maybe I can talk to them. Find out what their intensions are.'

Armstrong walks back to the front of the Embassy with McMahon.

'Oh my God!' says Wendy suddenly. 'I've forgotten all about Jamshid. I'd better go to him.' She runs to the flat where she finds Jamshid awake and watching the television news.

'Is it true?' he demands.

'Is what true?' she asks.

'That you have massacred peaceful demonstrators outside the Embassy.'

'Is that what the TV is reporting?'

'Is it true?' Jamshid demands again.

Wendy decides that she must give him an accurate picture of events from earlier in the day. She sits down next to him on the sofa and takes his hand in hers. She is unsure how to begin. She knows Jamshid will blame himself for Mary's death but also knows that he must learn the truth.

'Mary Bowyer was murdered in cold blood outside the Embassy this evening. She was shot in the head, probably on the orders of Rustram Abdulin. The crowd outside were stoning her and stoning the Embassy. Out soldiers fired over their heads to disperse them. Unfortunately, the Marines in the Embassy fired into the crowd. People were killed. It was a tragic mistake. A lack of communication. Now there are tanks outside the Embassy, so we have to get out of here. Everyone is assembled in the grounds. Come on.'

'Mary Bowyer has been killed?' Jamshid asks in a faraway voice.

'Yes,' Wendy replied simply; there is no other way to tell him.

'Because of me?'

'No. Because of Rustram Abdulin.'

She drags him to his feet. He is silent, stunned. He shakes his head, as if trying to shake the news out of his brain. She pulls him to the door. He does not resist but follows her like a dog on a lead.

Jim Armstrong and Captain McMahon stand at the Embassy gates, confronting the tanks. The two Keshevan officers regard them impassively. The huge red sun is sinking, bathing the world in a golden light.

'What do you want?' Armstrong calls in Keshevan.

The tank officers do not reply.

After a few minutes of silence confrontation, Armstrong says 'You'd better get your lads back, Captain. I'll tell the Marines to stand down. I don't think anything is going to happen. This is just Abdulin turning the screw. I assume he must know it was the American troops who fired on the crowd. He won't risk shelling the Embassy while they are inside. The American Ambassador is up to speed on the situation and is happy for his men to stay here for the moment.'

'I'm very glad to have them, sir. My lads are tough and very well trained, but not equipped to deal with armour.'

'Stand 'em down and get something to eat.'

'Thank you, sir.' McMahon calls his men and they retreat into the Embassy building in search of hot tea and sustenance. Armstrong follows, going up to where the American Marines are deployed on the first floor. He finds their commander, a major called Ed Zabrisky, talking on a mobile phone. When Zabrisky sees Armstrong he acknowledges him with a salute, terminates his call and slips the phone into a pocket.

'Sir!' he says.

'Major.'

'Sir, I have momentarily been in touch with my Ambassador. We offer our deepest regrets about the earlier incident. You have my deepest apologies. A terrible misunderstanding.'

'I've spoken to your Ambassador. What's done is done. What we have to do now is to resolve the situation.'

'Yes sir. Any suggestions, sir? I have been ordered to place my men fully at your disposal.'

'Rustram Abdulin wants the Dargan boy. While he is here, Abdulin will not lift the siege. He will ratchet things up and try to make our lives even more unpleasant. Ergo, Jamshid must leave.'

'Agreed, sir. How can I and my men assist?'

'I'm working on an idea. How are your lads at creeping about under cover of darkness?'

'Sir, it is what they are trained to do.' Zabrisky gives Armstrong a wolfish grin.

'Excellent. I need to put a few things in place and then I'll get back to you. In the meantime, I don't think our friends in the tanks are planning to do anything. I suggest you stand your lads down and get some food.'

Armstrong walks to his office and starts to make some phone calls on his mobile.

'Franz,' says Armstrong. He is talking to the German Ambassador, Franz von Rosenberg.

'Jim. How is it with you? Terrible business, the murder of that poor woman. And then the Yankees shooting at the mob.' Jim has earlier appraised his opposite numbers in the diplomatic community of the events leading to Mary Bowyer's death and their aftermath.

'I need your help.'

'Anything the Federal Republic can do for you, we will. Within reason,' von Rosenberg adds hastily.

'What is the current situation outside your Embassy?'

'Quiet. We had a few fanatics screaming and shouting death to the Infidels but I think they have all gone home for their supper. There are a few regular army soldiers hanging around and a few more, I believe, on the road between your grounds and ours. Basically quiet.'

'I need a vehicle.'

'What kind?'

'Something non-descript but with a large tank that can hold a lot of petrol. Ideally with local plates'

'You are making a run for it?' asks von Rosenberg astutely.

'Not me. But I want to remove the cause of friction.'

'You mean the Dargan boy?'

'Exactly.'

'How many people in the vehicle?'

Armstrong thinks for a moment. 'Four.'

'With food and water? For how long?'

'The nearest frontier is three hundred odd kilometres but I imagine that they can only travel by night. Say two days.'

'When?'

'Tonight. I have some more planning to do. Say for between one and two a.m.?'

'I'll get on it straight away.'

Pleased with the offer of co-operation, Armstrong goes off to find Paddy Winterslow and Captain McMahon.

'Is it safe to assume that the secure communications net to London is still uncompromised?' he asks Paddy.

'I'm pretty sure that the Keshevans can't hack into it. The Russians and the Chinese, maybe.'

'I'm not worried about the Russians and the Chinese. I need to talk to the FCO and the MOD. I'll need your input, Captain McMahon. What I have in mind is very much up your street.'

'Only too happy to help, sir.'

'What are you thinking?' asks Paddy.

'I'm thinking of a way to resolve this standoff. Now, let's talk to London. Speed is of the essence.'

40

Midnight. Franz von Rosenberg calls Jim Armstrong.

'I've got an old VW Passat. A fine German piece of engineering of course, despite its shabby appearance. Local plates. A full tank and we've put a spare can of petrol along with food and water in the back. Now what?'

'I've had the go-ahead from London. All systems are go. With a bit of luck, we'll be over to collect it in an hour or so. We need to distract our friends in the road between us.'

'Good luck, then.'

'I think we might need it. Whatever happens, thank you.'

'We are in this together. The Federal Republic is glad to help a friend.'

Jim has briefed the Marines on what he wants them to do and they have been having a lovely time blacking their faces and hands and filling socks with sand, effective but non-lethal blackjacks. Now Armstrong holds a final briefing for the escape party.

Paddy, Wendy, Jamshid and an SAS sergeant communications specialist called George Howard, a tough thirty-year old from Toxteth in Liverpool will constitute the escape party. The plan is to break out from Kesheva and head north, then to turn west and cross the frontier into the Koram Ghosh desert and cross the unguarded frontier into Turkestan. They will travel by night, using a military GPS system to navigate. George

Howard will handle the navigation and also keep in touch with the MOD in London, as well as providing an armed escort in case of trouble. He is more than up for it.

Paddy has an asset in the old fortress village of Ayam Kala, a smuggler of contraband electronic goods, whom, Paddy is sure, will help them hide up for the first day in exchange of a wodge of cash, which the Embassy will provide and for which Paddy has dutifully signed for.

Armstrong gives the Marines the nod and they clamber over the rear wall of the Embassy. The night is warm and most of the Keshevan soldiers are peacefully sleeping on the ground. Two soldiers, who must have drawn the short straws, are on sentry duty, slowly pacing up and down the length of the road behind the Embassy and casting covetous glances at their sleeping companions. Keeping to the cover of the wall, four of the Marines sneak up on them and dispatch them with blows to the head with the sand-filled socks, catching them as they fall. The other Marines swoop on the sleepers, disabling them with plastic hand-ties and gagging them. The Marine lieutenant slips back over the wall and gives the all clear.

'Someone has been a bit lax here, Sir,' he reports to Jim Armstrong. 'They should have been out there in strength. Always watch the back door.'

'A very lucky break for us, then,' says Armstrong. 'Thank your men for me.'

'A pleasure, Sir. We appreciate what you did for our people when the Embassy was bombed.'

The Keshevan staff of the British Embassy have rallied round and produced bundles of local clothing. Wendy's red hair is covered by a hijab headscarf and she wears a loose black cloak.

Jamshid is in a state of high excitement, both at the prospect of adventure and the prospect of escape. He has on a white skullcap and wears an embroidered waistcoat over his tee-shirt. Sergeant Howard is wearing a black, tight-fitting uniform and has his Heckler and Koch machine pistol strapped lightly to his chest. In his Bergan, he carries the all-important coms equipment and spare clips of ammunition. In the car, he will cover himself with a long, camel-coloured robe. Paddy has on the Keshevan version of a salwar-kammeez - baggy trousers and a long shirt. On his head, he wears a rimless felt cap. Unless they are subject to close inspection, they should be able to pass for locals.

They clamber over the Embassy wall and run across the road to where a light is shining on the German Embassy side. A gate stands open. They enter and are greeted by Franz von Rosenberg in person.

'This way,' Franz hisses and takes them to the front of the Embassy. Two cars wait on the drive, their Passat and a Mercedes sedan flying the German flag on a short staff fixed to the roof. 'My official car.' Franz explains, 'I have an urgent meeting with my French counterpart.' He winks.

The escapees get into the VW and the Ambassador, his driver and an aide get into the official car. The gates are opened and the Mercedes moves out slowly. Only to be flagged down by the Keshevan soldiers clustered outside the Embassy gates. All of the Western Embassies are guarded as a matter of course but the Keshevans have no real reason to suspect the Germans. The official car does not stop but inches forward, dragging the soldiers in its wake. When it is finally halted by an officer standing directly in its path, the Ambassador alights and remonstrates volubly, citing the right of unhindered movement for diplomatic vehicles. Paddy drives the Passat to the gates and makes a left turn as the soldiers are occupied with the Ambassador, who is threatening them with a Note to the Foreign Ministry. His driver has taken the opportunity to offer the Keshevan squaddies a nip from his flask and they go into a huddle to partake, unseen by their officer. It has been a thirsty few days for the soldiers since the alcohol ban was imposed and this offer is not to be missed. Driving as silently as possible in a low gear, Paddy slips away down the dark street, his lights off and his passengers ducked down low and out of sight. To all intents and purposes, he is a local staff member taking a sneaky trip home in defiance of the curfew.

Having established his right of unhindered movement, von Rosenberg and his companions re-enter their car and drive off noisily to the right. By the time the Keshevan troops take up their watch by the gates, Paddy has turned into another street and creeps his way towards the outskirts of the city through deserted streets.

As soon as they can, they turn off the highway and take a single-track road leading to the village of Beg Kala and the ruins of a hunting palace used by the Khans of the Nineteenth Century. Away from the city, they start to breathe easier.

'So far, so good,' says Howard, releasing his grip on his machine pistol. He had been quite ready to shoot their way out if push came to shove, up for a ruck. Wendy reaches to the front seat and gives Jamshid's shoulder a squeeze of encouragement.

'You're free,' she whispers.

'I can't believe it,' he says, his face flushed with excitement, 'it's like some kind of movie.'

'We're not home yet,' Paddy warns, putting a damper on the mood. 'Everything depends on how long Jim Armstrong is able to string Abdulin along into thinking he has still got Jamshid bottled up in the Embassy. I estimate we have about two more hours of darkness. We should be able to make Ayam Kala before dawn and then we go to ground.'

They reach Ayam Kala just as the dawn is breaking and the Faithful are at their dawn devotions. The village is a collection of small concrete houses with mud-brick outhouses for livestock. A young boy of ten or eleven is herding a flock of sheep out into the fields and after a cursory glance, ignores them. Paddy drives around to the back of the most imposing house of the village, a two-storey affair with a huge satellite dish fixed to the roof. A recent model four-by-four is parked outside.

'Business must be good,' observes Howard laconically.

A tall powerfully built man with a face like a hawk and wearing a sheepskin coat and hat, despite the rising heat, comes out of the house. Paddy gets out of the car and the two men embrace and kiss cheeks. The other fugitives get out of the car, stretching to ease their limbs after the tense journey.

'This is my good friend, Alisher Sobirov,' says Paddy, introducing the large man.

'Greetings,' says Sobirov in heavily accented English. He casts his eye over the motley crew, raises an eyebrow but says nothing.

'Alakum salaam,' Jamshid greets him.

'You are Keshevan?' Sobirov asks him in Keshevan. Wendy holds her breath; has Jamshid given himself away? Abdulin would be very well disposed to anyone revealing the whereabouts of the fugitive.

'From the city,' Jamshid agrees but says no more.

'He works for the Embassy,' Paddy says smoothly. 'He's my interpreter.'

'Ah,' says the big man and winks at Paddy. 'And the lovely lady? And the soldier?'

'My wife. This is our honeymoon but these are uncertain times and this gentleman is our bodyguard.'

Sobirov gives no indication whether he believes Paddy's story but gives him a mighty slap on the back that rocks him on his feet.

'Then you must come in and eat. When you telephoned me to tell me of your visit, I took the liberty of slaughtering a sheep. It has been roasting in honour of your visit. Come, eat and then you must rest. You must be tired and a man has duties to his wife on his honeymoon. You will need your strength!' He gives Paddy another lascivious wink and a nudge in the ribs with his elbow.

'Can you trust him?' Wendy whispers.

'No choice, but I think so. If the bribe is large enough. He has no great love for the authorities in his line of business.'

Sobirov guides them into a large, air-conditioned room. Cushions line three sides with low wooden table set in front of them and carpets cover the floor.

'Sit, eat, rest,' Sobirov commands. He claps his hands and two women enter the room carrying brass trays laden with dishes of steaming meat and rice and cold bottles of beer, dripping condensation.

'My wife and daughter,' he says but gives no further introduction. The women place the trays on the tables and shuffle out of the room. There is no cutlery, but the Brits take their example from Jamshid, who falls to with a will, rolling the rice into balls with his right hand and popping them into his mouth and pulling strips of meat off the joints. Wendy realises just how hungry she is after the short rations in the Embassy. Howard, too, digs in, the old military maxim of fill up when you can holds true. Out of the corner of her eye, Wendy sees that Paddy and Sobirov are whispering together, head to head. She sees Paddy reach into his shirt and the bundle of money changes hands.

The meal is over; the women of the house come to clear the plates. They will take them into the kitchen and eat what is left, as is the Keshevan custom. Sobirov shows them to their sleeping quarters, a room for Paddy and Wendy and another for Jamshid and Howard.

'Try to sleep, my friend,' says Sobirov to Paddy. 'After you have done your duty!'

'I never expected my honeymoon to be quite like this,' Wendy chuckles.

'We'll see what we can do,' says Paddy, pulling her down onto the bed.

41

Wednesday morning. The relief soldiers arrive on the road behind the British Embassy to find their comrades trussed up like Christmas turkeys. All hell breaks loose, gleefully observed by the SAS soldiers peering over the wall. Although they cannot understand what is being said, the sight of the night commander being repeatedly slapped by his daytime superior and the hoots of derision from the relieving squaddies at the plight of their unfortunate fellows is enough to lighten the heart of any professional soldier. The harsh reality, unbeknown to the Brits, is that the unfortunate commander of the night's debacle and all his family will be shot that same afternoon. He knows what fate awaits him and is on his knees pleading and weeping for the life of his wife and children; for himself, he knows he can expect no mercy. It will prove to be of no avail.

The commanding officer of the regiment assigned to the Embassy Quarter for that night calls for a report of any unusual activity from all his units. He is a close friend and fellow plotter with Rustram Abdulin and does not fear for his life. When he gets the report of the departure of the German Ambassador in the middle of the night, he smells a rat and immediately imparts this information to Abdulin.

Jim Armstrong is in his office, drinking a cup of tea and congratulating himself on a job well done. Paddy has contacted him from Ayam Kala to let him know the first part of the escape has been successful but has been careful to withhold their exact location.

His phone rings. He picks it up. It is a call he has been expecting and, indeed, looking forward to.

'Ambassador?' There is a ton of repressed fury in Abdulin's voice.

'Your Excellency! I trust you are well?'

'Where is he?'

'Where is who?' Armstrong asks innocently. He is going to enjoy this.

'The traitor Dargan!'

'I've no idea,' Armstrong answers in all honesty.

'You have helped him escape from justice. I hold you personally responsible.'

'Me?'

'Yes, you. He was in your Embassy.'

'And what makes you think he is still not here? As I have told you, he is under the protection of HMG. He applied for and was granted asylum.'

Abdulin actually splutters in rage, becoming incoherent.

'I'm sorry, I did not catch that.'

'You assaulted my troops!'

'I did no such thing. That would be beyond my remit as a servant of the British Crown. Besides, I'm far too old to be going around assaulting people.' Armstrong is loving this. He is sick and tired of being pushed around and threatened by Abdulin. 'Perhaps if you withdrew your troops from besieging my Embassy they wouldn't come to harm.'

'The troops are there for your own protection,' Abdulin snaps.

'They did not protect Mary Bowyer,' Armstrong says softly.

'Where is he?' Abdulin screams down the phone, all self-restraint lost.

'Search me. Having breakfast, perhaps?'

'You and the Germans are in this together!'

'In what?'

'The assault on my troops.'

'I can honestly assure you that no member of my mission has ever assaulted any member of your armed forces,' Armstrong replies with perfect honesty. 'And, I repeat, I have no idea of the present whereabouts of Jamshid Dargan.'

'You'll be sorry,' Abdulin shouts and slams his phone down.

'Temper, temper,' Armstrong chuckles as he gently replaces his receiver.

At ten o'clock in the morning, one of the huge battle tanks lurking outside the Embassy erupts into growling life with a dense black cloud of exhaust fumes. Jim Armstrong watches from his office window in the front of the Embassy building. On the ground, Captain McMahon and his remaining troopers brace themselves for what might come. Jim has sent the Marines back to the US Embassy with his profound thanks; he wants deniability of any involvement in the raid on the Keshevan troops during the night.

The great metal monster reverses backwards into the road that is now empty of troops and protesters, revs up its engine and rolls towards the Embassy gates, which are still blocked by the makeshift barricade of the Ambassadorial Rolls-Royce. The tank's tracks mount the body of the car and grind over it, crushing it flat before reversing to take up its previous position. The tank driver switches the engine off and the tank commander emerges from his turret to survey his handiwork. He appears to be well pleased with the result. With a smirk, he lights a cigarette and waves in the direction of Armstrong's office window.

'Abdulin, you petty bastard!' Armstrong says to himself. With a small sigh, he turns back to the pile of paperwork scattered over his desk. How was he going to explain to London that the Ambassadorial Roller had been totalled?

42

It is approaching sunset. Wendy is chatting as best she can with the Sobirov women as they make the evening meal. She is feeling much more relaxed after the flight from the city and is allowing herself a glimmer of hope that they might just pull their escape off.

The atmospheric conditions are good and George Howard is busy with the satellite phone, sending a message to the MOD reporting on their present situation and their projected destination for the morrow. Paddy is working on the car, releasing the air pressure in the tyres to give better traction in the desert. In the house, Jamshid sits in the main room of the house watching television. What he sees fills him with alarm. The television is broadcasting a message for all Keshevans to be on the look-out for him. He is labelled as a traitor and a human rights violator and it is the duty of all patriotic Keshevans to hunt him down and turn him in to the authorities. If he resists, he is to be killed. An eye-wateringly large reward is offered for his apprehension. So far, he has not been out of the house and has only been fleetingly glimpsed by the shepherd boy. He hopes he was not recognised. He must put his trust in Alisher Sobirov, a career criminal. The prospect somehow does not fill him with confidence.

The fugitives sit cross-legged on the cushions eating their evening meal of lamb stew and rice, washed down by cold bottles of beer. Alisher is in a good mood, making jokes and laughing loudly at his own wit. Jamshid is subdued, casting sidelong glances at his host. He expects the police to burst into the house at any time to arrest him.

'You are not eating,' Alisher roars at him. 'Is the food not good? I will beat my women for their failings!' He is speaking in Keshevan.

'I'm not really hungry.'

'You have a long journey. We have a saying: "*A long journey starts with a good meal*". You must know it?'

'I do. I just don't have much of an appetite. But the food is delicious. Please, thank your wife and daughter for me and the honour they do me.'

'Do not worry, young Dargan. I will not betray you.'

Paddy looks up sharply, he has been following the exchange. Jamshid looks stricken. Wendy glances at the men; she has recognized the use of Jamshid's name. Has their cover been blown?

'Did you think I would not recognise you? I knew your father back in the old Soviet days. I can't say we were friends, but I respected him. These bastards who have seized power will try to cramp my business. They will try to turn us into another Caliphate, banning alcohol…' He takes a healthy swig from his bottle, '…and music and joy in life. This is not for me. I like my freedom. I don't bother the police and they don't bother me. In return for a small consideration, of course. Live and let live, I say.'

A look of relief plays over Jamshid's face. Alisher slaps him on the back that nearly topples him over.

'Your secret is safe with me, boy. But the sooner you are on your way, the better for all.'

'What's going on?' Wendy hisses to Jamshid in alarm.

'Nothing. Really, nothing,' he reassures her. 'I think we can trust this man.'

Darkness falls. They pile into the car, Paddy and George in the front to share the driving and Wendy and Jamshid in the back. Paddy has topped the tank up from the spare jerry-can. They have a long night's driving to reach the frontier with Turkelstan, over rough terrain. The Passat is not a four-by-four and they will have to nurse it along at a slow pace. If they cannot make the border by sun-up, they will have to lie low and wait.

They drive north out of Ayam Kala for five kilometres and then turn west. The night is bright and clear, the stars a carpet of diamonds above them. Visibility is good, making the rough driving less fraught. The desert is flat, mostly hard-packed sand, but with treacherous drifts and gullies. There is little in the way of vegetation, scrubby knots of grass and thorn bushes. By day, there is no shelter, nowhere to hide. They must make as much progress as possible before dawn.

43

Ayam Kala is a small, sleepy, out of the way village, which is why Alisher Sobirov finds it perfectly suitable for his illegal business operations. Nothing much ever happens and life follows its slow pace, as it has for generations. Petty feuds are honed and polished and nurtured over generations, often long after the original cause has been forgotten.

The shepherd boy returns to his home as the dark creeps in. He tells his father of the strange car with its four occupants that he saw in the morning. The boy's great grandfather was killed by a great uncle of Sobirov over fifty years ago and the hurt still rankles and is unavenged. The boy's father sees a chance to strike a blow for the family's honour. He has been watching the television and makes a connection. He dials the number of the local police station in the small town twenty kilometres away and reports the sighting, while apologising if he is wasting the police's time. He neglects to give his name, calling himself 'a patriotic citizen of Kesheva'. The local constable passes the information up to his superior who, in turn, passes the tip up to Central Police Headquarters in Kesheva city. Who are *very* interested.

At ten o'clock, the dusty peace of Ayam Kala is brutally shattered by a column of armoured personnel carriers with their headlights blazing. They park in the maidan square of the village and a loudspeaker demands that all inhabitants of the village assemble outside their houses immediately. The villagers, most of whom had gone to their beds, shuffle out of their houses and stand around grumbling at the disruption to their slumbers. Troops disgorge from the vehicles and line the four sides of the square.

'There has been a report of strangers entering the village this morning,' announces an army major through his bullhorn. 'If you are not of this village, step forward and give an account of yourselves.'

Nobody moves.

'I repeat, step forward and give an account of yourselves.'

When he is met by the same lack of response, he gives the order to his men to search the village and all the houses. The villagers stand together in small knots, muttering and grumbling. They are wary of central authority; in their collective experience, outsiders never bode well.

Sobirov instructs his wife and daughter to plead ignorance and say nothing as the soldiers search his house. He sees the shepherd boy and his father talking to the officer and gesturing in his direction. He immediately knows they have given him up to the soldiers. There will be a pay-back for this, he promises.

The officer approaches him. 'You had strangers in your house.' It is not a question but a statement.

Alisher looks the man in the eye: 'Not that I recall,' he replies.

'They were seen. A group of people in a car.'

'And what did these people look like?'

The officer is at a loss and gestures to the shepherd boy to come over who does so with an air of extreme reluctance.

Sobirov fixes the boy with a stare and makes the sign of the evil eye. The boy quakes and wishes he had kept his silly mouth firmly shut. Sobirov is a powerful man in the district.

'You saw the strangers,' the officer says to the boy, 'describe them.'

'I didn't pay much attention; I was taking the animals out.'

'Just tell what you saw.'

'Some people in a car. I could not tell how many.'

'How were they dressed?'

'Just like people,' replies the boy, who has never left Ayam Kala.

'Men? Women? Young? Old?'

'I couldn't tell,' the boy wails, wishing the ground would open.

The officer realises he is on a hiding to nothing and dismisses the boy. One of the men who has been searching Sobirov's house marches up and snaps off a smart salute.

'Sir,' he reports, 'the house is full of contraband.'

'Such as?'

'Foreign cigarettes, alcohol, mobile phones and electronic equipment.'

'Well?' The officer says to Sobirov.

'I am a businessman. Ask anyone. Ask the local police. They know me.'

'So, you are a smuggler?'

'Your Excellency,' say Sobirov in a hurt tone of voice, 'that is such a harsh word. I am a businessman.'

'But are you a people smuggler, eh? That is the question. Have you been smuggling enemies of the state?'

'Sir!' Sobirov is outraged at the very suggestion. 'To even suggest such a wickedness!'

'Perhaps,' says the officer in a silky voice, 'if we shot your wife it might jog your memory?'

'Shoot her,' says Sobirov. 'She hasn't given me sons and if I divorce her I have to return the dowry. My father made me marry her.' While the truth is he married for love much against his father's wishes and still loves his wife deeply.

The officer is a city boy born and bred and has a low opinion of the hicks from the sticks, a prejudice that Sobirov has just re-enforced. These people are savages.

Sobirov decides it is time to make a concession.

'Your Excellency, I *may* have encountered some people in the course of business, now that I think about it.'

'That's better. Now, who were they and where were they from. Were they foreigners?'

'It depends what you mean by "foreign".'

'Westerners.'

'They *did* come from the west.'

'Ah!' Says the officer, scenting a result. You have to be firm with these peasants; show them who is the boss.

'From Nishkabad.'

'That's not the West. It's near the Turkestan border.'

'It is to the west of here,' says Alisher innocently.

'I mean Europeans.' The officer is getting frustrated.

'I've never been there. Is it a big city?'

It finally dawns on the officer that he is on a hiding to nothing. He could shoot the entire population of Ayam Kala and not get anywhere. He tries a different tack.

'How do you account for the contraband in your house. Did the strangers bring it?'

'I do have business people with many people, many of whom I do not know personally. But, please, Your Excellency, if I have paid the customs dues, surely it is not contraband?'

'And have you paid these dues?" The officer has a glimmer of where this might be heading.

'Not yet, but I have calculated the amount to pay and will pay it to the authorities in due course.' He pauses, as if hit by a sudden thought. 'Unless, perhaps, Your Excellency would be so good...' The money he received from Paddy Winterslow (or, at least, a chunk of it) should be enough to pay this pig off.

The officer, never one to look a gift horse in the mouth, and satisfied that he has merely uncovered a smuggling operation, is quite happy to take a backhander and forget the whole thing. The villagers are dismissed back to their homes, the soldiers pile back into their vehicles, the officer follows Sobirov into his house, money changes hands and the column roars off into the night.

Back in Ayam Kala an old feud acquires a new twist.

44

Paddy sits behind the wheel of the Passat, Wendy beside him. George Howard sits in the back giving navigational instructions and occasionally muttering into his Satphone, his words relayed by a secure and very secret military communications satellite. Jamshid scans the rear window for signs of pursuit.

Light from the moon casts shadows across the desert floor, masking potential obstacles and pitfalls. Paddy drives slowly, groping their way forward. Using the car's headlights are out of the question. In this flat and treeless terrain the beams would stand out like a lighthouse calling 'come and get me' to any potential pursuers.

'How are we doing?' Paddy calls over his shoulder.

'As far as I can tell,' says George, 'there is a depression about twenty more clicks to the west. We can lie up there. Should take us about an hour and there's still a couple of hours of darkness. We should be fine.'

'As long as Abdulin's men are not looking for us,' says Jamshid in Jeremiah-mode.

'Have you seen anything?' Wendy asks.

'No,' he admits. 'But in the daylight they might use aircraft to hunt us.'

'We'll meet that possibility when we come to it,' says Paddy.

'What's that?' Wendy says suddenly, pointing across the desert.

It is difficult to judge distance at night but over to the left of the car is a shape like a pill-box just visible against the night sky. Paddy slows the car to a crawl; George reaches for his weapon.

'It's a yurt,' Jamshid laughs in relief. 'The nomads use them to live in when they move around with their flocks looking for pasture. They are very basic. No electricity.'

'What about mobile phones?' Paddy asks.

'No reception out here. Much like parts of Wales,' says George, reflecting on memories of fun and games on the Brecon Beacons.

'You have reception,' Jamshid points out.

'This is a very special piece of kit. Not for the use of Joe Public.'

'So, we keep going?' Paddy asks.

'I think so,' says the soldier, making a command decision. He is the professional here although Paddy has overall authority. Wendy and Jamshid are passengers. Paddy speeds up, aware the sound of the engine will carry in the stillness of the night.

As they draw away, a figure emerges from the yurt, shines a flashlight over the animals, checks on the old Ford pickup truck parked behind the yurt, sees that nothing is amiss, shrugs its shoulders and goes back to bed. In keeping with his code of hospitality, the nomad would have been happy to offer a cup of tea and a slice of bread and jam to the travellers. It gets lonely in the desert and he would not have been averse to a chat and a catch-up of the doings of the world. His small family have not spoken to another living soul for weeks; the doings of the capital and the great and powerful of the land are a mystery to him.

'Two clicks ahead,' Howard announces forty minutes later. 'There is a depression where we can hide up. Keep your eyes peeled.'

Paddy risks increasing their speed and the car bumps and shudders over the ground.

'Is that it?' Wendy calls. Just over to their left is a lake of shadow.

'Spot on! See if you can find a way in, Sir.'

At that moment, Jamshid shouts: 'I saw a light!'

'Where?' Howard demands, twisting around in his seat to look out of the rear window, while at the same time urging Paddy to keep driving.

'There,' Jamshid points, 'very faint.'

'I see it,' Howard confirms, 'but it looks to be a long way off. Chances are they don't know where we are, even if they are looking for us. Could be anyone.'

The car gives a lurch as Paddy points its nose down a gentle slope and edges their way downwards. The depression is like a huge bowl some twenty metres deep and three or four hundred metres wide.

'Park the car as close to the lip as you can, Sir. I just need a few minutes out in the open.'

They tumble out of the car, stretching their legs in relief.

'Close your eyes, gentlemen,' says Wendy as she goes off to find somewhere for a pee.

'Can you handle one of these, Sir?' Howard asks, handing his weapon to Paddy.

'Yes,' Paddy replies. 'I did a course at Aldershot. Small arms and self defence.'

'Glad to hear it, Sir. I'd appreciate it if you took yourself up to the berm with the weapon and shoot anything that comes within ten metres of you. Here are some spare clips. That's all we have, so don't go banging away willy-nilly, if you please.'

Wendy returns from her comfort break in time to see Paddy scramble up the side of the bowl and peer over the edge. The sight reminds her of photographs of soldiers standing stag in the trenches of the First World War and a cold hand seems to close about her heart.

Jamshid is loitering about next to the car. Howard dispatches him to join Paddy on look-out duty.

'Give him something to do and take his mind off things, miss,' he whispers to Wendy. 'Bugger-all he can actually do.'

'What do you want me to do?' Wendy asks. She is experiencing a sense of helplessness in this world of action men. What will she do if it comes to shooting?

'Up to you. You can stay down here or go up and join the men.'

'What are we doing here, exactly, Sergeant? Why have we stopped? I thought the plan was to make a run for the frontier.'

'I've got friends in high places, miss,' he says enigmatically and taps the side of his nose. 'I've been chatting to them. We should be seeing them soon. Now, if you'll excuse me, I've got another little job to do.'

Wendy crawls up the slope and joins Paddy. 'See anything?' She asks.

'A flicker. Way back. Trouble is - distances are hard to judge at night.'

'What was George Howard talking about friends in high places? What's happening, Paddy? After all this, are we going to get out?'

Even as she speaks, she becomes aware of a sound in the distance. A sound like whomp-whomp-whomp.

'That'll be our friends,' says Paddy, a huge smile of relief spread across his face. 'The cavalry!'

'I don't understand.'

'Who do you think Sergeant Howard has been talking to all this while on his Satphone?'

'I can see more lights,' Jamshid shouts over the din of the approaching helicopter.

'Too late!' Paddy shout in triumph.

'Out taxi has arrived!' George Howard shouts. 'I've just got one more little job to do and then we can be off.' He makes it sound like a late-night taxi pick-up outside a nightclub.

And then the Chinook is hovering overhead and the rotors are kicking up a storm of sand and dust that gets into Wendy's eyes and mouth and nose. The aircraft touches down and a door opens. Wendy, still wearing her long, black robe tumbles down the side of the depression, her limbs flailing, looking for all the world like a wounded bat. Jamshid and Paddy fall after her. She staggers against the force of the downdraft towards the open door. George Howard is leaning into the door of the Passat and fiddling with something. He straightens up and makes a dash for the helicopter. No sooner has he been hauled aboard than the aircraft lifts off the ground. Seconds later, there is a dazzling flash and the Passat disappears in flames.

'My old Mum in Liverpool always said, never leave any evidence behind. Good advice. Lovely what a bit of Thermite can do.'

The helicopter gains height. From this vantage point, Wendy can see the lights of three vehicles closing fast on the depression.

From one of the vehicles comes a muzzle-flash as someone tries to shoot at the helicopter, but it is more a face-saving gesture rather than any kind of threat.

Wendy is astonished to find she has tears streaming down her face. Are they caused by the grit in her eyes or by something more? The end of her Keshevan adventure? The death of Mary Bowyer? Her utter relief at being out of danger and with the man she loves?

Probably all of the above.

A rush of relief that it is all over and she is safe washes over her in an almost physical sensation. She dabs away the tears and hugs Paddy and then Jamshid. Speech is impossible against the noise of the engines but her emotion is clear and does not need words to express it.

Part Three

45

Six hours later, she, Paddy and Jamshid are driven to Larnaca Airport and fast-tracked onto a BA flight full of holidaymakers returning home to England. George Howard stays behind until the Army makes up its mind what to do with him and he seems happy enough with the arrangement as he saw them off from the base.

'Let me know where your next posting will be and me and the lads will come and bail you out of that one,' he says.

'Not bloody likely, mate. I'm due a home posting. Safe in suburbia for me.'

'Well, mind how you go. And you take care, too, miss. And you, lad. Cheers.'

And here she is, seated in Business Class clutching glasses of something cold and fizzy with a flight attendant fussing around them.

'It's over,' says Paddy as he gives Wendy a hug.

'I can't believe these last few days. I'll never be the same again. Not after all that. And Mary.' She trembles and Paddy increases the pressure of his embrace, drawing her head down to rest on his shoulder.

'It's over, my love. It's all over. You are safe and we are going home.'

'And what next?' Wendy asks, broaching the subject that has been playing on her mind for some time. 'Where do you and I go from here?'

'I want to be with you, if you will have me.'

'Of course I want you. I love you. What we have just been through ties us tighter together than most couples will ever be.'

'I feel the same. Is it too soon to move in together? Do you need some space to sort your life out?'

'No,' she says passionately. 'What I need is the support of the man I love. I want to be with you. Now and forever! Christ, I sound like a Mills and Boon character. But I mean it. I don't want to be parted from you.'

'I've got a tiny one-roomer in Battersea that I bought years ago when I first started working in Vauxhall. I mainly use it as a base when I come back to London. It's a bit Spartan.'

'Then move in with me in beautiful Acton and experience the joys of West London. It's not huge but it is comfy and I like it. I was hoping the bonus I was due to get from Aslan Dargan would pay off the mortgage. No chance of that now.'

'I hate to admit it, but I suppose we should be honest with each other...'

'Don't tell me, you've got a mistress and an aged mother to support?' The question is only half in jest. What does he want to say?

'And half a dozen kids to boot. No, what I was going to admit to is the fact that I've been banking most of my pay for years while I have been abroad. We can throw that at your mortgage.'

Oh my God, she thinks, he's prepared to buy in with me. Now *that* really is love.

'Paddy. What can I say?'

'You could say you will marry me.'

'If you ask me.'

'Will you?'

'With the greatest of pleasure. But I get to keep my surname. I've published papers with that name. Paddy, this is the happiest day of my life. Listen to me. I'm talking in clichés and I don't care.'

She kisses him, unaware that the flight attendant has been eavesdropping on their conversation.

'More champagne, Sir? Madam?'

'Oh, I think so, don't you?' Paddy replies.

'With the greatest of pleasure and many congratulations.'

But as she goes off to open a bottle, Paddy injects a cold note of reality.

'What about him?' He nods his head towards Jamshid, who is sitting by himself across the aisle and staring silently out of the window at a world he has never seen before.

'I honestly don't know. I haven't given it much thought. I assume he will move in to student accommodation when he starts university, like most freshers do. Won't the Government do something about him. He is an asylum seeker, after all.'

'He is a very hot potato; that is what he is. His presence in the UK could sour Anglo-Keshevan relations for years. Abdulin is not going to let this go. Don't forget, he was prepared to sanction the murder of a British subject to get his hands on the boy. Jamshid is not just another foreign student studying in Britain. He is a potential rallying point for opposition to the new regime. And as such, will not be safe without protection.'

'He could stay with us. For the time being,' Wendy suggests tentatively, although this is the very last thing she wants at the start of her married life. But she has become very close to the young man over the months and the whole ordeal they have just endured has been for his sake. She does not feel that she can just abandon him now. Like her, he is starting out on a new life in a new and strange land with the trauma of the murder of his entire family to come to terms with. He has not spoken of the deaths but they must be eating on his mind like a cancer. At some stage, he will have to speak of it, either to a professional counselor or to a friendly ear that he trusts. And the only ear in town that fits the bill is Wendy's. She cannot, in all good faith, turn her back on him. She and Paddy will have to make compromises. She can do no less.

'You could be putting yourself at risk, you do realise that.'

'I know. And if we are going to be together, then I'm putting you at risk too, and that is the last thing I want. And maybe he won't want to live with us. Too many raw memories. Let him choose when he knows all the options. I suspect officialdom will be waiting for us at Heathrow. Let's leave worrying about it until then and enjoy our engagement.'

46

The plane touches down at Terminal 5 and two men in dark suits board and politely escort them off and down to a suite of offices somewhere in the bowels of the building, where a small group of men and women are waiting for them. The room is warm but windowless, Armchairs ring an oval table upon which someone has set out tea and coffee pots, cups and saucers with cream and sugar. A plate of biscuits sits invitingly by a small pile of side plates.

A blond woman dressed in a dark business suit and white blouse with a discreet broach at her throat steps towards them, her hand extended in greeting. Wendy judges she is much the same age as herself.

'Kitty Hamilton. I'm from the FCO and this,' she indicates a tall, thin man also in a regulation dark suit and wearing a striped tie over a pale, pastel blue shirt, 'is Peter Lovell from the Home Office. Let me start by saying how relieved we all are at your escape from Kesheva. It must have been quite an ordeal.'

'Has there been any news? From the Embassy?' Wendy asks.

'Indeed there has, Dr, McPherson. I'm glad to report that all are well. The siege was more or less lifted after the Keshevan Government discovered that their bird had flown. The worst damage was to the Ambassadorial Rolls-Royce but we won't be taking that out of Mr. Armstrong's pay.' She gives a little laugh at her own mild joke. 'There was a lot of pressure from the other Western Embassies on the new Government in Kesheva. Talk of economic sanctions, travel bans and so on. Rustram Abdulin saw sense. Now, can we offer you some tea? Coffee? And then we can get down to business,'

They indicate their preferences and a young man, who is not introduced, does the honours.

They sit around the table, Kitty Hamilton presides at the head and Peter Lovell sits opposite her, Wendy, Jamshid and Paddy sit on the left together and the unnamed minions sit on the right. A man and a woman sit with laptops ready to take notes while a third switches on a tape recorder of the sort used in police interviews with double cassettes.

'I know Mr Winterslow has already given an initial debriefing in Cyprus but we want to go into as much background detail as possible. I'd like to start with you, Dr. McPherson, if you'd be so kind. Right back to your first contact with Rustram Abdulin and your dealings with President Dargan. We know about your work for Mr Winterslow and have copies of your reports, so you can omit those.'

'What reports? Were you spying?' Jamshid demands, his voice shocked. Is this yet another betrayal by someone he has come to trust?

'They were just progress reports on how you were doing. I was sending them back to the university as well,' she lies glibly. Jamshid struggles to believe her; he desperately wants to. Without his trust in the one person remaining in his life who is on his side, he has nothing.

Wendy takes a moment to reflect on the events since she arrived in Kesheva, orders the points in her mind as she would her notes before delivering a lecture and then speaks fluently and succinctly for twenty minutes. The civil servants listen in silence while her words are captured by the tape recorder and the minions make occasional notes on their devices.

When she has finished Kitty thanks her and turns to Jamshid.

'First of all, Mr Dargan, I would like to extend the sincere sympathy of the Foreign and Commonwealth Office on behalf of the Government on your loss.'

'Thank you,' Jamshid says, not knowing what is expected of him.

'I'd like, if I may, to ask you a few questions about your father's plans for you and how he saw your role in the future of Kesheva.'

'I am,' he stops himself and then continues, 'I *was* the second son of my father. My stepbrother should have followed my father into politics but he made a big mistake in America and his life style when he came back to Kesheva was not considered suitable for a future leader. I think he was a disappointment to my father and so my father was going to try again with me. That was why he wanted me to come to England to study and why he arranged for Dr. Wendy to come to Kesheva. He did not really discuss politics with me. I think he was waiting for me to finish my studies abroad before he brought me in to his confidence. I know he wanted to open up the government. We inherited our system from the Soviets and traditionally Kesheva has been ruled by one person. Always a man, that is why he never considered my stepsister suitable. But he wanted to make reforms. Slowly, bit by bit and that would have included a greater role for women. Kesheva is a traditional society, as I said, and the extreme Islamists have been pressing for greater influence. He did not want this to happen, from what I know. He considered this a - what is the word? - a regressive step.'

Wendy smiles proudly - her language input is showing rewards.

'And what about Rustram Abdulin?' Kitty asks.

'I never liked or trusted that man,' Jamshid answers. 'He seemed to be absolutely loyal to my father and I believe did my father's dirty work. And from what little I know of his life style, was not particularly devout. He is an opportunist and is using the Islamists for his own ends. He will turn on them when he judges the time is right.'

'Interesting,' Kitty murmurs.

'That is all I can tell you. As I said, I was not a part of the politics. What will happen to me now here in England? You will not send me back, please. Abdulin will have me killed. He would probably take pleasure in doing it himself.'

'Don't worry on that score, Mr Dargan,' Peter Lovell assures him. 'You *have* been granted asylum. The United Kingdom has a strict policy in regard to deporting people to certain death. You have the right to remain in this country. It's just a question of what we do with you.'

'I would like to take up my place at university, if that is possible.'

'It is more a question of where you will live and how you can support yourself.'

'We have property here in London and bank accounts.'

'Ah, here is the thing. The new government in Kesheva have applied to take control of these properties as assets of the State of Kesheva. They have also applied to the courts here in Britain to freeze the bank accounts held by your family on the grounds that the funds they contain were siphoned off from state funds illegally. You see the problem?'

'So I have nothing?'

'Until the courts rule otherwise, I'm afraid it looks that way.'

'What can I do?' Jamshid wails. There are tears in his eyes. He turns to Wendy in mute appeal.

'Well,' says Lovell, 'usually we would suggest applying to Hounslow Local Authority for temporary accommodation and then see about claiming Benefits. Once you are settled and you still want to go ahead with university, you can see about getting Student Loans. We in the Home Office will do everything we can to expedite your resident status.'

'I don't understand? Am I a refugee?'

'Frankly? Yes.'

'I will take responsibility for him,' says Wendy impulsively, with a side glance at Paddy. How will he feel about sharing the flat in Acton with Jamshid when they are both feeling their way in a new relationship together? But she has no choice. She has bound her life up with both of these men and if Paddy truly loves her, he will understand her motivation and make allowances. She cannot bear to think of the alternative, that Paddy will present her with an ultimatum to choose between them. But he is smiling at her and nodding his agreement and the relief washes over her.

'So, Dr. McPherson, am I correct in understanding that you will take full responsibility for Mr. Dargan?' Lovell checks.

'Yes.'

He looks down the table at Kitty Hamilton, who gives him an almost imperceptible nod.

'That's settled, then.' As simple as that.

'Is that it?' Wendy asks, suspicious that the wheels of bureaucracy have spun so smoothly.

'For the time being. We will have to follow up the paperwork, of course,' Lovell gives a little chuckle - of course there will be paperwork; it goes without saying.

'And we are free to go?'

'My dear Dr. McPherson, there was never any implication that you were *not* free to leave at any time.'

'Am I coming to live with you?' Jamshid asks Wendy. He is bewildered by these developments and he is not sure he has fully understood what has been decided about his fate. And he has no idea what Benefits are. Do they include young women?

'Yes, if you would like to.'

Some of Jamshid's enthusiasm of a few weeks ago returns. He really is here in London and a new life is beginning. He does not want to think beyond the immediate future.

'Mr. Winterslow, you should report to your Central Asian Desk asap,' Kitty tells him, 'But I think we are done here. Mr. Hodgkin here will see you out. I wish you the best of luck in your new life, Mr. Dargan.'

The young man, Hodgkin, leads them along passages to the VIP exit. The paparazzi who habituate the area dazzle them with flash photography without having the faintest idea as to their identity. But if they are coming along the VIP channel, they are probably worth a shot.

'How will you get home?' Hodgkin asks.

'I managed to hold on to my purse, despite everything. A quick trip to the ATM and then it's a cab home.'

At the taxi rank outside Terminal 5 Wendy and Paddy embrace while Jamshid discreetly gives them space.

'Duty calls, I'm afraid. My master requires my presence. I'll call you when I can. I want to see the home I will be sharing with my wife.'

'Come as soon as you can. I'll text you the address. I love you.'

'Love you too. Welcome to London, Jamshid.,'

As Paddy's taxi drives off, Wendy turns to Jamshid. 'Let's get home. It's not what you are used to, but you'll get over it. Then I suppose we need to go shopping and buy you some clothes.'

47

On Monday morning Wendy is sitting in the office of David Rhys on her first day back at work. Already the events of the past weeks are taking on an air of unreality. To Wendy it seems like she has been living in a tale from the Thousand and One Nights: the exotic desert city of minarets and madrassas and bazaars; the evil Vizier and the deposed Sultan; the riots and the revolution; Mary's tragic death and the flight to escape. She remembers something her mother said at the Christmas dinner: "You'll be the Queen of Kesheva". That's it, she thinks –The Tale of the Queen of Kesheva with all its twists and turns with fantasy, tragedy and love. And now here she is back in reality sitting in her Head of Unit's office – the man responsible for setting the whole dream in action.

'Jesus Christ, Wendy, what a screw-up!' Rhys says, not the sympathetic welcome home she had hoped for

'Tell me about it, David. You think I was having a bundle of laughs?'

'Have you seen the papers?'

'Yes, I read the Sundays. We were woken up at the crack of dawn on Saturday by a media feeding frenzy on my doorstep. I spent two hours shouting "No comment. Go away" before they got the message.'

The paparazzi who snapped them at Heathrow had got

lucky. The siege of the Embassy and the murder of Mary Bowyer was hot news. And now here was a photogenic and courageous heroine bringing with her the son of the assassinated dictator of Kesheva. How the papers got the story, she did not know. She was hardly a well-known figure, unlike some of the female academic eye-candy who regularly appeared on the box. She suspected a well-placed leak for propaganda purposes from either Kitty Hamilton or Peter Lovell. A positive spin on what was otherwise a story of the British Lion being humiliated.

The headlines hands been broadly similar:

Brit Prof in Coup Flight - *The Sunday Redtop*

British Academic Escapes Embassy Siege - *The Broadsheet*

Islamic fanatics Fail to Hold Plucky British Hostage - *The Tabloid on Sunday*

And there was a picture of her and Jamshid staring into the cameras. Somehow, Paddy had managed to turn his head away and shield his face with his hand. Training, she supposed.

'How do you think this is going to reflect on the University?'

'Bit of good publicity. Gets our name out there,' she replies. 'Why, do you think it might have a negative impact?'

'Might be a bit early to tell,' he admits. In her experience, David has always been a natural pessimist. 'The question is what do we do about the Dargan boy?'

'What do you mean, "what do we do with the Dargan boy"?'

'He might prove a security risk. And what about his tuition fees? Where's the money coming from?'

Wendy reads between the lines: Rhys is mightily miffed that

the generous donation to university coffers that was promised by Aslan Dargan has gone up in smoke along with the Presidential Palace.

'The man from the Home Office that I spoke to promised to expedite Jamshid's permission to stay. I assume he can apply for student loans just like any other home student. The Dargan assets in this country have been frozen for the moment but if the freeze can be successfully contested, Jamshid will have plenty of money.'

'Lawyers don't come cheap.'

'True. But given the amounts I suspect are squirrelled away, I can image a queue of shysters prepared to work on a no-win no-fee basis for a healthy percentage of the loot.'

'Ah, the cupidity of man,' Rhys sighs, with what strikes Wendy as heavy irony.

'So, can we get him onto a Summer Pre-Sessional course? If it comes to it, I'll pay for him.

Rhys considers this proposal and then says: 'I'll see what I can do.' He mulls the idea over a little more. 'Here's a thing. We never got his IELTS score from Mary.'

'That's because Mary was too busy being kidnapped and murdered,' Wendy shouts, getting up and storming out of the office before she can hit Rhys in the face. She marches down the staircase and into her office. There is a young dark-haired woman in her mid-twenties sitting in her carrel. This is the last straw. Wendy is in a blazing temper at Rhys's total lack of sensitivity.

'Fuck off!' She shouts at the young woman, who looks up at her in terrified alarm.

'This is my seat,' she says.

'No it isn't. It's got my name on it.' Wendy points to the

printed strip of paper bearing her name sellotaped to the bookshelf.

'You're back, then,' Frank Brice notes from the other side of the office.

"Are you Dr. McPherson?' Asks the young woman.

'Yes,' says Wendy, calming down and feeling ashamed at her outburst.

'Oh, I'm very sorry. I'm on a temporary contract filling in on some of your classes. I was told I could use this desk while you were away.'

'Look, I'm terribly sorry. I've just had a row with David Rhys. I'm sorry.'

'Been up to fun and games, I hear,' says Frank, coming over to her and giving her a hug.

'Don't you start,' she tells him, laughing and glad of all the implied sympathy in his gesture.

'I'll move my stuff,' says the young woman, introducing herself as Polly Carrington.

'No, sit tight. I don't know what I'm supposed to be doing. I'll sit in the staffroom and calm down and then have a word with the Course Tutors to see if they've got anything planned for me. Nobody expected me to be back quite so soon. Where's everyone else?'

'Either teaching or not in yet. They'll be glad to see you're back safe,' Frank tells her. 'Was it bad?'

'Yes.' What more can she say?

'But you're safe now.'

'Yes.'

'Fancy going for a coffee in the SCR and having a chat?'

'Yes.'

48

Jim Smythe, Wendy's union rep, lobbies for her to be given a period of stress-related compassionate leave on full pay. David Rhys, prompted either by guilt or fear of what she might do to him if she snaps again, agrees. She is given the rest of the Summer Term off, coming back to work in the closing weeks of the term to assist in assessing students' end-of-year oral presentations, a job she can do standing on her head.

Paddy has moved some of his things in to the Acton flat and Wendy is experiencing her first taste of conjugal domesticity since That Bastard Tony walked out on her. She is loving it.

She buys Jamshid an Oyster Card and takes him on a tour of the sights of London to get him acquainted with the capital's transport system and then leaves him to his own devices to explore. He is loving it.

Paddy commutes to his work on the District Line and comes home to a cooked dinner and a woman who loves him and is prepared to wash and iron his clothes. He, too, is loving it.

On the Friday, Wendy arranges to meet up with her female colleagues for the customary end of week drink. Sheila, Jamila, Annabelle and Pauline are sitting in the Slug and Lettuce, getting stuck in to the Chardonnay when she walks in, She scans the room quickly with a flash of panic to see if Lucas, her seducer and robber, is in residence, but thankfully she sees no sign of him. Perhaps he has moved on to pastures new and fresh pickings. Or, hopefully, he has been arrested and banged up. She opts for the latter scenario.

Her friends greet her like someone back from the dead, firing questions at her about her adventures.

'It all started so well,' she says. 'And then it got darker and darker with riots and killings and then the bombing of the American Embassy and the assassination of Dargan and his family and then the siege of the British Embassy and then the killing of poor Mary in front of me. I feel so guilty.'

'It was hardly your fault,' Jamila tells her. 'How could you have prevented it?'

'I could have thrown Jamshid to the wolves.' She explains who and what Jamshid is and the role he played.

'No you couldn't,' says Annabelle, topping up Wendy's glass.

'The only good thing to come out of the whole mess is that I'm now with a lovely man.'

'Details!'

'He was the Cultural and Education Attaché at the Embassy.'

'Oh,' says a cynical and worldly-wise Shiela, 'the resident spook.'

'I couldn't possibly comment,' replies Wendy, with a grin that says it all.

'Was he the man in the photo with you?' Pauline guesses.

'Well, yes.'

'So, come on, tell us all,' Jamila demands.

And so Wendy does.

'What's going to happen to Jamshid now?' Annabelle asks.

'I'm hoping that he's going to enroll on the Pre-Sessional Summer course. One of you might have the pleasure of teaching him. I can't, I'm too closely involved.'

'I bet David Rhys was spitting feathers when he learnt that Kesheva wasn't going to cough up for a new library or whatever,' says Pauline.

'That reminds me, Annabelle, could you ask Carol if she can recommend a legal practice that might be prepared to challenge the freeze on the Dargan assets? Probably have to be on a no-win no-fee basis. Jamshid doesn't have any money and I'm hardly in a position to pay legal fees.'

'I'll certainly ask her; she's got lots of contacts. I'll get her to ring or text you.'

'That'd be great.'

'And what's the future with your lovely man?' Jamila loves a good romance, despite her own arranged marriage.

'He's asked me to marry him.'

'This calls for a real celebration!' Pauline announces and heads off to the bar to buy a bottle of champagne. The others are quick to add their own congratulations. They have long been aware of Wendy's single state and her loneliness in the love department and feel that she fully deserves a happy ending to her misfortunes in Kesheva.

'And what is the lucky man's name?'

'Paddy. Patrick, really. Paddy Winterslow.'

Pauline is back bearing a bottle and champagne flutes. She pops the cork and pours, passing the glasses around the table. 'To Wendy and her new love!' They raise their glasses in a toast. Wendy is swaddled in a blanket of warmth and love. She starts to cry.

'Marriage isn't that bad,' Jamila reassures her.

'I'm so happy. It was really awful at the end.'

'But you are here with us and you are safe.'

'And you screwed a bit of paid compassionate leave out of David Rhys. That's a victory in itself.'

'Thanks, you guys. What would I do without you?'

'Have you told your family?' Annabelle asks.

'Not yet. I'm going up to my brother's on Sunday. I'm taking Paddy and Jamshid. That'll be a surprise.'

'Time I was off,' Jamila announces, draining her glass.

Wendy remembers the last time she was here and there was just her and Mary left after the others had departed. As her friends make to leave, Wendy stands and raises her glass in a final toast.

'To absent friends.'

49

On their way back from her brother Jamie and her sister-in-law Rosemary's house on Sunday evening (they are both thunderstruck at the news that she and Paddy are to be married but pleased for her and very glad that she has returned safe), Wendy gets two messages on her smartphone. Paddy is driving so Wendy can access the messages. One is from Sheila Jones and the other, much to Wendy's surprise, is from Kitty Hamilton.

Sheila's message reads: Type "Orgush" into your search engine.

Kitty's message reads somewhat more enigmatically: Please come to the FCO at 10 am Monday. Ask for me by name at reception.

When she gets home, she fires up her desktop Mac and types "Orgush" into Google. Immediately there are a number of hits. She is directed to YouTube and clicks on the image. Footage obviously recorded on a smartphone fills the screen. Men and women can be seen demonstrating with hand-painted placards calling for the ouster of the Dargan regime. The sounds of angry shouting can be heard. A line of paramilitary police appear and without warning open fire on the crowd. Men and women can be seen falling as the crowd disperses in panic and the shooting goes on. A voice-over cuts in: 'This is the work of the discredited Dargan regime. Aslan Dargan, 'The Butcher of

Orgush'. The man responsible for the deaths of twenty-seven innocent people. The man who, for years, repressed the freedom of the people of Kesheva. He and his family exploited the people of Kesheva for their own gain. But now the people are free once more.'

Wendy is stunned and calls Paddy and Jamshid to see as she re-runs the clip. They watch in silence.

'It's obviously been posted by Abdulin's spin doctors to give some kind of legitimacy to their coup,' says Paddy. 'Notice the reference to the Dargan family.'

'And I am the only one left,'

'That's right, Jamshid. They are trying to smear you by association. Clever.'

Wendy clicks on to more sites featuring Orgush. They are full of shocked condemnation. Aslan Dargan is compared to Hitler, Stalin and Pol Pot as a mass murder of his people. Sites known for their radical Islamic sympathies praise the new Islamic revolution in Kesheva.

'Most of this is arrant bullshit!' Wendy says.

'We know that, but watch the proliferation of fake news on the social networks. Abdulin and his cronies are playing a clever game. Win enough popular support to your side and your own questionable actions are overlooked.'

'He murdered my family and some of my father's ministers as well as Dr. Bowyer.'

'Try posting that on Facebook and see what happens. Actually, don't. You need to keep a very low profile. If you break cover Abdulin might be able to find you and we don't want that.'

'Paddy's right. Keep your head down. You're safe here.'

'But it is so unfair.'

'So is life. Welcome to the real world,' Paddy tells him. 'And when all is said and done, your father wasn't exactly a saint.'

'He did what he had to do for the greater good of the country.'

'He had his Minister of the Interior boiled alive.' Wendy reminds him gently. 'That was a bit over the top. A cabinet re-shuffle might have done the trick just as well.'

Jamshid has no answer and takes himself off to his bedroom to sulk. Sometimes Wendy forgets that he is still a teenager from a very privileged background. It must be very hard for him to have lost everything and end up living in a small flat in Acton with little in the way of prospects.

On Monday at ten a.m. prompt. Wendy enters the august portals of the Foreign and Commonwealth Office and announces herself to reception. She is politely asked to wait and a few moments later the familiar figure of Rupert Hodgkin appears to escort her to a lift and a corridor that leads to Kitty Hamilton's rather smart and spacious office. Kitty sits behind a large paper-free desk with an impressive desktop computer on it. A small conference table and chairs take up the foreground of the office and Wendy is invited to sit.

'Rupert,' Kitty says, 'I wonder if you'd be so kind and sort out some refreshments. Tea? Coffee?'

Wendy has an instant mental picture of another grand office with a samovar and a young woman making tea.

'Coffee, please,' she says.

Coffee and biscuits are brought and Hodgkin silently departs. Kitty joins Wendy at the table.

'You must be wondering why I asked you to come here, Dr. McPherson.'

'Yes. Obviously.'

'I'm responsible for the FCO's dealings with Central Asian states. If you like, I'm Jim Armstrong's boss. Amongst others.'

'I thought you might be something like that,' Wendy smiles and sips her coffee.

'Ever since Rustram Abdulin's takeover of power I have been dealing with the Keshevan Ambassador here in London. You will not be surprised to know that he is Aslan Dargan's man, as are most of the senior appointees in his Embassy. His name is Mehmet Andreyev, by the way. To cut to the chase, Andreyev and his senior staff have been ordered to return to Kesheva pending the appointment of a new Ambassador of Abdulin's choosing. As you can imagine, Andreyev is not exactly raring to return to Kesheva. Mr Abdulin has been busy conducting a purge of any potential Dargan sympathisers and Andreyev doesn't fancy his chances.'

'I can understand that, knowing Rustram Abdulin. He'd murder his own grey-haired mother if it suited him.'

'Precisely. Anyway, Andreyev has applied for asylum for himself and his family and for a number of his senior staff and their families. It puts HMG in a bit of a bind. If we granted asylum to every Tom, Dick and Harry after every regime change in the less-than-democratic countries in this great family of nations, there would soon be standing room only. Fortunately, France takes the Francophone ex-dictators and Saudi Arabia takes the likes of Idi Amin and his ilk.'

'So how do I fit in to this?'

'*You* don't. Not exactly. Andreyev is keen to make a deal.

He knows where the bodies are buried, so to speak. One of the bodies is a very secret and very private bank account that Aslan Dargan set up for his son shortly before he was killed. These funds were to pay for Jamshid Dargan's education and very liberal expenses.'

'Jamshid isn't destitute?'

'Far from it. He is a wealthy young man. But this *is* where you come in. Aslan Dargan obviously trusted you. We know he did from the information he gave you to pass on to Mr. Winterslow. You are to be the trustee of the funds until Jamshid Dargan turns twenty-one or finishes his studies to your satisfaction.'

'Me?' Wendy is finding this news hard to comprehend.

'As I said, Aslan Dargan must have held you in high regard. He has made provision for a stipend to be paid to you for administering the fund that I think you will find generous. But, I need to stress, this fund must remain secret, otherwise Abdulin will seek to have it frozen and it could take years of legal actions to get it unfrozen. Think *Bleak House*.'

'How much is in the account?'

'Ten million dollars. That's a little over eight million pounds at the current exchange rate. Your stipend is fifty thousand dollars a year.'

'Bloody Hell!'

'We know the money is dirty. It can't be otherwise. But it is HMG's interest to turn a blind eye to its provenance. We have long-term interests in the region and if we have a pro-British asset like Jamshid Dargan onside who might make a return to Kesheva if and when the time is right. Well...'

'Bloody Hell,' says Wendy again.

'I take it you are not averse to the arrangement? You must stress on young Dargan to be very, very discreet. If he goes out and buys himself a new Lamborghini, he will attract interest. Abdulin will have sympathisers in the UK. We need to build him a new identity. He can't turn up at university with his real name. This is another thing we would like you to work on with him and with David Rhys. He must be low profile for his own good. You do understand?'

'Yes. It's entirely logical.'

'Good. And we can count on your full co-operation?'

'Of course. I've been through a lot with Jamshid and just want what's best for him.'

'I was counting on your co-operation. I'll have Rupert fill you in on the ins-and-outs. This is my direct line,' she says, handing Wendy a business card that just contains her name and a phone number. 'If you think of anything, anything at all, call me. Thank you for coming to see me.'

Wendy leaves the office in a daze. As if by magic, Rupert Hodgkin is waiting and takes her to his own, much less prepossessing, office, where she spends the rest of the morning going over the details of Jamshid's trust fund.

50

'Will a registry office do?' Paddy asks when he gets home on Monday evening.

'Will a registry office do what?'

'For you?'

'Paddy, what are you talking about? Will a registry office do what for me?' Her mind is so preoccupied with her meetings at the FCO that she cannot take in what he is talking about.

'Or are you a girl who likes a long engagement?'

The penny hits the floor with a resounding clang.

'To get married?'

'Isn't that what we agreed?'

'Well, yes. But I've not given the date much thought.' But in truth she has not dared to push things. What if their domestic bliss turns sour? What if he finds he is not happy with her? What if he was attracted to her as the only available female in his circle in Kesheva? She has been plagued with doubts and uncertainties. For her own part, she is absolutely sure of her feelings for him but previous romantic attachments have ended in bitter disappointment for her. She has not really, in her heart of hearts, dared to hope.

'That's a shame. I've made a booking in the Ealing Registry office for the second Saturday in June. Three thirty.

'You mean it? You really mean it?'

'If you are still up for it? Not having second thoughts?'

She flies into his arms, kissing him passionately.

'Oh, yes! Yes! Or do I mean no? I can't think.'

He holds her at arm's length. 'Which is it? Yes or no?'

'It's all I want. It's all I've ever wanted since the first time I met you, my darling.' She remembers her own news. 'I had a meeting with Kitty Hamilton from the FCO. It turns out Aslan Dargan set up a secret bank account for Jamshid. He is now a very wealthy young man. I'm to administer the trust.'

'Wow! They say good news comes in threes. I'm going to marry the woman I love; Jamshid can pay his own tuition fees. What's next?'

Jamshid comes into the living room from the kitchen.

'I have been learning to cook,' he announces, '*plov*. Has Wendy told you our news?'

'She has. And I've got some news for you. How would you like to come to our wedding?'

'You're getting married? Fantastic! When? I would be honoured. You are like my new mum and dad!' And he is only half joking.

Jamshid is on a high. Wendy has not seen him this excited or happy since the day he took his IELTS exam with Mary Bowyer, which was also the day his world fell apart and she certainly does not want to spoil the mood by comparing his culinary efforts to Ruthinna's. She and Paddy choke the scorched offering down while making approving noises. They discuss the plans for the wedding and the options for Jamshid's future as a man of means. He generously wants to give Wendy half of his fortune, but she will not hear of it, citing her fiduciary duty as a trustee. She repeats Kitty's warning to do nothing to attract attention to himself, stressing that although he is out of Kesheva, that does not mean he is out of danger.

More posts with highly negative comments about Aslan Dargan and his family, particularly Stas Dargan are proliferating on social media. Most damaging of all are snippets of film showing shots coming from the British Embassy and hitting members of the rent-a-crowd protesters. The British are portrayed as supporters of a discredited regime, anti-Islamic and imperialistic. No footage of the cold-blooded murder of Mary Bowyer has yet surfaced to balance the equation.

Nor is it ever likely to.

On Wednesday morning, Wendy is in the kitchen listening to *Woman's Hour* on Radio Four and teaching Jamshid to make a ragout sauce for their dinner. The doorbell chimes. She has learnt caution. She edges to the curtain on the window facing the street and peers out. A motorbike dispatch rider stands on her doorstep. He has removed his helmet so his face can be clearly seen; she reasons an assassin would not want to be exposed to the CCTV camera at the end of her road and judges it is safe to answer the door.

'Package for Dr. Wendy McPherson,' says the dispatch rider.
'That's me.'
'Sign here for it, please, madam.'
'Who is it from?' She is still a little wary.
'Foreign and Commonwealth Office. Do you want to see some ID?'
'No, there's no need,' she says as she signs for the package.'
'Ta-ra then. Have a good day.'

She takes the package into the living room and opens it. Inside there is a Russian passport in the name of Boris

Ivanovich Suslov, aged eighteen, born in Yekaterinburg. There is a British student study visa as well as several entry and exit stamps from a number of European countries. There is also a letter of authorisation allowing Boris Suslov to access his account at the small and very exclusive Credit Bank of Ghent branch in the City. Other papers and documents help build his legend, including a smartphone with pictures of his family back in Russia and a slightly pornographic sext picture of a blond girl in her late teens. He has a Facebook account with a number of posts and friends.

Jamshid comes into the living room to see what is going on.

'How's your Russian?" Wendy asks him.

'It's really my first language. I grew up speaking Russian and Keshevan. Why do you ask?'

'Because from now on you are Boris Ivanovich Suslov. Here, you'd better get to know him. Sexy girlfriend, by the way.'

'What girlfriend?'

'The one whose picture is on your phone.' She passes him the phone and is touched to see a blush appear on his cheeks.

51

For the next two days, it is like being back at school for Jamshid. He has to memorise totally all the details of his new identity. When Paddy comes home in the evening, Jamshid is subjected to a number of tests to see if he can be caught out. He is a quick learner and seldom makes a stumble after the first day. Both Wendy and Paddy have taken to calling him Boris. The Jamshid of old is dead and buried in the ruins of the Keshevan Presidential Palace with the bodies of the rest of his family.

Wendy also occupies herself with the practicalities of his new life. She makes an appointment at the Credit Bank of Ghent's London office and she and Jamshid head east across London to keep it on Friday morning.

The Bank occupies offices in the heart of the old City district in a building built in the heydays of Empire. Not for them the flashier parts of Canary Wharf and its ilk. A small brass plaque, set inconspicuously amongst a grouping of similar plaques admits that the Credit Bank of Ghent does, indeed, operate from these premises, as do three law firms and a number of brokerage companies. A uniformed receptionist guards the entrance lobby and, upon confirming that they are indeed expected, directs them to a lift, which whispers them to the second floor. They are met by a middle-aged man dressed in a discreet business suit. For a moment, Wendy was expecting striped trousers and a morning coat. There is nothing of a bank about this office: members of the public do not come here to pay in the night's takings, or come to discuss their mortgages. There are no glass cages containing tellers and Heaven forbid that an ATM should sully the premises. The man leads them down a short, brightly lit corridor and taps gently on the door, as if afraid to disturb the occupant within.

A voice calls 'Come!' and their guide opens the door with a soft swish as it glides over the pale blue carpet. The room contains a window with a view of the street outside, a desk with a telephone and Mac computer, four armchairs and a large blond man, similarly dressed to the other, holding out his hand to greet them.

'I am Peter Grant,' he tells them, shaking first Wendy's and then Jamshid's hand. 'I am the CEO of our London branch. Very pleased to meet you.' To Wendy's surprise, she detects a note of Estuary in his accent. But why not, she chides herself, not all the City boys went to public schools. 'Please, take a seat.'

They sit and decline offers of refreshment.

'Well,' says Grant, 'What do you know of us here at the Credit Bank?'

'Absolutely nothing,' Wendy admits.

'Good. Surprisingly, that is just how we like it. We pride ourselves on making the Swiss look like loud and pushy parvenus.'

'We were sent here by the Foreign and Commonwealth Office,' says Wendy, with a feeling that she is betraying a confidence; the office has that sort of effect on her.

'Quite so. We hold a certain account that was opened by a certain party in respect of a second party.' He makes a little steeple of his hands and beams at them, as if he has said something very clever. Just get on with it, Wendy thinks, impatient with all the enigmatic game playing.

'So we were informed.'

'As absolute security, and before we can allow access to the account, I must ask this young gentleman to take a small test to see if, indeed, he is the access-holder to the account.'

Here we go, she thinks. What was your mother's maiden name and date of birth and does this piece of memorable information mean anything.

Grant opens a drawer in his desk and produces a test-tube and cotton swab. 'If I may be so bold, I would like to take a saliva sample for DNA analysis.'

'What?'

'The depositor was very clear on this. Account details may be obtained under, how can I put this delicately, questionable conditions. DNA cannot be faked. As a further precaution, it must be given by a person present in this room. The criterion for access to the account must be a match of ninety-six per cent or better.'

Aslan Dargan, you cunning old bastard! Wendy thinks in admiration. She sees Jamshid is smiling. He must be thinking the same thoughts.

'Are you prepared to supply a sample, sir?'

'Of course. Please take your sample.'

'This will not hurt in any way,' Grant says as he comes over to Jamshid, who has watched enough cop shows on TV to open his mouth in readiness. Grant swiftly runs the swab around Jamshid's cheek, pops it into the test-tube, which he then seals and stashes away in a pocket. 'I will have this sent to a lab for testing this very morning, but even so, the results might take a little time to come back. Once we are happy that we have a positive match, I will personally get in touch with you. Of course, should the results prove negative,' he gives a little dramatic pause, 'then we will have no further communication. I trust that will not prove to be the case.'

And with that, the meeting is over. Wendy and Jamshid are politely escorted off the premises and deposited back on the street.

'Do you fancy a walk?' Wendy asks. 'I can show you some more of the sights and we can make our way west. I haven't shown you the University yet.'

'Are you going to introduce me?'

'No,' says Wendy. 'I don't think that is such a good idea. Remember, Boris Suslov and Wendy McPherson have never met. Of all the staff, only David Rhys will know who you really are.'

They stroll at a leisurely pace along the arteries of commercial London while people on a mission walk briskly past them, tutting with frustration when they are held up by the dawdling pair. The refrain of Londoners in a hurry 'Bloody Tourists' is on everyone's lips, but most are too polite to articulate it audibly. With a wry smile, she realises that she is prone to the selfsame syndrome when trying to negotiate Oxford Street on a busy Saturday afternoon.

52

They stroll on for another twenty minutes until they arrive in Bloomsbury, home to the British Museum and a number of Colleges and Schools of the University of London. The magnificent Art Deco tower of the University's Senate House dominates the skyline. Wendy's College, an Edwardian pile of five storeys, occupies a block between a Georgian square and a main thoroughfare. It faces a paved square with a small patch of lawn, much favoured by students in the summer, beyond the square. The College has spilled out over the years to occupy a number of the buildings on the north side of the adjacent Eighteenth Century square, named after the aristocratic landowner who commissioned it and whose family still enjoy its freehold and prime leasehold potential.

'This is it,' Wendy says, 'home, sweet home. I don't want to sign you in and have you go on record with me. There's a bunch of students hanging around the College entrance. You could go and have a mooch around, see what is going on. This time of the year there is always something happening. Let's meet up again in, say, thirty minutes. On the corner of the Square.'

Jamshid has been eagerly anticipating entering into student life and heads off in the direction of the activity. Wendy decides to have a look herself before going in to her office and touching base with David Rhys and keeping him abreast of developments on the Jamshid front.

Some of the students milling around are carrying placards and chanting slogans that Wendy can't quite catch. She moves closer, spies a young woman with close-cropped green hair and a number of visible body piercings. She is obviously a Home student and would have no contact with Wendy's unit.

'What's going on?' Wendy asks.

'We're protesting about the College's involvement in the murder of innocent people in Kesheva.'

'Where's Kesheva?' Wendy asks, all innocent.

'Asia,' replies the student.

'And what has the College done?'

'Are you from the media?' The woman asks hopefully. She can see her name in print already.

'I'm afraid not. I'm doing research. I use the College library.'

'Oh,' says the student, disappointment in her tone.

'So what has the College done?'

'Only sent a member of staff out to teach the Butcher of Orgush.'

'Who is that, and why would the College do that?'

'He's the King or Emir or something and he paid the College a lot of money but the cleaners are all on minimum wage.' She is getting close to the end of her attention span and wanders off to check her phone.

Wendy has suffered a severe jolt. She makes her way deeper into the demonstration. The crowd is basically composed of Home students. There are a number of female students in full hijab, abbiya and niqab. She knows these are Home students: female students from the Gulf make a great point of wearing jeans and tee-shirts with their hair uncovered. To each their own rebellion.

She accosts another group, a mixture of men and women. They are chanting: 'No Platform! No Platform!'

'What's the demo about?'

'One of the teachers here was responsible for the death of another.'

'What?' Wendy is gob-smacked.

'British soldiers fired on a group of innocent protesters. This teacher was part of the protest,' another student explains, shaking his placard that reads 'No Voice for a Murderer'.

'I'm confused,' Wendy confesses. 'Which teacher was part of the protest and how was he killed by another teacher?'

'She,' a third student corrects her.

'And the other one was a woman, as well,' a young woman chimes in.

'I'm lost,' Wendy confesses.

'I'm studying International Relations,' announces a tall young man wearing blue and white striped trousers and a green tank top. 'I can explain. See, the British Government was supporting this, like totally evil regime in this place called Kesheva and the College for, like, a ton of money sent this teacher out to work for the President to give lessons to his son, who was, like, another Uday Saddam. Like, totally evil. And this other teacher also got sent out but she got caught up in the Revolution and was protesting outside the British Embassy in solidarity with the People and the soldiers in the Embassy shot, like, loads of innocent people and this other teacher, she saw it and did nothing to stop it.'

'Thanks for putting it so clearly. Now I understand. But

what's this "No Platform"?'

'We are demanding that this teacher who let it happen cannot be allowed to teach here again,' says another young woman.

'What's this teacher's name?'

'Mary McPherson.'

'Thanks for explaining it all. Good luck with your protest.'

'Yeah! The Cause is Just!'

A very shaken Wendy McPherson makes her way to wait for Jamshid on the corner of the Square. He is already there, looking very upset.

'They are blaming you,' he says.

'Rustram Abdulin has got his retaliation in first, I'm afraid. This is the power of fake news spread on social media. These students have been fed snippets of information across a variety of sources and have come up with a garbled mish-mash. This is a very liberal College and I am sure they think they are acting with the best intentions. But it might make my life a bit awkward. Look, I need to talk to my boss. Why don't you go back home and I'll see you later. The Tube station is just over there.'

As Jamshid heads for the Tube, Wendy goes into her building and climbs the stairs to David Rhys' office. His door is open but she knocks anyway. Rhys is on his phone but sees her and beckons her in. She plonks down in a chair, uninvited.

'Actually, she's here now,' he says to the phone. 'Yes. I will. I'll get back to you.' He puts the phone down. 'Have you seen what's going on outside?'

'Yes. That's why I'm here.'

'I was just on the phone to the Vice-Chancellor. She's been

approached by the Student's Union and the NUS delegate with a view to having you fired.'

'Guilty until proven innocent, eh.'

'Look, *I* know it's a load of bollocks. So does the Vice-Chancellor. It will be a two-day-wonder but the media is bound to pick up on it, and, quite frankly, there is no way that the College will admit Jamshid Dargan now.'

'Then I have one piece of good news for you: Jamshid Dargan no longer exists.'

'What do you mean?'

'You might consider admitting a student from Russia by the name of Boris Suslov. FCO and Home Office approved. And with sufficient funds to pay his way.'

'Really?' Rhys says, intrigued.

'Untainted!'

'You must have friends in high places, Wendy.'

'Not me. Thank the geopolitical aspirations of HMG.'

'Then I don't see a problem. But what about you?'

'The students out there are baying for my blood. None of the ones I spoke to had the slightest idea who I was. Some of them couldn't even get my name right. What can I say?'

'It will blow over. The Finals are coming up and the Second Years will be thinking about buggering off for the summer. Our students on the Foundation courses don't tend to get involved in student politics. Having your Government dissuade you from political activity by driving tanks over you tends to concentrate the mind on other things. If you are worried, talk to Jim Smythe. See what the union has to say about it.'

'I'll do that. Thanks, David.'

She catches Smythe on his way to a meeting with the Unison rep and the NUS and Student Union reps.

'Wendy! I'm just off to talk about you with the other members of the College Soviet. I can only give you a minute or two. The Brothers get impatient if the Great Leap Forward is delayed. Loss of valuable drinking time.' Jim is a dedicated union man but not above having a laugh at the more ideological members of the Hard Left.

'And may the spirit of Trotsky move within you all. Seriously, Jim, where do I stand?'

'As far as the union is concerned you have done absolutely nothing wrong. You were sent to do a job in good faith. Apart from tutoring the son, you had nothing to do with the workings of the regime and there was absolutely nothing you could have done to prevent poor Mary's murder. This is all misinformation being disseminated by a regime that is likely to turn out as open and freedom loving as ISIS or the Taliban. It will blow over. There is no question of you losing your post. At the slightest whisper of any talk of dismissal, I'll be balloting for strike action. Go home; enjoy your paid leave. Come back for the oral presentations. Now, I've got to go and fight your corner with the Comrades,'

'Thanks, Jim.'

'Victory to the Masses!'

That evening Wendy, Paddy and Jamshid are watching the Channel 4 News. The demonstration outside the College is a minor news item towards the end of the running order. There is a brief re-cap of the events in Kesheva - the overthrow and murder of Aslan Dargan, the Embassy siege and the murder of Mary Bowyer. There is a comment on the flurry of posts on social media and speculation that they have their origin from government controlled cyber sites in Kesheva. What rivets the attention of the three watchers is the announcement from the FCO at the very end of the item: 'It is believed that the only survivor of the Dargan family, the youngest son, Jamshid, died while fleeing the country.'

There is a moment of silence in the McPherson household and them Wendy says: 'So that's it. Jamshid Dargan, Rest in Peace. Hello Boris Suslov.'

'I don't know how I feel about being dead,' says the late Jamshid. 'Pretty cool, I guess.'

'Congratulations on your demise,' says Paddy, shaking the ex-Jamshid by the hand.

'As soon as the Credit Bank can confirm that I am who I was,' says Boris, 'and release some cash, I will see about getting a place in student Halls of residence for the summer. You two newlyweds don't need me hanging around. There might be naked bodies around the place and I am far too innocent.'

'Not according to that picture of your girlfriend on your phone, you're not!'

'We are going to miss you,' Wendy tells him.

'Not you are not!'

53

The second Saturday in June is a perfect summer's day: a blue sky, sunshine and a pleasant temperature in the low twenties. In keeping with tradition, Paddy returned to his flat in Battersea for the night before the wedding. He has put the flat on the market and has already received offers in excess of the asking price. Their plan is to also put the Acton flat up for sale and look for something like a period terraced house with a garden. With the sale of both properties, two incomes and Wendy's fees as a trustee it should be feasible to stay in Zone Two.

Wendy's mother, Jane, is staying with Jamie and Rosemary and will come down with them and their two children for the ceremony. Frank and Belinda cannot believe that their exotic aunt is opting to be boring and actually get married. Wendy has invited her friends and colleagues from work, who have all faithfully promised to come. Paddy has no immediate family but has been making mischievous hints of mystery guests. The ceremony promises to be a low-key event but Wendy has high hopes for a rousing and raucous reception. Her hen night, last Friday week had been a disgraceful example of women of a certain age behaving badly and having a really good time while doing so. Paddy is reticent about his stag do and Wendy has no pressing desire to hear the details.

Shiela Jones has agreed to be her Matron of Honour and her brother will give her away, even though they are not, strictly, required at a civil ceremony and will not play a formal role. Boris Suslov, who moved out of the Acton flat and into student residences in King's Cross, has promised that even a second death will not keep him away.

And now here she is, about to get married. To a man she met six months ago on the other side of the world, whom she spied for, went through bombing and sieges and a desperate flight through the desert with. They have packed more intensity in the short time they have known each other than most couples do in a lifetime. Her doubts have gone. If they can weather Kesheva together, their marriage can easily weather the petty strains of peaceful domesticity in West London. Paddy has been confirmed in a desk job and a pledge that his days in the field are over and the kerfuffle over her involvement with Aslan Dargan and the death of Mary Bowyer forgotten as other issues occupy the minds of the students.

She has chosen not to go down the route of a traditional wedding dress but has chosen instead an emerald green silk dress with 1950's style swirling skirt. The contrast with her red hair is striking. She has managed to find, in a vintage clothes shop, a pair of ruby slippers to complete her ensemble. *If* things go pear-shaped, she can always click her heels and get back to Kansas.

Her doorbell rings. It is Sheila.

'Wow! You look like a million dollars!'

And Wendy will admit to herself that she has scrubbed up well.

She drives with Jamie and Sheila in the vintage Rolls Royce they have hired for the occasion and arrive at the Registry Office just as another couple are leaving.

OK, this is it. She swallows her nerves and goes to the chamber allocated to her.

The first thing she sees if Boris Suslov standing at the back of the room with a stunningly beautiful girl on his arm. She bears more than a passing resemblance to the lady in his phone photo. I hope he has had the sense to delete that photo, she thinks. Could land him in all kinds of shit!

The next thing she sees, seated further into the room are Jim and Phoebe Armstrong. She can't believe her eyes until Phoebe gives her a little wave and Jim mouths; 'Talk to you later.'

And then there is Paddy, dressed in a dark suit with a white carnation buttonhole, standing in front of the Registrar who is seated at her desk and then Wendy is standing next to him and the Registrar is reading through the terms and conditions of the civil ceremony and they sign the register and the job is done and they are officially man and wife. As simple as that.

Arm in arm they walk out of the Registry Office, trailing their guests behind them.

'God, I'm a lucky man,' Paddy says as the two of them climb into the Rolls. 'You are so beautiful. Let's dump this pack of freeloaders and go straight home to bed,'

'Not an option, you randy goat. Be patient. I'll make it worth your while,'

'That's a promise, then?'

'I do believe it is customary on your wedding night. But tell me, how did you get Jim and Phoebe here? It's wonderful to see them.'

'They got back last week and when I told them we were getting married today, well, you couldn't have kept them away. I'll let them tell you all about it.'

They have hired a reception room in a nearby hotel and somehow the guests have got there before them. Strong drink is flowing freely, canapés are being nibbled and everyone is shouting to be heard over everyone else shouting.

A good time is being had by all.

Wendy works her way through the happy people who are there to share the happiest day of her life with her, dispensing kisses and hugs. She is crying with happiness and doesn't know it and no-one tells her. She finds the Armstrongs and hugs them both.

'You look a lot better than when we last saw you,' Jim beams at her.

'You look fabulous, my dear. Much better than when you were covered in blood and dust!' Phoebe agrees.

'What happened at the Embassy after we left?'

'Rustram Abdulin had my car crushed in a fit of pique.'

'I heard. But how did you get out?'

'When they realised their bird had flown and the international diplomatic pressure started to mount, they gave over playing silly buggers. We were due to come home any way and as soon as London sent out a replacement, back we jolly well came. I believe I am persona non grata in Kesheva now. Not that I have the least wish to go back. Abdulin is in trouble. He released the fundamentalist monster and thought he could control it. Looks like he can't and a civil war is looming. Can't say what the outcome will be. We were sad, though, to hear that young Dargan is dead. But we did meet a nice young Russian lad at the Registry Office. We got on like old friends. Oh, here he is now. We won't keep you.'

'Wendy, I'd like you to meet Maria. She is from Chile and

will be studying Law at Queen Mary's next year. She has a room in the Student Halls. I have been showing her London.'

'Hello, Maria.'

'How do you know Boris?'

She has been dreading this question but prepared Boris for just such an eventuality.

'I was his teacher on a language course at the University in Russia.'

And with that, Maria's curiosity is satisfied.

'I have something for you and Paddy. For your honeymoon.'

'That's so nice. What is it? Nothing naughty, I hope.'

'It's this.' He gives her an envelope. 'I hope you like it.'

Paddy has materialised at her elbow.

'Boris has given us a wedding present,' she tells him.

'Open it, please,' Boris urges, like a kid who has brought his mother a Christmas present. She does. Inside there is a photograph of a villa with a swimming pool and palm trees.

'It's for your honeymoon.'

'Oh Boris, that is so thoughtful. We didn't get round to booking a holiday.'

'You can go any time.'

'What do you mean?' Paddy asks.

'It's for you. I bought it for you. To say thank you. It's in Granada, in Spain. I had to argue with Mr. Grant but I won in the end. Do you like it?'

'You've bought us a *villa*!' Paddy cannot credit it.

'Don't you like it? Did I do wrong?' Boris asks anxiously.

'Boris, most people buy a toaster or a set of bath towels. I *love* it!' Wendy shrieks and hugs him.

'I've never been to Spain. Can I come and visit?'

'In Spain they say: *Me casa est su casa*. It means my house is your house. In this case, it is literally true. Of *course* you can visit any time you want.'

'But not on our honeymoon!' Paddy warns.

'I wouldn't dream of it,' Boris says. He raises his glass of Champagne in a toast. 'To the happy couple and my best friends!'

THE END

Plov

Ingredients

- 1 kg moderately fat lamb, shoulder or ribs
- 1 kg medium grain rice (paella type)
- 200-250 ml vegetable frying oil
- 1 kg carrot
- 2-3 medium size onions
- 1-1.5 tbsp cumin
- 2-3 whole heads of garlic, the younger the better (optional)
- 1-2 long hot chillies (optional)
- salt to taste
- 5 liter heavy cast-iron dutch oven or bigger, preferably round-bottomed

Method

- Wash the rice under the tap until clear, cover with cold water and let it soaks for a while. Cut the meat with bones into match-box pieces. Cut the carrots into 0.5x0.5 cm thick sticks. Slice onions into thin rings or half-rings. Clean heads of garlic from the remains of roots and dirt.
- Heat oil in the dutch oven on a very high flame, deep-fry meat until golden-brown, in 3-4 batches. Fry the onions until golden, add meat to the cattle, stir well to prevent onion from burning. Add carrot, stir from time to time, until it starts to wilt and browns a little (15-20 min). Add 2/3 of the cumin - rub it in your palms a little to release flavor, stir gentliy to keep carrot from broking.
- Lower gas to moderate, pour hot water just to cover all the goods, add salt and let it simmer for 40 min to 1.5 hours until almost all water evaporate and meat became tender and juicy. Do not stir.
- Turn gas to max. Drain rice well, place it on top the meat and vegs in one layer, stick the garlic and whole chillies in it, and carefully pour boiling water over it (place a spoon or ladle on top of the rice to keep the rice layer from washaway). Cover the rice with about 2 cm of water, let it boil. Add salt to make the water a bit over-salted. When water will go down the rice, reduce the gas

a bit, keeping it boils rapidly. Check when it will evaporate and absorb into rice completely - rice should remain rather al dente. Make a holes in the rice to the bottom of a vessel to check the water level.
- Reduce gas to absolute min, cover tightly with the lid and let it steam 20 minutes. Turn of the heat, remove the garlic and chillies on the separate plate. Carefully mix rice with meat and carrots, if the rice tastes a bit blind add some salt, mix and let it stand for 5 minutes. Pile the plov on a big warmed plate and serve with garlic, chilies and plain thinly sliced tomato-sweet onions-chili salad

Acknowledgements

Thanks to my friend and editor, James Essenger and to Annie Kimber for helpful proofreading and feedback. Thanks to Charlotte Mouncey for painstaking typesetting and her brilliant cover designs. Also to Paul and Joanne Serrellis at www.eazy_print.com for publicity. And, of course, to my wife, Liane, for help, advice and patience above and beyond the call of matrimonial duty!